FICTION

STREET JUDGE

STREET JUDGE

JUDGE GREG MATHIS

SBI

STREBOR BOOKS

NEW YORK LONDON TORONTO SYDNEY

Strebor Books
P.O. Box 6505
Largo, MD 20792
http://www.streborbooks.com

ISBN-13 978-1-59309-172-9
ISBN-10   1-59309-172-9
LCCN 2008929335

Jacket design: © www.mariondesigns.com

First Strebor Books hardcover edition September 2008

10 9   8   7   6   5   4   3   2   1

Manufactured in the United States of America

For information regarding special discounts for bulk purchases, please contact Simon & Schuster Special Sales at 1-800-456-6798 or business@simonandschuster.com

DEDICATION

I dedicate this book to the great City of Detroit,
and all of its citizens whose strength and tenacity prepared me,
and inspired this book.

ACKNOWLEDGMENTS

I am very grateful to the voters of Detroit who believed in me enough to elect me in 1994, and who inspired so many of the stories in this book. I thank my wife, Linda; my children, Jade, Camara, Greg Jr. and Amir, for their support of everything I do, and for being my pride and joy. To Clarence Tucker, my law school classmate and my attorney who helped make it happen; A.P. Richard for his brilliant assistance in crafting this book; and a very special thank you to Zane, the queen of authors, and now publisher, for her willingness to sign this book to her publishing empire.

PROLOGUE

I t seemed that everyone responsible had gone the extra mile in putting together what was to be a very memorable evening. Cobo Arena's ballroom was the designated spot where my specially invited guests were to assemble. To me, the building selected to celebrate my historic accomplishments served as a reminder of how far I had come.

Just a few short years earlier, in the midst of a concert featuring the Average White Band, who were performing before a capacity crowd, I jumped from the second level of the auditorium onto the stage, in four-inch, glass-heel shoes, nonetheless. On that evening, my boys, a group of rabble-rousers known around the city as the Errol Flynns, and I, would turn a night of fun and jubilation into one of intimidation, which eventually led to panic.

Our planned robbery created such chaos that most law-abiding citizens of the city and its surrounding suburbs refused to attend any functions slated to take place in that building. This included the annual North American International Auto Show.

The city was hit hard because the auto show was a cash cow—for the nine or so days that the event was under the roof of Cobo Arena's Exhibition Center, turnout was at an all-time low; and the Errol Flynns were credited for that drop in attendance.

Public leaders mandated that stricter security be put in place at and around the arena any time an event was scheduled. They then devised campaigns geared to inform the public that it was safe to attend functions at the 2.4 million-square-foot complex.

Although time had passed and people were no longer afraid to travel to the heart of Detroit, I couldn't help but think that at one time I was a vital part of the problem—now I would be a stabilizing force and lead the way toward the solution.

Mayor Aaron Dennis, along with the Who's Who—the crème de la crème of the Motor City—were dressed to the nines. All the gentlemen attending the gala sported black-tie, while their dates would put any red-carpet affair to shame in their stunning gowns.

I watched as Assistant District Attorney Carolyn Otto approached Detroit's top man. Rumors had been circulating around town that the mayor and the stunningly attractive prosecutor were secretly seeing each other. It would not only have been a blow to the Honorable Aaron Dennis's career, but to his marriage as well—if it was proven that he was, in fact, sleeping with the power-hungry, green-eyed brunette.

I turned my attention to the elegantly adorned dinner table next to where my wife, four children and I sat. I could clearly see what only could be described as a murderous glare emanating from the eyes of Mrs. Cynthia Dennis. The mayor's wife of fourteen years looked as if she were attempting to burn a hole through the blue sequined Oscar de la Renta, which covered the shapely figure of a woman she thought to be cheating with her husband.

I figured that it was simply a matter of time before Cynthia would snatch that fancy, lace white tablecloth from under the centerpiece and fine china, and use it to hang her husband from the rafters.

My table afforded me a perfect view of the tuxedo-clad, handsome gentleman who attempted to camouflage his age with the help of Grecian Formula 44. The mayor and prosecutor stood several feet to the right of a podium that was positioned directly in front of my table. He was attempting to politely excuse himself from Carolyn Otto's conversation. However, everyone who knew the ADA understood how difficult it would be for him to step up to the podium and give his scheduled speech as long as she had something to say to him. Her personality was strong and demanding, especially when it came to something that she wanted.

The girl was a pit bull in Prada—and if she didn't like you, watch out.

I knew how Carolyn felt toward me; she was none too pleased that I was in my current position. The University of Michigan Law School grad was with the prosecutor's office for several years. The woman was extremely ambitious. I'm not one for rumor, but it was said that she would do any-thing to achieve her political aspirations, and I do mean *anything*.

I was told that in college she manipulated her way into the beds of her dean and two professors to assure that she would attain success in law school. After entering the prosecutor's office, she attempted to use her feminine wiles on DA Joseph Monahan in an effort to control her assignments.

In her quest for a judgeship, she only wanted to be assigned cases she thought would enhance her resume. But, once it became evident that she wouldn't be able to manipulate Monahan, she turned her spider web toward the mayor.

Carolyn had her eyes set on becoming judge. In fact, she lost to me in the race for the very seat for which the evening's celebration was meant. And of course, like so many others, she felt that I lacked the experience necessary to do the job. Ms. Otto felt that I hadn't paid my dues.

The way she peered at me—man, it was a jealous fury that could have cut clean through the earth's surface, and destroyed the planet's core. Some would ask why I had even bothered to extend an invitation to her. My response was, why not?

The mayor finally stepped to the podium—he didn't say a word until the prosecutor made her way to her table. When Carolyn sat, Aaron Dennis tapped lightly on the microphone in an effort to draw everyone's attention.

"Excuse me, everyone," he said while gazing across the impressive assemblage. The mayor cleared his throat before he continued. "I'd like to thank you all for coming. This is a very historically rich evening. Tonight, we will be paying homage to a young man who has come a very long way. At one time, new security measures around this very building were imple-mented due to his propensity to incite violence." He glared at me and smiled. "Our guest of honor has redirected his energy toward ensuring that the youth of our community have more opinions than what were available to him. We're really not here to honor him for those outstanding works, but I would be remiss if I didn't take this opportunity to say to him... thank you."

There was a round of applause; it was kind of a bizarre moment for me. People praising me would have been a stretch several years prior. If anything, they would have all gotten together and pitched in to have me whacked.

"I want you all to understand what this night is about." The mayor pointed toward my beautiful family and me. "This young man has just been sworn in as the youngest judge who has ever donned a robe in the state of Michigan. As an African American, I must say that Judge Greg Mathis makes me proud."

Aaron Dennis spent the next several minutes going over my life. Every word that came out of his mouth seemed to trigger a smile from my gorgeous wife. I glanced over at her several times; she looked unbelievable. Linda's form-fitting, red evening gown, her light-red lipstick and perfectly styled hairdo contributed to my baby being the finest woman in the building.

The mayor concluded his verbal communication with the introduction of someone who attended law school with me. The next speaker, Mr. Gram Olson, was a so-so student in law school. He never really had the drive and hunger necessary to become a successful attorney—pursuing a career in jurisprudence was his parents' dream. Gram ended up leaving school after meeting the love of his life—Ms. Barbara Poindexter, daughter, and only heir of billionaire philanthropist Edward Poindexter.

My old classmate certainly married well.

Barbara and Gram Olson shared a table with the mayor and his wife. When it came to wealth in the city, the couple were at the top of the aristocratic food chain. Barbara was in a class of her own when it came to charitable causes. The heiress was determined to continue her family's benevolence, which extended several decades. With the death of her father several months prior, Barbara became the last of the Poindexter bloodline and the wealthiest individual in the state.

Gram stepped to the podium. I could see the majority of the women

THE BODY

Playful at times, yet very protective of the family, he had been acting strange all day—digging with a sense of urgency, running in circles and barking for several seconds at a time as if he were rabid. He'd jump up and down like a bull attempting to buck a cowboy before stopping suddenly and staring intently at the fence as he panted incisively, his tongue hanging, dry—in desperate need of moisture.

The sun was a gas-pilot light producing a searing heat, but he wouldn't take a second to go to the porch and take shelter under the wooden steps, his usual place for shade on hot days—or even quench his parched throat, his water dish no more than ten yards away, resting on the last step.

Without warning, he would break into an all-out sprint and attempt to jump the five-foot-high homemade corral.

He repeated each act several times.

The dog was beautiful, dark-brown, well groomed, a full-bred canine with a snow-white chest. He had been a part of the family for three years, and in that time, no one had ever seen him so agitated.

Wrecks's constant barking, whining and feverous clawing at the back door was not his customary call for yard time. Because of the ruckus, the boys were told by their father to let the usually sedate, housebroken animal out.

The boys spent most of the morning watching cartoons, but periodically, during commercial breaks, they would check on the family pet. On one such break, the thirteen-year-old twins were drinking a glass of water while looking out of the kitchen window when they saw their German

Shepherd slip under the fence through a hole he'd spent all day digging.

The teens darted through a back screen door in need of repair, one that barely hung by a hinge and swung back and forth like saloon flaps. Their father worked two jobs and hadn't had time to fix the door, but he had every intention of repairing the only property blemish he hadn't addressed.

Terry and Perry Johnson headed straight to the wood-and-chicken wire fence that enclosed the backyard of their home, which was located on the poverty-stricken Eastside. They hopped over the enclosure in time to see their sixty-pound pet sniffing around a pile of broken bottles, cans, and an assortment of other discarded trash at the far end of the alley. The filth-laden alleyway hadn't seen a garbage pickup in sometime. The city was on a tight budget and garbage pickup on that side of town was not seen as a priority.

Perry called for the dog, and Terry did his trademark whistle, but Wrecks was determined to get at something. The boys briefly stared inquisitively at each other before deciding to investigate.

It was built in 1954, the first in the neighborhood. Ms. Ethel Frazier had had the wooden barn-type garage constructed behind her modest, gray wooden home so that she could protect her new car from the harsh Michigan weather. At the time of its construction, it was perfectly safe to pull into the alley, open the double doors of the garage, and back the car in.

Over the years, others in the area followed suit, but during the riots, most of the homes and garages were destroyed. Ms. Frazier's property was virtually untouched.

Upon her death, the property was neglected and began to decay. Weeds grew as high as the uncut grass that surrounded the paint-peeled eyesore There was very little evidence that a wooden picket fence once separate the property from the alley.

The closer they got, the stronger the stench. And the flies—it seem that every fly in the city had congregated in that area of the alley.

They were used to the odor of garbage and rodents, but this was much harsher than discarded food or diapers, more severe than the combination of dead rodents and dog feces.

As Perry and Terry approached the back of the decomposing wood that once sheltered Ms. Frazier's Dodge, they realized that whatever it was that Wrecks wanted was covered by cardboard boxes, milk crates and a few garbage bags.

Perry, the more outgoing of the identical twins, cautiously made his way to the pile of trash leading from the oblique structure. Terry grabbed Wrecks by his collar and pulled the excited Shepherd back, but the dog continued to wildly express his feelings about the pile of rubbish.

The curious teen threw aside two crates and several trash bags. He then reached for the long cardboard strip that lay atop whatever it was that his dog was trying to reach. Perry hesitated; he peered at his brother, who continued to struggle with the dog. Terry nodded, prompting his twin brother to redirect his attention back to the discarded trash.

Perry let out the breath that he'd been holding, then inhaled once again, as if he were bracing himself. When he pulled the cardboard back, his eyes opened as wide as an owl's, and he nearly jumped out of his skin. Paralyzed, his mouth suspended open, the teen turned just in time to see Terry screaming while running in a terrified outbreak with flailing limbs.

The confused dog barked and howled while jumping up and down, as if he were trying to tell both boys, *I told you so.*

❂❂❂

The story, as written by Darwin Washington of the *Michigan Chronicle*, was the first thing that caught my eye as I sat at the kitchen table with the paper and a cup of coffee. The hideous murder of a young woman and the discovery of her body by two young boys overshadowed the nervous excitement I felt.

This was to be an historic day, a day that defined my journey—but it would mean nothing if I couldn't make a difference. My city was living up to its billing as the "murder capital." I was disgusted with the direction in which the city was headed. For the second consecutive year, we had been given a tag reflecting the ultimate crime, the sin of all sins.

People were moving from a city that was portrayed as a place that was not safe to raise a family. It was reported that one could not walk the streets without having to look over their shoulders. Although it was the truth, I didn't want to accept it. But that truth was in the paper every day.

I folded the day-old newspaper before my eyes veered toward the wall clock. It was time for me to get ready for my first day. I was still a little tired from the celebration the previous night, but I had to do what I had to do. Still in my robe, I rose to my feet, finished my coffee and headed for the shower.

❂❂❂

I stood at the corner of Macomb and Beaubien, marveling at a building that is as well known in Detroit by its address as the White House is in Washington, D.C. I couldn't help but be reminded that the architectural makeup of the "Motor City" could be attributed to the same man who constructed the nine-story edifice towering before me.

There is literally no place where you can go in my hometown without seeing Albert Kahn's contributions. In 1923, Kahn, the son of German immigrants, completed construction of this particular building at 1300 Beaubien.

I was a hardheaded, rambunctious youngster who grew up in the jungles of a declining metropolis. However, hearing that address briefly made *me* think twice about the direction in which my life was headed.

In my youth, Detroit Police Headquarters was no joke, not even for someone who was said to have been as hard and incorrigible as myself. The traffic entering and exiting this building was, and continues to be, as consistent as New York's Penn Station.

It was said that you could enter the station looking like Elvis, but exit with the face of the Elephant Man. Back in the day, police brutality allegations weren't brought to light by the media, as it would be today, so everything that you heard was word of mouth—an "urban legend," you might say.

The horror stories surrounding the complex were enough to dissuade most of the youth of my time from a life of crime, but it served as a badge of honor for the young hoodlums of Herman Gardens, the housing development where I grew up. In my 'hood, your street credibility was enhanced if you survived being taken to 1300 Beaubien.

"Scoey…is that you? Hey, man. Yo…Scoey…help a brother out. You a judge now, man…get me out of this."

With the activity taking place in front of police headquarters, and the spots in my eyes created by God's lamp, I couldn't identify who was trying to reach out to me from my hoodlum days. No one had called me by my nickname in years, so I immediately used my hand to fend off the blazing noon sun in an effort to identify the person who screamed out a moniker that very few knew.

It wasn't until I saw the doors to headquarters open that I noticed.

He stood six feet five inches tall. His dark-chocolate skin tone and shiny bald head, along with his muscular physique, reminded me of actor Tommy "Tiny" Lister.

I couldn't remember the brother's name, but he was so big that two sets of cuffs were used to secure his hands behind his back. The arrogant high school dropout, sporting a white Tommy Hilfiger track suit, was being dragged into the station by two of Detroit's finest.

For years the brother had worked as an enforcer for one of the most notorious drug suppliers in the city. Funny thing is, that drug dealer was once a very close personal friend of mind.

Andre's *yes man* was one of the guys who followed Dre's way of life instead of searching for his own. Andre was somewhere in the federal system doing fifteen to thirty, and his subordinate looked to be on his way to a reunion.

Andre and I first met in the Seventh-day Adventist Church that I was forced to attend by my God-fearing mother. *God rest her soul.* At one time we were really close; our criminal destinies mirrored each other—until mine took a turn into Judge Kaufman's courtroom.

The day that the judge told me to get my GED, or go to jail, was the day that my friendship with a man who would eventually come to be known as Detroit's most notorious narcotics dealer began to drift.

Any chance of me remembering the guy's name that shouted out my childhood label was circumvented by a uniformed officer's inquiry as he shoved his open notepad in my face. "Hey…aren't you Judge Mathis?"

A slow nod of acknowledgment was all he needed.

"Can I have your autograph?"

It was hard for me to imagine that several years prior I was signing a personal property form given to detainees after they'd been released. Now, I found myself signing autographs for the very people for which I had disdain as a youth.

"I wanted to congratulate you on having won a seat on the Thirty-Sixth District. No one thought that someone with your record would stand a chance. Especially since your incumbent held that seat for over twenty years," the officer conveyed.

I slyly snuck a peek at the law enforcement officer's nametag before I responded. "Thank you so much, Officer Roby…"

I scribbled my name on his pad, then handed the officer my autograph.

Roby stuffed the notepad in the back pocket of his blue uniform before he continued, "Judge Mathis…your campaign was a bit unorthodox…but it was the reason that I voted for you. I'm thinking about running for Wayne County Sheriff. Since you ran your campaign on very little money, I could use your advice."

"It's really about your constituency. You can always find a way to reach them without spending a lot of money. Use the *grass-roots* approach. Get out there and knock on doors, meet with your constituency. Listen to their concerns and tell them how you would go about addressing them."

The heat was beginning to take its toll on me. I loosened the black-and-gray tie that I had chosen to accent the pin stripes in my black, double-breasted suit.

"We started our drive for that seat several months before anyone else because I had a lot to overcome. I was confident in my chances of pulling off an upset; despite my criminal background."

I extended my hand to the inquisitive policeman. "I'm sorry…but I'm late for an appointment with Commander Daly."

Roby shook my hand. "Thank you for taking the time to chat with me… and once again, congratulations, Judge Mathis."

Being addressed as "judge" was still new to me. A prideful smile instantly materialized. "I thank you for your support."

❁❁❁

Commander Ronald Daly, with his bifocals resting on the end of his nose like a perturbed schoolteacher, sat at his desk sipping on a cup of java. This gray-headed, twenty-five-year law enforcement officer of Irish ancestry had played a big part in my conversion from criminal to judge. It was his arrest of me that culminated in my standing before Judge Kaufman. So you can imagine how I felt when informed that he was unable to attend my celebratory function the previous evening.

"Judge…why are you pacing? You're gonna wear a hole in my carpet. What could you possibly be worried about? The campaign is over and you've just been elected the youngest judge in the state."

When the police commander realized that his statement fell on deaf ears, he whispered, "Judge, what's wrong?"

Daly's concern was evident. The short, heavyset head of Special Crimes rose to his feet, removed his glasses, and headed toward me as I continued trying to get a grip on my situation.

Being a judge can make one feel that the weight of the world is on his or her shoulders. Taking on the responsibilities of deciding one's fate after they've committed a criminal act is no small task, even if the statute is clearly defined. As a judge, you sometimes use your digression on whether the offender stands a chance at rehabilitation without incarceration; and I thank God that I was given that chance. So, I totally understood what I was getting into, and appreciated the responsibilities. But what I wasn't cognizant of was how family and so-called friends would try and take advantage of my new position.

Daly placed his stubby hands on my tension-filled shoulders. "Talk to me, son. Are you upset with me because I couldn't make it last night?"

When I directed my attention toward him, I had every intention of opening up, but for some reason I chose subterfuge.

"Yes…I was a little blown away that you couldn't attend. But I got over it when I realized how much time you put into my campaign." I paused for several seconds while gazing into his compassionate green eyes, and then I rambled. "Ron...you promised that you would accept my lunch invitation. You and Jesse Jackson had a lot to do with me getting elected. Jesse is not around. I can't extend an invitation to him, so it's you and me."

"Judge, the pacing; the intense look, the wondering eyes... I know all of that was not about me going to lunch with you."

I knew that my hunched shoulders and awkward expression wouldn't convince the professional investigator that I was oblivious to what he was alluding to. I also knew that he wouldn't press me about what was really on my mind; he would allow me to open up when I was ready.

I mumbled, "Grab your jacket and let's go get a bite to eat."

My friend didn't budge until I dropped eye contact. Commander Daly walked over, then grabbed the green blazer to his J.C. Penney single-breasted suit, which was draped over the back of his seat.

Daly wasn't a frill-and-thrills kind of guy. He would have been happy picking up a hot dog from a vendor. Because of his low-key attitude, I wouldn't dare tell him that I had made lunch reservations at the Pontchartrain Hotel, because I knew he would have objected. The Pontchartrain has one of the finest restaurants in the business district of the city—it's definitely not a place that Daly would frequent.

The restaurant was packed when we arrived. As the maitre d' escorted us to our table, Daly noticed Tommy "Hit Man" Hearns having lunch with several patrons.

Now, in the decade or so that I'd known Daly, I'd only seen him excited on two occasions: when I won the election, and the night that he and I watched as Hearns defeated Virgil Hill for the WBA light heavyweight championship title. The commander was a big Hearns fan, so you can imagine his reaction upon spotting the "Hit Man" pouring A1 sauce on a porterhouse steak. He was like a child seeing Santa Claus for the first time.

"Judge...look over there." Daly eagerly pointed toward the far end of the establishment. "It's the 'Hit Man.' Let's go over and say hi."

I put my hand on his shoulder before whispering, "Ron, let the man eat. Besides, I need your advice about something."

It must have been the look in my eyes, but Daly was no longer interested in shaking the hand of the man that he considered, pound for pound, the best fighter on the planet.

We made ourselves comfortable at our table before the maitre d' placed menus before us. "I'll give you gentlemen a few minutes to look over the menus. Would you like coffee?" she asked, while filling our glasses with water.

Daly picked up his list of lunch options. "Yes…black, no sugar."

"No, thank you," I replied as she turned her attention toward me.

When she stepped away, Daly, from behind his menu, began the conversation with small talk. "You didn't have to bring me to such a fancy place." He flipped the page before he continued, "By the way…wasn't this supposed to be your first day presiding over cases?"

"Yeah, but I decided to postpone my docket. I wanted to sit in on my colleagues to see if I could pick up some pointers. I plan on doing the same thing after lunch."

Placing my menu atop the white lacy tablecloth, I interlocked my fingers and rested my elbows atop the table before getting straight to the point.

"Ron, I have a close family member who's dealing crack. I realize that as an officer of the court I have an obligation to report this, but I think that I might be able to fix it before it goes too far."

Daly spoke matter-of-factly while placing his menu next to his water glass. "Be sure that the way you handle this is above reproach. The press is already talking about your criminal past and how you should not have been allowed to hold your seat. You don't need them thinking that you're using your position to cover for family. Judge…you know damn well they'll equate this situation to you still having criminal ties, especially if they find out that you had knowledge—and didn't report it."

He spoke the truth. The talk going on around town was that it wouldn't take long for me to become a corrupted judge. I knew in my heart what I had to do—and I knew that I had to do it fast.

While I was soaking in the commander's words, his text pager went off. Daly's message was urgent, so we had to leave the restaurant before having a chance to order.

That wasn't a good thing for me, because I was extremely hungry. So, I grabbed breadsticks from the basket atop the table just so I could have something to snack on.

As we made our way back to 1300, Daly informed me that a drug dealer had been arrested on assault charges—and that his victim was in stable condition. I didn't understand why a routine assault case had required us to miss lunch.

Immediately upon stopping at a traffic light, I directed my attention toward my passenger. "Ron, what's so urgent about a routine assault case?"

"A few days ago, we got a call that a citizen had run across the decapitated body of a black female. We found the head yesterday in an alley three blocks from where we discovered the body. The dealer that was picked up today wants to make a deal. He wants to provide us with the name of the person responsible for this crime...but he won't speak to anybody but you."

My response made it obvious that I was baffled. "Yeah...I read about that in the *Chronicle*. But why the hell would he ask to speak to me?"

"He says that he knows you—and he won't say a word to anyone but you."

❋❋❋

Immediately upon returning to headquarters, Daly escorted me to a room about as big and just as drab as an eight-by-ten cell. I was asked to wait in the room typically used to conduct formal, thorough investigative questioning, for a chance to speak with someone. Whomever it was felt they could lead authorities to the individual responsible for the decapitation of a female crack addict. I was puzzled. Why did this person refuse to speak to law enforcement; and even more puzzling, why did he feel that he needed to speak with me?

During my time alone, I realized that I was absorbing a third mental view of the walls around me. Recollections of being a teenaged knuckle-head, who spent the majority of his youth being grilled in a room like the very one I was seated in, caused me to shake my head. It was a moment of disbelief.

From a youth offender, to a defense attorney, and now a judge—from the one being questioned, to the one asking the questions, and now, the one mediating, my evolution was truly a blessing, and I knew that my mother was proud.

I regret that I'd spent so much time disappointing a woman who did nothing short of her best in trying to raise my three brothers and me. Giving her a hard time at every turn was something I wish I hadn't done. She worked hard; two jobs most of the time. All she ever expected from us was that we did our best, and that we believed and trusted in God.

My mother always brought a sense of comfort to my siblings and me, so you can imagine that my biggest regret came when she informed me that she had cancer, and I was unable to bring comfort to her, because I was locked up.

"Momma, I did what I promised the day you told me you had cancer. I promised you that I would change. I did…I changed…and I'll make you another promise. I'll help as many people as I can," I whispered, hoping that if she didn't hear my declaration, that God himself would pass it along to her.

Before I had a chance to go into prayer, the door opened.

Daly escorted into the room the cuffed suspect of a drug-related assault case. Entering the interrogation room was the man responsible for interrupting our lunch. He was also the same man who had shouted out my nickname, as he was being forced into headquarters upon my arrival.

Daly led him over to a small desk that was positioned between me and another chair. At that moment, his name finally hit me. "Eugene Scott," I mumbled under my breath.

"What up, Scoey? How's it going, baby?" the mammoth drug dealer inquired as he lifted his cuffed wrists toward the head of Special Crimes, hoping the officer would remove his restraints. His beady, dark-brown, bloodshot eyes caused the police officer to hesitate.

Daly glanced at me. A quick head gesture alerted my friend that I felt safe, so he removed the handcuffs. Eugene immediately began to rub both of his wrists in an effort to get the blood flowing. The pusher of illegal narcotics, then extended a hand to me. "You done good, man. I mean… with yo life and everything."

I got to my feet; we shook hands. "Eugene, besides the obvious, what's going on with you? The last time I saw you was during Jesse Jackson's campaign."

We both took a seat before Eugene continued, "I know. Me and Dre were in the club when you came in passing out flyers."

"Yeah, you boys thought it was a joke back then." I crossed my legs and waited for him to open up. I never really liked him. I knew that he was aware of that fact, so I was even more curious to know why he wanted to speak with me.

Eugene sat back before crossing his legs.

"I guess the joke was on us." He glanced over at Daly, then back at me, an obvious signal for me to clear the room.

I directed my attention toward the officer. "Ron, would you give us a couple of minutes, please?"

"I don't know about that," Daly said with concern.

I made eye contact with my friend. "It's okay, Ron."

Eugene waited for Daly to exit before he would uncross his legs. The new kingpin sat forward and rested his arms atop the table. He glanced at the two-way mirror before he whispered, "Scoey…what can you do to get me out of this?"

I paused several seconds before asking, "What do they have on you?"

"Possession with the intent…and assault. This punk-ass bitch tried to short me, so I beat the shit out of him." He once again allowed his eyes to veer toward the mirror before he continued, "My attorney tried to make a deal with that prick from the DA's office, but he said that he had me on some three-strike shit."

"So you're trying to use the information you have about that woman to make a deal with the DA's office?"

The dope dealer stood and nonchalantly made his way to the mirror. He stared at it as if he were trying to look through to the other side. The conceited taskmaster began to toy with his thinly trimmed mustache before whispering, "Yeah…but Sanders's white ass said that he wouldn't give me a deal. He said that he didn't care about no crackhead losing her head—no pun intended. He also said that I was more of a coup for him. That man don't give a shit about what goes on in the 'hood... I need you to pull some strings."

I was incensed. "What...look here. I'm not about to try and pull any strings for you or anybody else. You sell drugs to women and children in the 'hood. You claim you have information that could help the police get a sick bastard off the streets, but you won't say anything unless it benefits you. It's all about *you*...So don't go telling me that some ADA doesn't care about what goes on in the community...when you're the one killin' the 'hood." I got to my feet before I continued, "If pulling strings for you is why you asked to speak to me, then you wasted a phone call."

As I headed for the door, I had one more thing that needed to be said. "Eugene...for once, do something for someone else besides Dre or yourself. The person who decapitated that woman is sick. Help the police to get his ass off the streets."

"Fuck you, Scoey..." Eugene countered in anger, while peering at my reflection in the mirror.

That arrogant bastard continued grooming himself as I left, as if he were preparing for a night out on the town.

Upon returning to Daly's office, I explained to the police commander that there was nothing I could do to convince Eugene Scott to cooperate with law enforcement.

The veteran cop handed me the file on Sheila Morgan. Immediately upon opening the folder, I had to take a seat. Nothing in my criminal past had prepared me for what my eyes were viewing. I could barely stomach the crime scene photographs.

"Oh my God, Ron... Reading about someone being decapitated, then actually looking at photographs depicting it... I gotta say, I have a new respect for you guys," I declared while thumbing through the collection of high-quality, graphic pictures.

Daly made himself comfortable on the edge of his desk. He pointed at the snapshot I was holding. "What sticks out to you in this photo?"

I examined the picture for several seconds, and believe you me, if I had eaten, my lunch would have been all over Ron Daly's office.

I briefly glanced up at my friend before redirecting my attention toward the poor woman whose headless torso lay sprawled out, half naked, in an alley. "What is it that you want me to see?"

"Blood…where is the blood?" Daly countered as he placed his finger on the depiction of the woman's body. "With the carotid being severed, there should be blood all around here."

My eyes widened. "So, she was murdered someplace else, and her body dumped here."

"We haven't been able to locate where the murder was actually committed. We came up with absolutely nothing within the first forty-eight hours, which decreases our chances of ever solving this case without someone coming forward. Right now, Eugene Scott is our only lead. If we can't get him to talk, I'm afraid that this case is going to go cold," Daly said as he got up and walked over to his picture window.

My friend didn't have the answers, and that was killing him. With his back to me, while staring out the window at a city he loved, Daly continued, "I can't get ADA Sanders to budge."

After getting to my feet, I responded, "I don't know him. As an attorney I handled juvenile cases." I closed the folder and placed it atop Daly's desk. "Let me see what I can do."

THE PACKAGE

The premium-grade, wall-length, red-stained woodwork. The genuine black leather furniture, the small built-in bookcase to the right of my desk, and a full-wall-length cherry oak entertainment center on the left side. The large beautiful picture window that allowed sunlight to introduce the décor made it clear that my chambers were missing but one thing, my personal touch.

The plaques, certificates and diplomas that I'd earned, along with photographs of me and several prominent political powerhouses, had to be strategically hung, so I spent the first fifteen minutes upon my return from lunch playing interior designer.

After hanging the last photograph, which depicted me posing with Coleman Young, who served as mayor of Detroit for two decades, I stepped back and marveled at my surroundings.

A sense of pride overwhelmed me; I was very proud of what I had achieved.

At that moment, a strange, yet wonderful cosmic-like energy filled the air. It felt as if someone, or something, had wrapped a loving arm around me. A sense of comfort besieged my being. I whispered with all sincerity while continuing to scan my chambers, "Momma…you're here, aren't you? I feel you."

Without warning, a tear found its way out of the corner of my eye. My mother was proud. I could truly feel her love. The tear slowly continued down my face before I would give in to the feeling. "I love you, too."

After a brief moment of reflection, I made myself comfortable at my desk and began going over motions in an effort to prepare for the following day. It would be my first day presiding over cases.

I hadn't been a judge long enough to assemble my own staff, so two individuals were assigned to me from the clerical pool. One of the designated clerks entered my chambers with documents and a manila envelope in hand. She walked over and placed the papers and bulky package atop the beautiful oak desk left behind by my predecessor.

The list that Maggie Thornton had laid before me was a comprehensive breakdown of the thirty-one judges elected to fill the seats in the 36th District. I pushed up on my reading glasses and began to carefully scan the spreadsheets.

While watching as I went over her work, Maggie communicated, "Those printouts list the judges slated to preside over cases this afternoon, along with the prosecutors who are scheduled to represent the people of Wayne County during this afternoon's sessions."

Maggie waited for several seconds before she politely asked, "How was lunch, Judge Mathis?"

"Didn't have a chance to eat," I half-heartedly responded as I continued to use my finger to guide me through the documents.

"Hmm... okay, here we go."

Looking up over my glasses toward my diligent temporary assistant, I continued, "Maggie, please, take a seat. Tell me what you know about ADA Geoffrey Sanders..."

Maggie sat and relaxed in one of the two chairs positioned in front of my desk. Although she was conscientious and methodical, for over two years she'd found herself buried in the clerical pool, serving as a temp replacement for the assigned legal assistants who were out sick or on vacation.

The clerk who was assigned to me had graduated from the University of Chicago Law School, but the young woman looked as if she were summa cum laude from RNU (Revenge of the Nerds University). Her plain Jane, nerdish appearance led to rumors that she lacked confidence and passion. These assertions were the raison d'être which most judges used to justify not extending her an opportunity on their staff. So it was no surprise that the chief judge made it a point to have her assigned to me.

He didn't like me, and he certainly didn't like the fact that I now occupied the office of his poker buddy of twenty years. It was made obvious that the chief judge didn't feel that I should hold the position for which I was elected. He let it be known that the citizens of Wayne did the county a disservice by electing someone with my past.

His first attempt at disrupting the success of my office was assigning me the two clerks whom he felt were the weakest in the pool. My guess was that her early-nineteenth-century librarian disguise also had something to do with it. The thick oval glasses which overwhelmed her colorless face, and her silky brunette hair being pushed back into a bun made her stealth-like. She came in under the radar—no one seemed to be able to get past her appearance. If they had, then I'm certain that they had been able to see what I saw. Upon meeting Maggie, I could tell that she was going to be invaluable.

"As you know, the men and women who take on the responsibility of representing the People in our judicial process are a competitive bunch. Nevertheless, just as in any profession, the dedication level of these individuals varies. Geoff Sanders is District Attorney Monahan's obvious choice when it comes to spearheading high-profiled cases—he's considered one of the more feared members of the district attorney's office. I don't see him as being loyal to Monahan, though. I think that everyone but Monahan knows that he wants to be district attorney."

She smiled at me. "Can I be blunt, sir?"

"Always…"

"He's a true asshole, Judge Mathis. But he's considered a tough-minded and aggressive legal wizard. As far as cases, he never takes pleas. He'd rather not prosecute a case if making a deal is required…and he won't initiate an indictment if he doesn't feel that he has a slam-dunk. So, he and the police have bumped heads on many occasions. If they were unable to gather sufficient evidence, Sanders would ride them until they came up with what he deemed necessary to prosecute, if you know what I mean."

I was curious. I knew what she was insinuating, but I wanted to hear her say it. "So you're telling me that he would prosecute with tainted evidence?"

"If he feels that he could win…and get away with it."

I had to let her know that she was pushing the envelope. "Those are very strong accusations."

"I'm not the one making them. I've worked for enough judges around here to know how they feel toward some of the cases that he's prosecuted. They themselves can't prove that he's done anything unethical. But some of the evidence that he's presented has raised eyebrows. While some of his evidence has been considered questionable by the appellate court, none has been reversible under appeal."

My new clerk's appearance wouldn't exactly induce confidence that she could be an aggressive litigator, but anyone would have been impressed by her knowledge of jurisprudence.

"Maggie, why haven't you taken the bar exam?"

"To tell you the truth, Judge Mathis, I'm scared. My two years working here have tested my resolve. I truly believe that I would pass the bar on my first try, but what do I do after? When I first got out of law school, I couldn't make up my mind whether I wanted to work as a defense attorney, or for the prosecutor's office. Now, I question whether I want to practice law at all."

"Why?" I asked. I thought I knew the answer; the look in her blue eyes spoke volumes. It seemed that she lacked faith in the individuals responsible for maintaining judicial integrity.

"When winning becomes the prosecutor's and defense attorney's main focus, then true justice takes a back seat to what our forefathers had in mind when faced with signing the Constitution. Since I've worked here, I've seen a handful whose prosecutorial conduct has weighed heavily on Lady Justice. They made it difficult for her to keep the scales of impartiality balanced. So, do you work as a prosecutor and put the innocent in jail because of evidence you know is tainted, or work as a defense attorney and try to free a person you know to be guilty? I don't know which is worse out of the bunch—the defense attorneys, or the prosecutors."

I removed my glasses before sitting back in my butter-soft leather chair. Maggie Thornton was someone whom the legal profession could not afford to lose; her dilemma was something I was very familiar with. Having dealt with life on the wrong side of the law, my perspective was all encompassing, so I felt she needed to hear it from me.

"Maggie, as you know, they're both a necessary evil. In my case, as a youth offender, I clearly relied on the defense attorney to represent me with all the vigor that he could, whether it meant that he had to stretch the boundaries of law, or not—because I felt that I was just another statistic to the prosecutor. He was going to do what he had to do in order to put another black man behind bars. But, who would have thought that my saving grace would be a judge? When I stood before Judge Kaufman, in this very building, I had no clue what to expect."

I spent several minutes edifying Maggie on Judge Kaufman's profound influence on my life's course, and what his decision, which forced me to get my GED, meant. Kaufman also changed the way in which I viewed White folk; he made me think twice about the conspiracy theories I was convinced besieged our nation.

I stood, then walked over to my coat rack and grabbed the matching blazer to my suit. "As a youth, I was certain that the bureaucrats who made up the hierarchy of our judicial system had one agenda—to confine as many young Black men as possible."

While putting on my jacket, I continued, "Laws had been adjusted to effect more stringent punishments for offenses known to be prevalent in African-American communities.

"As a teen, I was very much aware of Whites who had been convicted of murder getting less time than some of my homeboys who had been convicted of distributing narcotics. Thus, my conspiracy theory, that the government would do anything to ensure the destruction of Black men.

"But, Kaufman's unorthodox way of handling the law gave me a new perspective. He inspired me to put myself in the position to do the same. He made me feel that White America as a whole was not plotting against me. Maggie, change comes from within. Okay, you've seen things around here that you don't agree with, but they'll go on if you don't put yourself in a position to initiate change."

I fiddled in wonderment with the long black robe that hung from my coat rack. The majesty was captivating. Although I found myself lost in its aura, I managed to say, "Look, I want you to ask me questions, follow me around…and after a while of working with me, if you still aren't sure about law being your life's destiny, I'll do my best to help you with anything else that you decide to do."

Surprise and excitement infused her reply. "Are you saying that you're offering me a position on your staff?"

I directed my attention toward Maggie. The look of appreciation was in her eyes—her excitement was refreshing.

"If you can be true to yourself and commit to helping me stay grounded, the job is yours on a permanent basis."

I felt that she was receptive to my suggestion. She had a smile that stretched from ear to ear. "I'm going to sit in on Judge Kelly. After the trial, I'm going home, so I'll see you in the morning."

"You'll get a chance to see Geoff Sanders. He's prosecuting a murder case in her courtroom, but I guess you saw that on the spreadsheets."

Maggie stood before she continued, "Thank you so much, Judge Mathis, for extending me an opportunity."

Call me crazy, but it seemed as if my new assistant was flirting with me from behind the fish bowls that covered her eyes.

It wasn't until Maggie left my chambers that I remembered the package she'd left on my desk. I curiously picked up the envelope and examined it. It was addressed to me, but there wasn't any postage. My name was type-written, and there wasn't a return address. The item inside the package felt familiar. I opened, and then pulled from it a VHS cassette tape; a white envelope, which obviously included a letter; and a note.

I immediately turned my attention to the note. It read:

Before you view the tape or read the letter, it is important that you follow the instructions contained in this note. First, you should view this tape in private. Second, please don't read the contents of the white envelope until you have viewed the tape.

After reading the simple instructions, I picked up the tape and stared at it. I wondered whether it was some sort of new-judge orientation that no one had bothered to tell me about; or for that matter, some kind of hazing from the judges who sat on the bench of the 36th District. At that moment, I had nothing but conjecture, but the latter brought about a smile because if it were some sort of initiation—that meant that I wouldn't be working with a bunch of stiff shirts, which was my initial assumption upon being sworn in. Then again, depending on the type of prank, I could have been walking straight into hell.

Enough was enough. I didn't have Superman-type X-ray vision, nor did I possess the ability of foresight by touch, so I walked over to my entertainment center and pushed the tape into my VCR. I turned on the television, picked up the remote from atop the TV, and returned to my seat.

❂❂❂

The bedroom was shrouded in pink lace. Scented candles of various colors and dimensions were strategically placed throughout. A beautiful orange-blue illumination flickered unsteadily at the tip of their wicks. Two champagne flutes sat on a nightstand next to a bucket containing a chilled bottle of Dom Perignon: The ambience was set.

Shadowy figures, which were created by a variety of stuffed animals, seemed to dance about the walls. Stunning, well-placed trinkets adorned the shelves and dressers. Decorative fluffy pillows lay atop a black silk bedspread. The décor left no doubt that the bedroom belonged to a woman.

Without warning, the door was forced open.

Stumbling through the entrance were the elongated shadows of two people entangled in an embrace. The silhouettes, which were cast on the walls, were without a doubt sharing a very passionate moment. The figures spun and twisted their way toward the bed as if they were dancing an erotic waltz.

The pair began seductively jostling at each other's clothing, disrobing one another, as they got closer to their destination. The profiles continued to display sensuality as the shadowy outline of a garment flew to the left, followed by another piece of attire tossed to the right.

What was obviously the silhouette of a very shapely female, pushed her dance partner, forcing him to fall backward onto the bed. She stood before the man who lay atop the black silk that was draped over the queen-sized mattress and seductively removed her bra. The image of a full set of perky breasts cased a shadow on the wall.

The woman straddled her lover and began planting soft tender kisses over his body.

"Okay...what the hell is this," I said with interest. I wanted to fast-forward the tape so that I could get an understanding of what was going on. But I decided that I needed to be patient and let the tape play out. I watched a no-holds-barred exchange of intimacy, but because of the camera's angle, I was unable to see the participants' faces, which was a bit frustrating. I convinced myself that whoever wanted me to see the video was more interested in me knowing that the two depicted in the tape were involved, rather than me playing witness to the entire encounter—so I decided to fast-forward.

I stopped the tape at a point where the two individuals who were knocking boots had gotten out of bed and were standing in front of a dresser mirror. I could clearly see Assistant District Attorney Carolyn Otto, but couldn't immediately make out the man who was standing behind her. He had his arms draped around Carolyn's nakedness while kissing her neck.

I picked up the white envelope and split my attention between the letter and my television. I still didn't fully comprehend what the hell was taking place—the sex part was clear; but I didn't have an understanding of why someone would think that I would be the least bit interested in who Carolyn Otto was fucking.

Just as the mysterious man looked up is when I was taken aback. At that moment, I wanted so badly to open up the envelope. I thought to myself, *why shouldn't I open it—there is no one in my chambers but me?*

I pulled the paper from its wrapper, unfolded it, and began to read:

Judge Mathis, if you're reading this letter, then you have viewed the tape of your friend Mr. Gram Olson. His affair with ADA Otto is something that will ruin him in a lot of ways. Now, I know that you must be saying to yourself, what does this have to do with me? Well, it's like this. I know that you don't care what people say about you because your life is an open book. But you have a propensity to throw caution to the wind when it comes to your friends. I know how close of a friendship you have with Gram Olson, and we both know what will happen to Gram's marriage, and his standing in the business community, if this tape is leaked to the media, and/or to his wife. After all, Gram's power is a direct result of his wife's purse strings.

Now, here's where you come in. I have a few things that you must do. Only someone in your position is capable of seeing that these things are accomplished. I don't want money; after all, if that were what I was after, I would have sent this package to Gram Olson himself.

Judge Mathis, I also realize that your first thoughts will be to not look at the big picture... But I assure you that this is something that you need to take serious, because it will have great implication, not only for your friend, but for you as well. I'll be in contact when I need you. It could be tomorrow, next week, or next month—who knows. But I will be in touch soon.

He was a good-looking man with a lot of money, and with money came power, so it stood to reason that women came on to him—albeit they were aware that his fortune was a result of his marriage to Barbara. Upon his father-in law's death, my friend's wife handed over to him the reins to the entire Poindexter empire, which instantly catapulted Gram into Camelot status.

With his newfound prominence, Barbara Olson's husband became a very influential force in business, as well as the political arena. Gram was a very powerful man because of his beautiful wife, so I was surprised to see that he would take a chance on giving all of that up just for a night with Carolyn Otto.

When I witnessed her intimately stroking at his chest in a dark corner of Cobo Arena the previous night, I thought that he would surely put her in her place. Women far more attractive than the assistant district attorney had attempted to seduce him; I knew that as a fact. Although she was beautiful, I was certain that he wouldn't allow that black widow to ruin his marriage. But I guess I was wrong. Thing is, I thought that Gram was smarter than that. His wife was one of the kindest, most generous people that I knew, and she loved her husband to no end. She was the key to his power, to his ability to move heaven and earth. If she found out about his adultery, it would be like Superman being hit with Kryptonite; Gram would lose all of his power.

"Carolyn, this can't happen again," he said as he stood by her bed while putting on his pants.

"What do you mean? It's not like I'm asking you to leave your wife."

Like a naked Cleopatra, Carolyn lay on her stomach atop the black silk which covered her bed. She crisscrossed her legs like a teen at a slumber party while grazing at Gram as he adjusted his belt.

"Look, I made a mistake. I disrespected too many people tonight. This was Greg's night… and I leave his reception and go home with you. Then my wife…I love her so much. I've never done anything like this before. She doesn't deserve this." The sincerity of his words was evident. He lowered his head in shame and stood motionless for several seconds. At that moment, I felt for him— he'd made a mistake, and he was beating himself up.

"Who gives a damn about Greg Mathis?"

Gram angrily grabbed the jacket to his tuxedo, which was draped across a white chaise positioned in the corner of her bedroom. *"You see, that's another thing. I can't spend time with you knowing that you hate one of my dearest friends. I'd do anything for Greg."*

I stopped the video, picked up the note, and began to wonder what the hell was going on. For approximately two minutes, my mind was a complete blank. Seeing Gram susceptible, unable to pull himself free of Otto's web in time to prevent the biggest mistake of his life, was upsetting to me.

A quick glance at my watch and I realized that I had to put Gram's situation on hold if I stood any chance of catching the last part of a trial that was taking place in Judge Karla Kelly's courtroom. But first, I needed to retrieve the tape and put it someplace safe. I also wanted to set up a meeting with Gram; he needed to know what I had.

SHE'S DESERVING

Immediately upon stepping from the elevator, I noticed several reporters huddled around the chief judge as he stood fielding questions in the middle of the hallway. The man was definitely in his element; the senior judge never saw a camera or microphone that he didn't like. He gravitated to the limelight with the ease of a professional athlete.

I played witness to the sixty-six-year-old judicial juggernaut performing his signature move. It was said that at the peak of his arrogance, in all public venues, he would causally run his fingers through his salt-and-pepper hair as if it were the source of his strength, or defined his macho persona.

His self-made public image was Herculean, for sure.

But, my boss wasn't as confident as he would lead one to believe. The chief judge's superior mind-set fit the psychological profile of a man attempting to avenge the ridicule that plagued his adolescence. His short, slender stature and authoritarian attitude reinforced everyone's hypothesis that he suffered from a severe case of Napoleon complex.

Several reporters standing before him noticed me attempt to manipulate my way through the chaos. Three of the journalists immediately maneuvered through the crowd and headed straight toward me.

"Judge Mathis...please...can I have a moment of your time?" someone yelled.

Anticipating an onslaught of questions, I checked my watch—time was on my side, so I stopped. I needed to be accessible, but at the same time,

I didn't want to appear that I was seeking press. I wanted to ensure that my wife and children didn't have a microphone constantly stuck in their faces because I didn't make myself available.

The first to approach were Darwin Washington, a journalist on staff for the only black-run newspaper in the city, *The Michigan Chronicle*; and Carl Croom, a popular home-bred beat writer from the *Detroit Free Press*.

"Judge Mathis, I'm Carl Croom of the *Detroit Free Press*. First, congratulations on unseating someone who was considered to be a hallmark in this building. Of all the seats relinquished to new blood, his was the last that I expected."

"Thank you…" I replied as I slid my right hand into my pants pocket.

Pulling a notepad and pen from the breast pocket of his wrinkled suit, the reporter asked, "Judge Mathis, how does it feel to be elected the youngest judge ever in the State of Michigan?"

He had asked a question that I hadn't really thought about, so I paused for a second before attempting to answer.

"Well, Carl, I'm not sure if I can answer your question intelligently right now…because I haven't really given that much thought. My goal was to win the election—so I'm still basking over the fact that I was sworn in."

Michael Darcell, a Caucasian beat writer from the *Detroit News*, shouted as he forced his way past Washington and Croom, "Judge Mathis…Judge Mathis."

The reporter shoved a tape recorder in my face. "Judge Mathis, I'm Michael Darcell of the *Detroit News*. As an African-American judge with a criminal background, do you think that you'll find it hard to be a judge in cases involving young African Americans?"

How dare he suggest that I couldn't be impartial, I thought to myself. I was a little annoyed with that question, but I wasn't about to run from it.

"I'll apply the law as defined in the statute, on a case-by-case basis, as is the responsibility of every other judge, and not based on race…and I'll use my discretion when appropriate."

I peeked in the direction of Napoleon and could see antipathy emanating from the chief judge's eyes. The man responsible for supervising thirty county judges was clearly upset that I was receiving media attention. He looked at my judgeship as a novelty—one he hoped would quietly fade. He just needed to convince the media that they should ignore it.

At that moment, there was nothing that he could do. The press felt that I was newsworthy. I was the new kid on the block, not just any kid. I was an *Inner City Miracle*, a young man who took full advantage of a second chance. Now I was ready to make a difference.

For a split second, the chief judge and I locked eyes, but I quickly diverted my attention from him and back to the group standing before me.

Something had crossed my mind. I was a bit upset. If I were truly to make a difference I felt that I needed to start at that moment. It was my turn to ask the questions.

"I have a question for you guys. There was a twenty-seven-year-old woman who was decapitated a few days ago. Why aren't you guys running her story? Why aren't you putting any emphasis on her brutal slaying? Is it because she was a drug addict? Do you not believe that her life and death is worthy of coverage? I read the papers every day. The only story about her murder was in the *Chronicle*."

Not waiting for a response, I forced my way past the reporters and headed toward the entrance to Judge Karla Kelly's courtroom.

Room 219 played host to a first-degree murder case that was being prosecuted by Geoff Sanders. It was a tribunal that was closed to cameras, and the jurors had been sequestered for fear of having the verdict affected by public opinion.

The morning session had been adjourned for lunch, so everyone stood outside the courtroom waiting for the trial to reconvene.

I stood at the entrance for several seconds ingesting a new perspective of the courtroom. Closing my eyes, I took a deep breath and released it slowly—that moment was truly surreal.

After opening my eyes, I walked toward the front of the vacant room before taking a seat directly behind the prosecutor's table. I wanted a closeup view of Geoffrey Sanders as he prosecuted this high-profile case. I wanted to see if I could learn his tendency, and I wanted to see if he were really as good as advertised.

While immersed with the thought of sitting on the bench in my own courtroom, someone eased open the door of Room 219. I never turned to see who had entered; my hope was that whomever it was had the decency not to disrupt my daydream. But my optimism was short-lived when a mysterious intruder of contemplation sat directly behind me, and then whispered, "Judge Mathis, I'd like to thank you."

Sincerity was evident in his softspoken statement, which prompted me to slowly turn around to face him. "Thank me for...?"

The heartbroken expression in his eyes touched me. I could see that this man was truly hurting. He dropped eye contact and began to slowly shake his head.

"I didn't get a chance to introduce myself in the hallway. I'm Darwin Washington of the *Michigan Chronicle*."

He looked up, and then extended a hand.

We shook before I responded, "Mr. Washington, why are you thanking me?"

"She was my cousin...it didn't seem as if anyone cared that she was murdered. I've run several stories in the *Chronicle* about her life, and death. My family and I are at our wit's end because the police don't seem at all interested in solving her murder."

I'd spent much of the past hour being dragged into the epicenter of one of the more gruesome murders of my time; and now, seated before me was a family member of the victim. Was this a coincidence—or something spiritual? Whatever it was, I couldn't walk away. I couldn't just act as if there wasn't a reason why this homicide had fallen into my lap.

My mother always told me that God works in mysterious ways, but I would never have imagined anything like this. I think that even my mother would have been questioning this situation.

No more than twenty minutes earlier, I had made a promise that I would help as many people as I could, and I had every intention on living up to that pledge. After all, the very reason that I was in Karla Kelly's courtroom was to observe Geoff Sanders. I needed to try and talk him into making a deal with Eugene Scott. I figured that I would try and talk with the ADA first. If that gesture of respect proved to be unsuccessful, then I would go to his boss.

Meeting one of Sheila Morgan's relatives wasn't something I expected to happen. But, as Momma would say, *"HE WORKS IN MYSTERIOUS WAYS."*

Getting straight to the point, I asked, "Darwin, how long had your cousin been involved with drugs?"

The reporter was pissed at the implication. "What are you talking about? I heard you say that in the hall…," his mind seemed to drift for a split second, "but I wasn't thinking. I haven't been thinking lately…"

Darwin quickly caught himself. With all sincerity, he continued, "My cousin didn't do drugs. We had the damndest time getting her to take prescribed medication. Sheila would never take drugs; she has an aunt who is a junkie."

I realized that the autopsy information hadn't been released to the public, but I was under the impression that the coroner's office had at least informed the victim's family of its findings.

"The coroner's report indicated that she had ingested illegal narcotics—cocaine to be more specific."

Darwin was shocked. He stared at me as if he were under hypnosis. The newspaperman blinked his eyes inquisitively several times before he managed to ask, "How do you know what the autopsy revealed? They haven't released it yet."

Court was to reconvene in a matter of minutes. I had just enough time to explain to Darwin Washington, of the *Michigan Chronicle*, how I'd become involved in his cousin's case. I assured the journalist that the police were working diligently to solve Sheila's murder.

Darwin was angry as hell that his cousin's name was being dragged through the mud. "Judge Mathis, I just wanted you to know that you were wrong about the other papers. They did do a story on her, the day her body was discovered. I think that they were under the impression that she was a prostitute, so they didn't do any follow-ups."

The journalist paused for a brief second before he whispered solemnly, "The stories they ran were done only because of the horrific nature of the crime, and not because of whom she was."

It suddenly hit me why I hadn't seen her story in the *News* or *Free Press*;

her murder was around the time of the election. I hadn't read the paper for a few days because I didn't want to see any negative press.

People started entering the courtroom, so Darwin and I promised that we would continue our dialogue after the trial.

Karla Kelly's courtroom filled up as fast as a Michael Jackson concert, standing room only. I watched as ADAs Sanders and Otto made themselves comfortable at the table directly in front of me. Carolyn immediately noticed me—boy, did I get the evil eye.

I was kind of relieved when the bailiff said the words, "All rise!" because Carolyn was forced to turn her attention toward the woman in the black robe.

The judge of four years looked stoic as she entered, then sat perched in her black leather chair in lawful grandeur. The forty-nine-year-old blonde immediately took control of her surroundings.

Seated next to me was one of the best courtroom artists that I had ever seen. His depiction of the judge and the courtroom as a whole was extremely detailed. I didn't have to look around the jam-packed courtroom in order to know what was going on. I couldn't seem to take my eyes off of the drawing.

The trial that she was presiding over was preparing for deliberation—and she was about to address the jury. Karla Kelly turned her attention toward the jurors. "Ladies and gentlemen of the jury, before we adjourn for deliberation, I'd like to remind you that the defendant has been charged with first-degree murder. Michigan Penal Code, 750.316 states that a person who commits any of the following is guilty of first-degree murder and shall be punished by imprisonment for life.

"Murder perpetrated by means of poison, lying in wait, or any other willful, deliberate, and premeditated killing. If you find that the prosecution has met its burden of proof beyond a reasonable doubt, then you must return a guilty verdict of first-degree murder as brought forth in the indictment."

I didn't get a chance to see Sanders in action, but I was going to make it a point to talk with him after the proceedings.

Prosecutors determine if they have the necessary evidential ammunition to bring forth an indictment against individuals accused of committing a crime. If law enforcement does not provide the necessary evidence, then the prosecutor has the authority to use other methods, such as making deals with the criminal element in order that the proof they require to prosecute is brought forth.

The ADA agreed to stay after the proceedings so that he and I could discuss Eugene Scott. We both made ourselves comfortable at the prosecutor's table. Although we kept our words to a whisper, both of our voices seemed to bounce off the walls of the empty courtroom.

In our discussion about the death of twenty-seven-year-old Sheila Morgan, I found it appalling that the man seated before me didn't feel it necessary to strike a deal with a narcotics dealer in order to identify her assailant.

"Geoff, I don't like it, either, but if Eugene Scott won't say anything without a deal, then at least think about it. The symmetry of our judicial system relies on many things, and we depend on the legal experts who represent the citizens of this county to spearhead that balance. This woman's children and the rest of her family deserve to have the person responsible identified, and prosecuted. The police can't identify that person without your help."

Geoffrey Sanders had served as an ADA for Wayne County for nearly a decade, and rumor had it that the forty-six-year-old Harvard alum was posturing himself to become the head man.

Sanders crossed his legs and leaned back in his chair. He gazed at me in complete silence for several seconds. "Okay, so what did this guy have to say to you?"

"He told me that you wouldn't make a deal."

I studied his expression—he was a hard man to read. I did get the impression that he was an arrogant bastard, so I just went at him. "Why won't you at least agree to talk to him...let's just see what your take is... what you think that he would go for. He might bend if you take the assault with a deadly weapon charge. Or is this case simply not high profile enough for you?"

I could tell that I had rattled his chain, but he was not going to budge. I think I drove him further into his arrogance. "Mathis, I am not going to make a deal with the very person who could have contributed to her addiction. Just as I told your drug-dealing friend, he gets no deal from me."

I needed to be calm. The man had lost his damn mind, but I couldn't allow his ignorance to affect my demeanor. "He's not my friend. Look, Sanders, that woman's family seems to think that the coroner made a mistake on her autopsy. They claim that she didn't do drugs."

"I'm not surprised that they would say that. It's hard for people to deal with family issues like that." The ADA sat up in his chair, and rested his elbows on the table. "Tell me something, why did Eugene Scott refuse to say a word to anyone but you?"

"Evidently, he felt like he was dealing with a bunch of pricks in the DA's office." My sarcasm quickly turned to anger. "How the hell would I know? My God…some sick bastard chopped off the head of a woman who had three children. He left her body in an alley, and then discarded her head several blocks away. If he's capable of killing her…he'll do it again, unless we stop him. "

"Look, Mathis, I don't have to explain myself to you," Sanders insisted as he rose to his feet. He packed his briefcase, and the man never made eye contact—I think he could tell that my eyes would have burned a hole through his soul. The prosecutor closed his brown leather attaché case.

I didn't budge. "First, let's get one thing straight, you arrogant bastard. It's *Judge* Mathis to you. I know that you don't consider that woman as being a person. You think that she sold her body for drugs; you think that she neglected her children because of dope. Even if that were the case, your job is to fight for her rights; she had the right to live. *She's deserving*…you owe it to her family, regardless if you agree with her lifestyle or not…or the color of her skin."

"Wait a minute. Don't you dare try and play the race card with me. My decision to not make a deal with Eugene Scott has nothing to do with race. That woman…"

I quickly interrupted, then demanded that he refer to her by name. "That woman's name is Sheila Morgan. And if it turns out that she was not a drug addict and simply a hardworking mother, there goes your opportunity to be elected DA." I got to my feet, and then stormed out.

RESTLESS NIGHT

The warm breeze's strife with a dull flickering bulb, which dangled from a lamp pole behind several dilapidated dwellings, caught my attention. For a fleeting moment it seemed as if crickets crooned to the fluttering glow that briefly illuminated an otherwise dark alleyway.

I was in an area that was marred in bureaucratic red tape—a place of neglect, poverty, and a sense of hopelessness. There were more abandoned shacks than legally occupied dwellings. I wouldn't hesitate to bet that there were more people occupying the forsaken tenements than in the homes for which taxes were being paid. The desolate individuals who occupied these shacks had already surrendered to their situations. These forlorn families could not care less that they had to be without the basic necessities, like running water, heat, or electricity. They were satisfied to have a roof over their heads.

The neighborhood dumping ground smelled of garbage, rodents, manure, and urine. I even caught whiffs of foul odors that my sensitive nose couldn't distinguish. The eeriness of the atmosphere was unnerving; it was beginning to take a toll on my usually calm demeanor.

The shadowy figure that I was following picked up his pace. He moved with a sense of urgency as he made his way toward a wrecked fence that barely stood upright behind an abandoned house. The silhouette rushed up to the boarded, unkempt property, and headed straight for the basement.

I had secretly followed this person through the trash-filled alley—over broken bottles, around discarded furniture, and past rats as big as full-grown chihuahuas. For some reason, I felt that this individual was the key in solving Sheila Morgan's murder.

The sudden burst of sirens startled me as police cruisers sped through this low-income neighborhood, located on the city's Eastside. Area dogs immediately expressed their objections to the noise created by the marked police cars; their barks and howls unsettled me even more. The residents were obviously accustomed to the blue and red flashing lights, as no one appeared to peek from their windows.

After standing frozen for several seconds, I decided that it was time for me to make my move. I cautiously made my way across the vacant lots toward the gate while keeping a sharp eye out for anything suspicious.

When I touched the fence, it seemed to fall another few inches or so. I was a bit unnerved because I was sure that the noise caused by the enclosure's collapse had alerted the man whom I was following. If the fence hadn't warned him, I was certain that the dogs surely would, as they continued barking, even though the racket created by the police cars, which triggered their aggressive behavior, had subsided.

Upon entering the musty tenement, a place in which the city neglected to demolish, I slowly descended the decaying wooden steps. But, no matter how careful, I couldn't eliminate the creepy Alfred Hitchcock squeaking noise caused by my weight on the weakened flight of stairs. I could see the glow of candlelight, and the shadow of someone as it reflected off the dirty cellar wall. The individual was holding a crack pipe to his lips as he feverishly paced the basement. Upon filling his lungs with poison, the man would react in the true vein of a drug addict, mumbling—while moving his hands erratically.

The man babbled as he continued to pace. "I need to know the number… and you're gonna tell me the number." With junky precision, he placed the pipe back to his lips. He had to flick his cigarette lighter several times before the flint, and what was left of the fluid, would combine to ignite into a barely noticeable flame.

I stood in a dark corner and watched as he inhaled. Several seconds later, he slowly exhaled, filling the area with white smoke. The man was extremely agitated. Suddenly, he stared in my direction. I was sure that he had spotted me. My mind was spinning; what was I going to do if he approached me? I felt that I could take him, but people on drugs have been known to garner supernatural strength. Plus, if he were a killer—someone who could decapitate a human being—then I was in trouble, serious trouble.

"I told you that you gotta give me that bank ATM number, bitch. I ain't playin' with yo ass," he said as he walked over to a corner and knelt.

I was relieved that he didn't see me, but I was curious to know what or whom he was talking to. Like a Navy SEAL in a war zone, I eased closer, and positioned myself to get a better view. To my surprise, bound and gagged, sitting in the corner was a very frightened black female whose face seemed familiar. But I was so caught up in the admission of defeat, which seeped from her dark eyes that I couldn't pinpoint where I had seen her.

"What the hell...what am I gonna do? Shit...I think she spotted me," I whispered to myself before quickly pulling my head back into the cover of darkness. My thoughts spiraled as I nervously contemplated whether I should peek again. I can't lie, I felt panicked.

Her muffled mumbles intensified, and that's when I knew she really did see me. I decided to peek back at her, and when I did, her agitated state besieged my heart. I quickly placed an index finger to my lips; she needed to calm down, because I had to think.

Her eyes were begging for my help. A tear eased its way down her cheek as she continued to struggle.

Without warning, the man began to blow smoke into her face. "I told you, bitch, I need the numbers," he asked while in an obvious state of euphoria. "You gon give 'em to me?"

She nodded her head in compliance.

"Okay, I'ma take the tape off your mouth, if you scream," the man lifted an ax, then reverted back to his demonic demeanor, "I'ma chop your damn head off. You got me?"

With her face covered with fear, she nodded, which sparked the man to violently snatch the tape from his victim's mouth.

"AWWWW..." she screamed in agony. The frantic woman stared in my direction before she yelled, "MISTER...PLEASE HELP ME..."

The man dropped his pipe, immediately erected himself, with both hands firmly gripped on the ax handle. He reared back, then viciously swung, completely severing the woman's head. Blood gushed everywhere as her head fell to the floor and rolled in my direction—her body twitched like a Halloween prop.

"NOOOOOO…." My scream immediately revealed my position.

The unsuspecting ax murderer, without delay, turned his attention toward me. "Who the hell are you? Whatcha doin' here…" He rushed toward me while recklessly flailing his weapon.

I was spooked by the nightmare figure that approached me with lethal purpose. He was like a crazed psychopathic Paul Bunyan. His whirling rage caused my anxiety to swell into panic, so I stepped backward. In my haste to distance myself, I stumbled and fell to the cool, cracked, concrete floor. My eyes veered to his elongated shadow as he stood over me with the ax perched high above his head. I put my arms up in a defensive position, expecting the blood-stained, jagged edge of the cold steel to slice my bones as easily as a knife through melted butter. Closing my eyes, I braced myself for the impact.

Covered with perspiration, my heart beat like a bass drum as I managed to crack open my eyelids just enough to see—nothing. My eyes darted around the room, but I couldn't find him.

As hard as I tried, I couldn't remember what the person wielding the ax looked like; I don't really think that I ever saw his face.

"Shit…" I whispered as I immediately sat straight up and frantically examined my body for injuries.

It took several seconds before I could gather myself and realize that what I had just experienced was instituted by my imagination. Sheila Morgan's horrific murder had played in my head like a Wes Craven film. The dream felt so real—she was asking for my help; she was trying to tell me something.

On the previous day, I'd begun having gained knowledge of Sheila's brutal slaying through a newspaper, but before the sun had a chance to set, I'd found myself smack in the middle of her murder investigation.

My mind was racing at a hundred miles per—anxiety filled my gut. But

Sheila Morgan wasn't the only reason why I had tossed and turned in bed for half the night.

The video I'd received that depicted Otto and Gram was hard for me to expunge from my mind. Someone was going to try and use my friend's situation to gain some sort of favor from me. I wasn't really sure what their plan was—but I was certain that whatever the plan, the blackmail request was bound to be something extremely unethical.

To add to my fretfulness, in a matter of hours, court would convene in Room 201. It would be my first day officially holding a gavel and presiding over cases in Wayne County's 36th District, so I had to find a way to relax. There was no way that I could go into court for the first time without being sharp.

Fluffing my pillow and repositioning my head turned out to be just what the doctor ordered. For a little more than a decade, my source of comfort in times of distress was lying right next to me—my wife, Linda, the love of my life. Linda's presence has always reminded me of how far I have come; she is my source of inspiration.

She looks so cute cuddled up next to me, I thought.

A loving sigh seemed to be the key that started my mind on a comfort journey, a voyage westbound, up I-94 toward Ypsilanti, Michigan. Dropping anxiousness off on the side of the road, this would be a trip sure to relieve the uneasiness that had kept me from sleeping.

My thoughts sped past the signs and markers, which led me from the horrors and worries that plagued my restless night, and directly toward a day that has always put a smile on my face.

It was my sophomore year, 1979, in the recreation room on the campus of Eastern Michigan University. My hustling partner, a guy by the name of Stone, and I were running a three card-Monte scam trying to pick up a few extra bucks to supplement our non-existent income. Stone had just played to the audience, and he'd won a few bucks by picking the red card It was something that he had done every day that we ran the scam.

"All right, who's next? Step up and get yo money. I know that some of you need it... After all, ya'll ain't all got money. Some of ya'll from the hood, too. You know you need this paper," I hollered as I slowly maneuvered the three cards.

Several students stood before me; it seemed as if they were trying to decide whether to risk some cash. I enticingly revealed the red card, hoping this would reel in the big fish. Times were tough, I was barely surviving. I tried to hold a job but it interfered with my studies, so hustling was my only option if I were to continue at Eastern.

This nerdish-looking brother was feeling around in his pants pockets. I smiled because I knew he was digging for cash. "Hey, sir...how 'bout you?"

The guy placed an index finger on the bridge of his glasses. He pushed them back into their proper position before pulling a Lincoln from his pocket. I had already calculated what I was going to do with the five bucks before it hit the table.

"He's going to risk a cool five," I broadcasted while speeding up my pace in maneuvering the cards.

After presenting my mark with the object that could lead him to his prize a final time, I said, "Here's the red card." I then moved the cards so fast that I almost lost track.

With the three cards resting atop the table, I was confident that his eyes had played tricks on his mind. "Okay, big fella, if you pick the red card, you get paid; if not, I get paid."

The guy's four eyes examined the cards as if he had X-ray vision. Thing is, he had no clue. I began to rub my hands together—that dead president was as good as mine. At least until this mini Phylicia Rashad stepped up to the table and flipped over the red card.

"This is it," the foxy co-ed said as she glared at me.

My anger was evident. I blasted, "What the hell you doin'? You ain't got no damn money on the table..."

"You and your boy," she pointed toward Stone, "...been running this scam and taking people's money for a few days. Why don't ya'll get a job or something?"

I countered with a few expletives; I said things to her that no man should say to a woman. And it wasn't as if it were between the two of us. Everyone who played witness had to feel that I was a coward for coming down on her the way I did. With every profanity, my foot went deeper and deeper into my pie hole. At that moment, I wasn't ashamed; I should've been. I was trying to embarrass her because she was taking food out of my mouth.

The fire in my eyes made it impossible for me to see how absolutely gorgeous Linda was; her beauty eluded me due to my rage. It wasn't until I began to calm that a feeling came over me. It was as if I was being told that Ms. Thang was going to have a significant role in my life. So, two days after my initial explosion upon her intervening in my card scheme, I apologized. It was a combination of beauty and her poise under fire that attracted me. From the day of my request for forgiveness, I pursued Linda Reese to no end.

Sleeping was no problem after my mind was ingratiated with thoughts of my wife, lover, confidante and best friend. I slept so well that before the vault of my past could be opened to 1985—the year Linda and I married—my alarm clock went off. It was six a.m., and although I didn't have to be in court for another four hours, I did have an errand to run. So, I would save that wonderful memory, one of the happiest days of my life, until the next time I found it difficult to fall asleep.

My eyes veered from the digital alarm atop my nightstand and toward the empty spot next to me. Linda had already started her day. I could smell the Oscar Mayer bacon she was frying, and the rich aroma of Taster's Choice brewing in the coffeepot. The incredible Mrs. Mathis wanted to ensure that I had a solid breakfast. She knew how busy my day was to be.

During the previous evening, I had explained to her my intentions of meeting up with Darwin Washington at the coroner's office. It shocked her of how the reporter had lost his cousin in one of the more horrific crimes ever committed in the city, and how Sheila's case had fallen into my lap. I explained to Linda that Darwin and I were going to review her autopsy report and make a few queries about the findings.

My wife was very much aware that if I got caught up in something important, eating would be the furthest thing from my mind, so she got up earlier than usual to prepare me a hearty, nourishing breakfast.

Upon entering the kitchen, I found myself still in awe with the woman sitting at the table with a cup of coffee to her lips.

"Good morning, gorgeous..." She looked extremely sexy in her blue silk robe.

"Hey, baby," Linda said as she got to her feet and immediately began adjusting my blue tie.

"I didn't expect you to get up so early." I gave her a peck on the cheek. "I know that you have a busy day ahead of you. I could have eaten a bowl of cereal, or something."

"Cereal...not a chance, not today. Anyway, the kids and I are going to meet you at the courthouse. We want to take pictures with you sitting on the bench."

"That'll be great."

I made myself comfortable. There was no room on my plate for anything else. It looked as if my wife's goal was to ensure that I wouldn't be hungry for the rest of the day. Several pieces of bacon, scrambled eggs, pancakes, oatmeal, and a glass of orange juice along with a cup of steaming hot coffee were before me. I had absolutely no idea where to begin, so I picked up my fork and stared at my plate.

"Linda, this is just too much food, baby. If I try to eat all of this, I'll fall asleep in the middle of court."

She smiled. "Greg, I'm just afraid that you'll miss lunch again."

"I won't."

"Are you excited?" she asked as she sat next to me.

"I'm a little jittery."

"I dreamt about us last night."

Her loving smile sparked my curiosity. I laid down my fork, picked up my coffee, and then turned my attention toward my wife. I found it fascinating that she'd had a night of relaxational reflection. And from the smile on her face, her memories were just as delightful as those that played on the silver screen of my mind.

I'd already believed that she was my soul mate, and that our connection was a spiritual one, but her dreaming of us on the same night that I had dreamt of us, confirmed that.

"I dreamt about how we met, and how my girlfriends told me that I was a fool for even thinking about you after you cursed me out. They let me have it after you took me out the first time. Remember, you were supposed to take me shopping before the movie?"

"Yeah, but you know that I wasn't going to do that. I didn't have no damn money…you made sure of that when you gave everyone the four-one-one on my hustle."

"I wasn't going to let you take me shopping, anyway. I just wanted to see what made you tick. My girlfriends used to see you spinning records on campus. They thought you were really cute, but they also felt like you were a thug. So they weren't really surprised that you cursed me out. Even so, all of them would have jumped your bones if given the chance," my wife said about my working as a popular disc jockey around campus. Spinning records was my second hustle.

I countered with a blush, before expressing, if I had only known, "Really…!"

Linda snapped a Muhammad Ali-type jab to my shoulder which caused the smirk on my face to turn into a playful grin. "Baby, come on…" I grabbed her hands before she could let loose with a flurry of combinations.

My next statement was filled with all sincerity. "After all these years that we've been together, I still can't believe that you were interested in me. Especially after the way I acted the day we first met." I pulled the cruiser-weight champ toward me and kissed her—the display of affection worked like the bell between rounds because my wife relaxed her clutched fist and wrapped her arms around me.

"Greg, that look in your eyes…it was the look of someone who had God's grace. You didn't understand who you were back then, but your eyes spoke to me."

I was so lost in her loving gaze that I didn't get a chance to tell her that I also had dreamt about us, that I was unable to rest until my mind turned to our love.

"Judge Mathis," she said with a smile, "I'll be holding an open house at YAAT. Barbara is going to meet me there."

Three other brothers who had pulled themselves out of an impoverished situation had joined me to start Young Adults Asserting Themselves. It was a program set up to help empower and provide a sense of hope.

"Barbara was in attendance yesterday. She's impressed with the job and community development workshops. She and Gram really love you. Barbara has strong opinions about the programs. I didn't realize that she's so hands-on with most of the charities that she's involved with." My wife looked at me with a smile. "Honey, she wants to help financially."

"Really…"

"Yes. She was very impressed with the flyers that you had printed when you first started the program in 1986."

I remember exactly how those flyers read. We were looking for young adults ages seventeen through twenty-eight who were in search of jobs, training programs, and a college education. We asked that they attend our first career development workshop that was scheduled to take place at the University of Detroit School of Law.

After several years of holding these seminars in churches, recreation centers, and any other place where we could conduct them, we eventually found a location we could afford. However, we were still in need of support. We paid for everything out of our own pockets, and that couldn't go on but for so long. Donations were and continued to be what kept the program going.

Linda continued while giving me a bear hug. "She was impressed with how you got started, and even more impressed with what you have achieved. I don't know why you never told them about the program. Barbara Olson wants to make a substantial contribution. She also wants to open the doors to their companies as possible places of employment for some of the young people attending the program."

"That's great, baby. But I never told them because I didn't want them feeling obligated to help out due to our friendship."

"Well, I think that she made the offer because it's a worthy program. She also wants to help with the rehab center. She asked if you could stop by her estate."

"When…?"

"She wants you to stop by as early as you can…this morning."

"I'm supposed to do something this morning before going into work." I paused. Having a chance to speak with Barbara Olson about my personal projects wasn't exactly something that I had planned. Raising money was essential, but I didn't want to use my friendship with her husband to do so. But since Linda had already had discussions with Barbara, I didn't see a reason not to meet with her. "Okay, but I need for you to do me a favor. Contact her and let her know that I'll stop by around eight fifteen. I have an appointment at seven thirty."

My wife sipped on her coffee before asking her by-the-way question, "Were you able to get some help around the office?"

"Yeah, wonderful girl. Kinda librarian nerdish, but very smart. They also assigned me a young man. It seems as if he might have a little sugar in his tank. But both are going to be a big help," I whispered. For the next several seconds, I said nothing, just picked at my food. My thoughts were ripping away at my gut because I had some very damaging information—data that could destroy Gram's marriage, yet I was about to accept help from his wife. Was I wrong if I accepted that help?

"What's going on, baby?" Linda asked. She obviously could tell that I was deep in thought.

Of course, I was evasive. "Nothing…just thinking about my first day."

"Everything is going to be okay. Don't worry." She winked at me lovingly. Then, suddenly, as if something sparked her memory, my wife uttered, "Oh yeah, by the way, don't forget that the program director at the radio station WCHB wants to talk to you about hosting a new show." She gave me a passionate kiss.

MATHIS PRESIDING

I always felt that the individuals who choose to examine cause of death as a career were a strange breed. To be so intrigued in the investigative techniques that lead to the circumstances in which someone died is admirable, yet strange. They seem so comfortable working in an environment that appears to be deficient of compassion and respect. The bizarre thing to me is how these individuals become so accustomed to death that they eat around carved-up cadavers.

Both Darwin and I cringed as we watched the forensic pathologist stuff a croissant into his mouth with one hand while digging into the bloody remains of a young man who had died under mysterious conditions with the other.

The ten-thousand-square-foot workspace was something that I could never get used to. For me, it was bone chilling. Fifty or so vaultlike drawers built within the dull, gray concrete encasing the room were all occupied with the bodies of individuals who had recently lost their lives.

In the middle of the white, glossy, highly polished concrete floor sat several stainless steel carts of various sizes. Some of the pushcarts were used for the corpses, while others had the equipment required by the pathologist resting atop them.

"The toxicology report says that it was cocaine," the coroner firmly stated.

"Tell me something, I heard that codeine can be misconstrued as cocaine," I asked while Darwin read over his cousin's autopsy.

"If cocaine is not the focus of the screening, it could be," the pathologist responded as he placed the heart of his subject onto a scale.

Darwin paced the cold examination and storage facility with his eyes fixated on the preliminary summary of autopsy. He read it aloud. *"The hair is brown and approximately twenty inches in length. The skin is blackened and bruised, consistent with blunt force trauma."*

Based on our similar physical attributes and attire—gray double-breasted suits and blue ties—anyone seeing us would've thought that the reporter and I were related, and had talked the previous night of dressing alike, but, believe me, it was a coincidence.

The reporter's voice cracked as he continued, *"The head is symmetric and the eyes are closed. The irises are brown and the pupils measure 0.4 centimeters. There is evidence of inflammation, which is noted around the eyes and mouth. The head was severed between the C1 and C2 vertebrae. With the dura removed, the base of the skull shows a hairline fracture."*

The report indicated that the oral cavity showed signs of inflammation but the mucosa-associated lymphatic tissue was intact. There was no sign of obstruction in the airway. Time of death was estimated based on larva development.

I could see a bit of relief in Darwin's eyes when he read that the decapitation was probably not the fatal wound. It was revealed that his cousin might have already been deceased prior to the severing of her head. The medical examiners were hoping that further toxicology results would provide additional information.

I requested of the coroner. "I would like for you to ensure that no mistakes were made with the determination that Ms. Morgan had ingested cocaine. Also, could you have toxicology clarify whether she suffered, and whether her death was the result of the decapitation? That's very important for the family—if you know what I mean?"

While writing down the weight of the heart he was examining, the pathologist glanced at the dismayed reporter. "He family…?"

"Yes, they were very close."

"I'll see what I can do."

Darwin's eyes began to water. He shook his head slowly—as if he couldn't convince himself that reality was before him. His cousin's life was reduced to notations on a medical examiner's report.

When we exited the pathologist's work area, it was obvious to me that the reporter's thoughts were conflicting—battling whether to allow his strength of character to be stormed on by the dark cloud of righteous anger, which hung over him. Darwin blamed himself for not being there for Sheila during her time of need.

"This is like a bad dream, man. I can't believe that this happened to someone who was so sweet and full of life. My cousin would have given her last to anyone. If she had the money, she would've fed and housed all the homeless in the city—that's the kind of person she was. She didn't deserve this; nobody should be subjected to this. I should've been there for her."

"Sounds to me that you thought a lot of her…"

Out of nowhere, he blurted, "I felt it."

"Felt what?"

Without warning, he stopped abruptly in the crowded hallway before grabbing me by the arm.

"I felt that something was wrong the night she came up missing. I knew something was wrong, but at the time, I couldn't put my finger on it."

"Look, Darwin, you can't keep beating yourself up about this. There was nothing that you could do." I placed my hands on his shoulders before continuing, "If we're gonna have any chance of finding out who did this, then you're gonna have to focus on bringing that person to justice. We're gonna find that sick bastard."

I guess he saw sincerity in my eyes, and heard it in my statement, because he offered, "If there is ever anything that I can do for you, please don't hesitate. I really appreciate what you've tried to do."

I smiled at him.

It was obvious, based on the awkwardness behind his expression, he could tell that I had something in mind. "What?" he questioned.

"You really want to do something for me?"

"Sure."

My hope was that discussing the mentoring program would be a way to get his mind on something other than the tragedy he'd lived over the past few days. I was playing amateur psychologist. "I run an organization called

Young Adults Asserting Themselves, and it's a mentoring training program."

"I'll do it."

"You will?"

"Sure."

I was shocked; he'd read my mind. I couldn't believe how easy it was to get him to agree to become a mentor. I guess that I should not have been surprised—Darwin Washington, of the *Michigan Chronicle*, was a good guy.

Immediately upon leaving the coroner's office, I made my way to the Olsons's extravagant six million-dollar mansion, which was located in suburban Detroit. Barbara was expecting me—and was aware that I had to be in court early, so she knew that our meeting had to be quick and to the point.

Her butler had escorted me into a study; it was literally as big as the Detroit Public Library. Barbara, seated in a tan leather chair, never allowed her eyes to stray from the documents atop her beautiful, antique, hand-crafted, mahogany, hardwood desk.

"Now that you're a judge...do I address you as such, or is it still Greg to me?" she asked politely.

"It's the same as it's always been for you, Barbara."

"How are the children?"

I smiled. "They're doing great. I'll bring them by to see you sometime soon."

Although Barbara Olson had financially backed the reelection bid of my incumbent, she didn't seem at all bothered that her support had gone in vain. While Gram and I were friends, she felt that it wouldn't be in good taste to forgo her support for a man whom her father had helped to put into office.

The heiress was considered a fixture on the campaign circuit. She spent most of her time trying to ensure that the right civil servants were elected. It didn't matter to her whether it was a city council seat, a judge, the mayor, or for that matter, the school board—she took every election as serious as any politician running for public office.

"Greg, I'm thinking that I backed the wrong man. But, as you know, my family was responsible for him holding that seat for as long as he did. So regardless of your relationship with my husband, I felt obligated to continue with what my father had started. I was a little surprised to find out that your incumbent—a man whom my family supported for years, because of his integrity—had suddenly resulted to character assassination by having the media peg you as one of John Gotti's henchmen. But, it didn't seem to matter how you were being portrayed; the people chose to support you. And it seems that the citizens of Detroit made a wise decision." She smiled at me. "Greg, you're truly a credit to hard work and perseverance."

She always intrigued me.

Gram's wife was a very special lady, a real humanitarian. She donated millions out of her multi-billion-dollar inheritance to charities and was on the board of almost every special interest group in Detroit.

Combating the escalating drug epidemic that was wreaking havoc on the inner city had become a priority to me. To tell the truth, I had no idea how it would be possible for me to open, in a timely manner, a drug rehabilitation center, as a way of addressing that epidemic. I had located a suitable building, one large enough to house thirty drug addicts, but the money was much harder to come by. I had no intention of using my friendship with Gram to raise the money, and my wife knew that. She was also aware that if I didn't, there would be no way I could get the money in time to purchase the building. There were two other groups vying for the same property.

"Your wife told me that you wouldn't approach Gram or myself for donations. Why not?"

"I just didn't want to take advantage of our friendship."

"Nonsense, that's what friends are for. Now, how soon do you want to open?"

"I'd like to open Sheila's House as soon as possible."

As she continued scanning the documents, she asked, "Sheila's House... where did that name come from?"

"It's a long story. I'll tell you about it one day."

"Well, how about you telling me over dinner?"

"Sure."

"I'll speak with Linda. We girls will come up with the time and place."

"That would be great," I whispered, but I was having second thoughts about her donation. "Barbara, I really feel bad about taking money from you."

"Greg, I love this city. For all its faults, it's the place that my father chose to raise me. This city meant so much to him that he wouldn't allow his advisers to talk him into moving our family to Connecticut. My father refused to desert this city because my great-grandfather helped to build this place into an industrial powerhouse. He was even more determined to stay after my mother passed away of cancer. He wanted to stay close to his beloved Eleanor's crypt. So when I see someone fight to try and help the city regain respectability, I'm going to help in any way I can."

I continued to walk around her study, marveling at the memorabilia that was reflective of her father's life—a man who made billions in oil and technology. There were photographs of Barbara at various stages of her life, several with the handsome philanthropist who had raised her with the values of a saint.

Her father strongly believed that having wealth and power meant absolutely nothing if those with the riches were not willing to ensure the economic success of the consumer.

The awards recognizing Edward Poindexter's contributions—not only to his community but to the world—were many, and they were very impressive. One corporate award was the brilliantly tapered, optically perfect, crystal circle presented to Edward in recognition of his special efforts in leadership and commitment to success. Another truly noteworthy award was the fourteen-inch Inspiration Crest, which is presented annually to the head of an organization who inspires those around them. But I could stand in that study all day looking at Edward Poindexter's achievement and not find a honor that would blow me away like the Humanitarian service medal that was displayed in a glass-encased shrine. That award is not handed out all willy-nilly—you really would have to be giving of yourself, beyond the call of duty, to have a president present you with that honor.

The only heir to the Poindexter fortune followed in her father's footsteps. She gave of her free time in helping children. Awards reflecting her contributions were also prevalent throughout the room. It was said that she spent a lot of money and time on children because she was unable to have any of her own. Whatever the case, Barbara was a blessing to others and well deserving of her accolades.

Sophistication, with an elegant beauty, is how I would describe the poster child for aristocrats in the Michigan area. Her golden-blonde hair and petite frame made her look much younger than her forty years. Gram was three years younger than his beautiful wife.

Every few seconds, she would split her attention between me and the documents placed before her—paperwork necessary for me to purchase the property that would allow me to give a helping hand to those seeking another shot at life.

"I'm hoping that this rehabilitation center will effect change in the drug users' mindsets," I blurted. "If we're able to deter one person from losing his or her way in drugs or alcohol, I look at that as a start."

I picked up a picture, which depicted Barbara standing hand in hand with her father, in front of the Fox Theater. They were both immaculately dressed. From the activity portrayed in the background of the photograph, the two were attending a very elegant gala. "When was this picture taken?"

"In 1963, my father was honored for a groundbreaking scholarship program that he'd developed. That picture was taken the night he was honored."

"You must be very proud of him."

"What my father instilled in me was rudimentary…a desire to give back to a society which rewards success to those who put in hard work. Look at you…you put in the work, so you've been rewarded."

"I am truly blessed," I said with a smile.

"Gram and I believe that in order for us to really make a difference, we would have to do it from within the infrastructure. So, my husband will be running for mayor in the next election."

My eyes widened. Gram and I had never had any discussions about his political ambitions. *Mayor*, that was really news to me.

Barbara must have noticed that I was surprised. "I guess my husband didn't share his desires with you."

"No, he never said a word about running for public office."

"Well, he really likes Aaron Dennis. We've backed Aaron during both of his campaigns. So discussing his desires with anyone, especially those who back Dennis, is a touchy subject. I guess that you and Gram are alike in many ways."

"What do you mean?"

"My husband didn't want to take advantage of your friendship by asking you to help him in his bid to become mayor. He knows how you feel about Aaron." She turned her attention back to the paperwork before she whispered, "Now that I feel no obligation toward any one judicial candidate, I'll be supporting you throughout your career in public service."

"I really appreciate that," I said. After placing the picture I was holding back in its proper place, I casually made my way back to her desk. "I sincerely appreciate you helping with this project. I've been working with several individuals over the last couple of months trying to get this underway. You and your husband are definitely a godsend."

"With the money, and our influence with all the agencies waiting to approve your application, how soon can you open Sheila's House?"

"I'm really not sure. We have a lot of work to do internally in order to bring that place up to code."

"I have a construction company. I can have them get that place up to code in a matter of days."

"I can't ask you to do that."

"My husband wants this for you...and so do I. Gram asked that I apologize to you for his not being here. He needed to address a problem at his pet company."

Gram was once the vice president of communications for Poindexter Technologies. The heiress had turned over the reins of that firm to the love of her life as a wedding gift. Upon taking control, he immediately renamed the company Olson, and then quickly took his wife's gift to new heights. Gram didn't have the same hunger for law as he did for business. He felt that business was his calling, and that he had wasted three years in law school.

Barbara smiled before handing me the paperwork. "Here you go, Greg.

And if you should ever need anything else, please don't hesitate." She stood, and then extended her hand.

I took her butter-soft hand into mine. "Thank you so much, Barbara. And if you should ever need anything from me, I'm here for you."

"Linda also told me about your mentoring program. I'd like to help out with that also."

"Your generosity knows no boundaries."

Barbara smiled. "I'll be sure to talk with Linda about us sharing a lovely evening out."

"I had planned on taking Linda to dinner this coming weekend. She wants to dine at the Renaissance Center, you know, at the revolving restaurant on the seventy-second floor."

"I love that place."

"So, allow me to treat you and Gram."

"That would be nice."

❂❂❂

After spending more than forty minutes at the Olsons' estate, I wasn't able to arrive to the office until nine fifteen in the morning. I was kind of baffled that my office door was open but neither David nor Maggie was in sight. I glanced at David's desk and realized that he had already arrived. The twenty-three-year-old flamboyant clerk was obsessively neat, but at that moment, there were law books and files scattered atop his desk. He'd more than likely left the office abruptly.

I glanced at Maggie's desk and noticed a purse sitting atop it, which baffled me. In the short time that I had known my clerk, I hadn't seen her with a pocketbook—just that little grandma-type change-purse that she carried. Actually, she was the only woman I could think of who didn't bother with that particular accessory—that sort of thing wasn't who Maggie was.

With briefcase in hand, I walked through the receptionist area and toward my chambers. When I opened my door, to my surprise, there was a woman standing and rifling through files atop my desk. This woman's silky brunette hair flowed down the back of her light-gray, power pantsuit.

"When you're going through people's things, you shouldn't leave evidence that'll let them know you're around. You left your purse on my assistant's desk," I said nonchalantly.

My comment startled the woman. She flinched but didn't bother turning around. I closed the door behind me, then slowly made my way toward my uninvited guest.

"Why are you going through my things?" I questioned as I slowly approached.

When she turned, I immediately noticed her ocean-blue eyes—they were stunning. Her makeup was flawless—just enough liner to accent the metallic shine on her lips. At first glance, I didn't recognize her. I couldn't put my finger on it, but something about her seemed so familiar. It wasn't until she smiled that I realized who was standing before me—and, I just couldn't believe it.

Astonished, I managed to utter, "Maggie…"

Her makeover showcased everything from her beautiful unblemished face to her eye-catching shapely figure. I was interested in knowing why Maggie Thornton would want to camouflage all those curves under the baggy librarian-type clothing that she wore upon our introduction.

From behind her delightful grin, Maggie said, "Good morning, Judge Mathis. I hope you had a nice evening. I know I did." She redirected her attention back to my desk and once again began rifling through the files. "I thought about how nice you were to me. When I got home, I decided that I needed a change." There was a sassy excitement in her voice. "What do you think?" She held her arms up as she slowly turned the three hundred and sixty degrees necessary so that I could get the full picture.

I rested my briefcase at the side of my desk before removing my brown double-breasted blazer. "You look absolutely amazing…" I said while hanging my jacket on the coat rack.

I tried not to be too obvious, but I couldn't help but think how remarkable my assistant looked as she stood before my desk. Maggie once again picked up her search for whatever it was she was browsing for in my manila folders.

There weren't very many people who could have done so much for someone in such a short period of time.

I wanted to meet whomever it was responsible for Maggie's metamorphosis from studious librarian to the attractive, self-confident young woman standing before me. Her new look was minus the lethargic posture, the slouched shoulders, and mundane persona that was once her calling card. Maggie Thornton appeared as if she had spent ten years in Ms. Angus' School of Charm.

Before I could make myself comfortable, both Maggie and I redirected our focus toward my door. The chief judge entered unannounced. He almost froze in his tracks when he laid eyes on the gorgeous bombshell in my office. Knowing him as I did, I knew it was just a matter of seconds before he would jump on his opportunity to flirt with her.

"Excuse me, Judge Mathis," he managed to say although his eyes were locked on Maggie as if he were a lustful schoolboy.

My assistant's eyes veered from the chief judge back to the file she held.

"Whom do we have here?" he asked in what he had to feel was his sexiest monotone. His cockeyed gaze was followed by his signature move; the arrogant prick ran his fingers through his hair as if he were Arthur "Fonzie" Fonzarelli of *Happy Days*.

Maggie made it painfully obvious that she was offended by my supervisor's flirtation. She scrunched up her face as if she were haunted by a nauseating smell. "Oh my God…no he didn't," she mumbled under her breath before closing the file and briskly heading for the door.

"Who is she?" he questioned. My nemesis' attention never wavered from Maggie until she closed the door behind her. "I've never seen her before."

I quickly asked, "What is it that you need?"

He somewhat adjusted his demeanor. "You have a bad habit of going against my orders." His horny ass was still not fully focused on me until his next comment. "I just wanted to tell you personally—"

I interrupted, "Tell me what?"

"It's just a matter of time before I put the screws to you." An egotistical smile materialized after his self-indulgent warning.

Before I could assure him that his threats were meaningless dribble, coming from a foolish little town crier who felt that he could intimidate with what amounted to high school theatrics, my phone rang. I answered immediately. "What is it, Maggie?"

My clerk informed me that everyone was waiting on me in my courtroom. I was to have my picture taken with my wife and children prior to my session convening.

"I'll be right in," I assured my clerk.

❁❁❁

Linda and my four children sat with me in my chambers after having spent ten minutes taking pictures in my courtroom. The children were excited, but I don't think that they were as excited as my wife and me. The smile that was on my face seemed to be a permanent fixture. I was so proud to have my family sharing this moment.

"Dad, you gonna put somebody in jail today?" my eight-year-old son, Amir, asked as he walked around soaking up the décor.

Camara, my gorgeous eleven-year-old daughter, quickly intervened. "Boy, Daddy's trying to help people. He's not trying to put them in jail."

My daughter was right, and I was so proud that she understood my objective. "Amir, we want to try and steer people in the right direction. I want to hand out tough love."

Before I could continue my lecture, all eyes were drawn toward the door to my chambers. Someone was knocking.

"Yes," I answered.

Maggie, my dedicated law clerk, entered. "Sir, it's time."

The sudden hush, which instantly cascaded over the room after Maggie made her announcement, seemed to awaken the butterfly within my stomach. But I was determined, my nerves had to know their place; there was no way that they were going to get the best of me. I'd worked too hard for this moment, I'd dreamt of this moment.

My eyes veered in Linda's direction in time to see her place both hands

62

to her mouth as if she were trying to stop an overflow of emotion. I stood, and then smiled; my black robe hung in judicial splendor.

Greg Jr., Jade, Amir, and Camara were set to hug me when Linda mumbled from behind her hands, "Don't...don't wrinkle your father's robe." My wife got to her feet and headed toward me. She kissed me gently on the cheek, and then whispered in my ear, "You didn't describe your assistant as being beautiful...as a matter of fact, I was under the impression that you were working with Jane Hathaway from the *Beverly Hillbillies*."

All I could do was turn up the corners of my lips slightly, because I had led her to believe that Maggie was some homely woman looking for her chance at a full-time position, and that I saw something in her that made me want to extend the woman an opportunity. Now, my wife was left to believe that I wasn't completely forthright. In one short day, Maggie had transformed herself into the complete opposite of what I had described—and I do mean, the *complete* opposite.

❂❂❂

My bailiff announced, "All rise...Court is in session, the Honorable Judge Greg Mathis Presiding..."

When I entered the large, windowless courtroom for the first time in the capacity of a judge and headed slowly toward the bench, my predecessor's frozen steely eyes were locked on me. A large photograph of the man whose gavel doled out justice for two decades in the very courtroom that I had inherited was mounted on the wall enclosed in a stained wooden frame. Albert Fitzgerald's nickel-colored hair—mind you, a full hairline—and square chin, was intimidating. It was like this man would be there to judge me judging others for as long as I held my seat.

Suddenly, it hit me. There were people standing, waiting on me. My blank expression veered in the direction of a packed courtroom. If I hadn't known better, I would have thought that the entire city was waiting to be arraigned. No one move. I had to control myself. I wanted to lift my hands up to the heaven and scream to my mother in joy. My dream had come true—I was a judge. As I stepped to the bench, I fought to turn the corners of my mouth down, but seeing that gavel as it lay atop my mahogany work surface made it difficult.

I had to catch myself.

I didn't want to let those who were awaiting my brand of justice to think that it would be easy—so I quickly took another glance at Fitzgerald, which immediately caused the smirk to disappear. I made myself comfortable and lifted my gavel before striking once. "You may be seated."

I laid my gavel down, and then picked up some papers that sat before me; this was done for effect. I needed to do something with my hands.

"All right, let's get started. What's the first case on the docket?"

After everyone had taken his or her seats, David, my wiry, thin clerk, read from the docket. His voice was timid. "Case 4673B; the state versus Ronald Blackmon, grand theft in the first degree. Edgar Martinez for the defense, and Carolyn Otto for the People..."

There she was—in her form-fitting, black pantsuit. The woman looked smug, and played with her legal pad so she wouldn't have to look me in my eyes. I would have bet anyone that she would rather have been in any other courtroom in the universe.

❊❊❊

Going out to lunch was not an option. I had twelve arraignments left on my docket and I wanted to use my lunch to better prepare myself for the afternoon sessions. Besides, I still had a bit of a problem with first-day jitters. There was no telling how my stomach would have reacted if I had gone out to eat. Thankfully, my assistant was kind enough to pick me up a sub.

"Come in," I ordered in response to a knock at my door.

Maggie entered my chambers; as usual, she had her hands full. I still couldn't get over what a beautiful girl she was. My clerk walked over to, and then placed a sandwich, a large Coke, and several manila folders on my desk.

"Thanks for the sandwich and drink."

"No problem. A part of my job is to ensure that you keep your strength up."

I immediately picked up a file and began browsing. "What's this?"

"My due diligence…"

"You've done what I asked already?"

"Otto is out for blood. She's going to do whatever she can to stop you from making a difference. If she hasn't yet, you best believe that she'll recruit Sanders to help her make you look bad. She wants your seat."

Carolyn Otto had represented the People during my first arraignment, and the woman did everything she could to get under my skin. Her attempt at challenging my knowledge of the law put her two seconds from contempt charges.

Seeing Otto and Sanders huddled up in the back of my courtroom after the arraignment sparked my curiosity. The tape that I had viewed in my chambers also helped to make me curious about the goings-on of that woman. So before the next case could be called, I gave my assistant a project. I didn't expect that she would be capable of completing it for several days, so I was shocked to see what she had obtained in just a couple of hours.

Maggie was to provide me with any and every little thing she could on what Carolyn Otto had been up to over the past couple years, and dig up anything else she could on Geoffrey Sanders. I was still determined to find something—anything—that could give me leverage in my pending argument with the DA.

"Judge Mathis, several prosecutors were quick to speak off the record. They reiterated what you already knew. Geoffrey Sanders's arrogance and strong-arm tactics, coupled with the manipulative ways of Carolyn Otto, create friction around the prosecutor's office. You're also aware that Sanders and Otto both have reputations of being assholes, but it isn't confined to the prosecutor's office. They're referred to as 'Bonnie and Clyde' throughout law enforcement. The detectives whom I spoke with, of course on the condition of anonymity, said that they cringe whenever Sanders's and/or Otto's names are associated with their investigations."

Maggie had come across several detectives who requested to be removed from investigations that involved either. All of the detectives claimed that they were involved with evidential chain of custody issues regarding Sanders's cases. They also stated that Otto's tactics with suspects led to confessions from innocent individuals. The detectives insisted that on several occasions, Ms. Otto was well aware that she had coerced a confession from an innocent, and that the forced admissions sometimes stalled ongoing investigations. In some cases, the mayor ordered police not to continue their search for the truth, which of course, allowed the real perpetrator to elude justice and put an innocent behind bars. These investigators wanted to be relieved because they didn't want to go down with the proverbial ship when the shit hit the fan.

Everyone was aware that Ms. Otto's only concern was trying to convince the public that she was a hard-nosed crime fighter, and the best possible candidate for judgeship, but I ruined that.

My law clerk made it clear that each of those dedicated investigators who spoke up were later disciplined for one reason or another—coincidence, I didn't think so. My clerk also reminded me that the female prosecutor had some very powerful friends.

I spoke while continuing to thumb through files, "I see that Sanders has an outstanding conviction ratio."

"As I told you before, Sanders finds ways of pushing cases that he feels are not rock-solid convictions off on the other prosecutors. He doesn't want to tarnish his record. He hasn't lost a case in over three years," Maggie said as she sat and relaxed.

I couldn't believe how easily she had obtained her data; then again, *look at her*, I thought as I glanced up. It was as if she were a mild-mannered librarian who had stepped into a phone booth and exited a super diva.

While continuing to browse the information provided, I asked, "How were you able to get so much information, so fast?"

She quickly responded, "Favors…in the two years I've been here I've done a lot for the police and several prosecutors. Plus, it's really easy to obtain information on individuals with attitudes like those two have. They're hated. I also think that my new look might have something to do with it. It took me a few minutes to get some of the guys to stop asking me out, before they would answer my questions."

"Yeah...about that. How were you able to change your appearance so quickly?"

"I've been dressing down for two years because I wanted to get my position based on my efforts...not on what I looked like. When you extended me the opportunity yesterday," she smiled at me, "I realized that I could be myself around you."

Maggie paused for several seconds. "Did you know Ms. Otto prior to her appearance in your courtroom today?"

"Yes. When I was an attorney, we had several run-ins. Our dislike of each other was rekindled during the race for this seat."

"Oh yeah, I would imagine so."

Silence filled the room for several more seconds before she blurted, "From the way she acted in court today, I guess she hasn't gotten over losing to you. She doesn't like or respect you very much, does she?"

Ignoring Maggie's question, I mumbled, "As far as I'm concerned, Joseph Monahan supervises two of the more disruptive individuals ever employed under the banner of public service. But for anyone looking in from the outside, Sanders's conviction ratio is impressive."

"If I were weeding through cases and had the ear of the DA, I could accomplish the same thing. Judge Mathis, he's a fraud. And she's a black widow spider."

"I need you to continue to look in to the both of them, but for now, get me what you can on Monahan."

"Monahan...why him?"

I looked up from the file. "If Sanders is a fraud, then what does he have on Monahan? How could he and Otto get away with so much? Why is Monahan protecting them?"

I removed my glasses and stared at my assistant. "I need to get him to overrule his star—and in order to do that, I need to know what the hell is going on in that office. So tell David that he'll be working in the courtroom again this afternoon. You do whatever you need to do, but I need the DA to make a deal with Eugene Scott. That's the only way that we'll be able to get the psycho who murdered Sheila Morgan off the streets."

"Judge Mathis, what do you think I'll be able to find that will help you with Monahan? I need to know what to look for."

As I closed the file, I whispered, "I don't know, Maggie. I don't know."

"I'll get on it right away," she said as she got to her feet. Maggie smiled at me. "Judge, make sure you eat. I don't want your wife angry at me."

As soon as Maggie stepped out, I unwrapped my turkey sub and went to town.

Trying to put something on my nervous stomach was paramount. Just as I sunk my teeth into the lean turkey with mayo, lettuce and tomatoes, my phone rang.

I grabbed a napkin, wiped mayo from the corner of my mouth, and then took a sip of my Coke before picking up the receiver.

"Mathis..."

Terry Arnold, the senior program director at the most popular radio station in the city, WCHB, was on the line. Arnold wanted to know if I were interested in his pending offer to do a community affairs program.

It was an easy decision for me because the radio show would allow me to reach the public. I thought it might be possible for me to get someone to come forward with information about Sheila's murder. Thing is, I didn't want the executives at the station to think that it would be easy to bring me aboard. I was fearful that if they knew I wanted to do the show as bad as they wanted me, they would limit my input in the show's direction. So, I quickly turned Arnold's idle chitchat into meaningful dialogue about control over the show's dynamics and content.

"As I stated, the programming that I envision will assist the community in finding job opportunities, affordable daycare facilities for single parents, outreach programs for wayward teens, and emergency assistance for families in need of financial support. I'll cover topics that educate and enlighten the audience. The program can also be used as an outlet for citizens who play witness to crimes committed within the city. It could be like a confessional; we gather the information that will help law enforcement without putting the caller at risk of retaliation."

Arnold was very receptive of my vision—he was anxious to get started.

"Send the contract to my attorney," I said. "His name is Clarence Tucker. You can reach him at 555-6231."

Terry Arnold asked me if I would be willing to come in and be a guest on one of his radio programs called "Keepin' It Real." However, he didn't want me as a guest until I had already established my show. He wanted to give me at least a month before I appeared on "Keepin' It Real." I'd never listened to that program, so I wasn't aware of its format. I guess it didn't matter because Terry just wanted to give me as much exposure as possible.

"I'll do the show."

He asked that I report to the station the next afternoon to fill out paperwork.

"I'll see you then," I said before ending the call.

THE CRIME SCENE

The weatherman predicted that a stifling heat wave would wreak havoc on the city for several more days. I couldn't believe that we were expecting another week without precipitation, just Arizona-type dry heat. For fourteen days, the only water to hit the city streets came from the fire hydrants, which children used to cool their overheated frames.

If the high temperatures persisted, the asphalt, which had been laid to cover the damage caused by a harsh winter, would oxidize, thus, leaving the street blanketed with what would amount to molten tar.

An unexpected mid-day's breeze brushed against my face; it was refreshing. The exhaust created by the stop-and-go traffic was adding to the heat index, but that gentle wind felt good, much more relaxing than the artificial air, which eased through the vents of my Ford Explorer. I left the windows lowered because I was hoping for another gust of Mother Nature.

There was very little evidence that the street I traveled was at one time considered the Wilshire Boulevard of the Midwest. I saw very little proof that the surrounding area was once the center of a bustling economy, a booming financial hub fueled by the automotive industry. It was hard for me to believe that well-paid factory workers spent millions of dollars in the decaying structures that aligned the once popular avenue.

The Fox Theatre was the only evidence of that once booming economy. Seeing the historic building immediately reminded me of another unique entity that had graced my beloved city—Motown.

Nostalgia is a very powerful human characteristic. As I was being held up in bumper-to-bumper traffic, which had placed me right across the street from this legendary house of entertainment, our version of New York's famed Apollo, my thoughts drifted to opening night. I wasn't around on September 21, 1928, but I had heard plenty of stories of how 5,000 invited guests were lined up in front of the new building constructed at 2111 Woodward Avenue.

I pictured the bright lights of the marquee and a line that stretched for blocks, an assemblage of women with an array of fancy hats that accented their Bernard-Hewitt apparel.

Women eagerly chatted with their male dates who sported single- and double-breasted wool and tweed—all-linen crush suits that they purchased for six dollars and ninety-eight cents. Adding to the grandeur were the velvet ropes, which led from the curb to the entrance. In my mind, the star-studded event had all the glitz of a Hollywood premiere. There were two valets dressed in tuxedos standing curbside.

A green 1928 Chrysler Imperial 80 coupe drew everyone's attention as it came to a halt, its passenger door in perfect line with the velvet runway leading to the entrance. The commoners watched in envy as photographers' bulbs flashed when Charles Howard Crane stepped from the vehicle. Mr. Crane, who designed the marvelous structure that was now the toast of the town, was once the right-hand man of famed architect Albert Kahn.

As Crane made his way up the walkway to the delight of the opening-night crowd, a brown-and-tan 1927 Packard Single 8 Dual Cowl Phaeton pulled up in the very spot that was previously occupied by the Imperial coupe. A larger contingent of the press pushed and shoved its way closer to the robes used as a security barrier. William Fox, famed film producer and founder of Twentieth Century-Fox, stepped from his car resplendent in a black-and-white tuxedo, as bulbs flashed and reporters screamed out an onslaught of questions. The owner of the new theater studied his new building with a smile. Several seconds later, he reached into the car, and the hand of the millionaire's lovely wife was extended to him.

Eve Leo was responsible for the magnificent interior. At that time, the ten-story structure for which so many waited patiently to enter, had a décor which consisted of a combination of Far Eastern, Indian and Egyptian styles that was the most exquisite in any theater to date. The Fox was also the second-largest theater in the world.

The blood-red marble columns each held its own jeweled figures, which represented various Asiatic gods. Subdued tones of gold contrasted a multitude of colors. In the lobby, golden damask and stage draperies combined with regal-red velour was set off by festooned drapery with wide silken fringe.

My mind quickly drifted to a time that I could more relate to—the winter of 1964. I could see the snowcapped ground and the lights flashing from the marquee which immediately put me in the holiday spirit. My family used to tell my brothers and me stories of how Berry Gordy started a Christmas tradition by having the Motown Revue light up the stage at the Fox. This musical odyssey packed the theater for ten straight days, from Christmas to New Year's—with several performances by the likes of the Four Tops, the Temptations, the Originals, the Supremes, and Smokey, just to name a few. I could see my mother and other family members standing in line in anticipation of seeing their homegrown favorites singing such hits as "Baby Love," "Come See About Me" and "The Way You Do The Things You Do."

Following the riots, the Fox was in ruins; it was left for dead. For a couple of decades, no one seemed interested in keeping its splendor intact. In 1987, the owners of Little Caesars Pizza, who just happened to also own the city's hockey team, the Detroit Red Wings, stepped up and purchased the Fox along with the adjacent office buildings. With that purchase, Mike Ilitch and his wife, Marian, began the revitalization of a once-proud city.

I was pleased that that particular stretch of Woodward was on the fast track to recovery. But I wasn't about to fool myself; just a block up the road the riots of '67 could still be felt.

Someone leaning on his or her horn quickly snapped me out of my daydream. I peeked through my rearview mirror. An elderly man was upset that I hadn't noticed that the traffic in front of me had been moving for several seconds. He was cursing me out. I was holding up travel, so I gave the man a hand gesture of apology before accelerating.

I hadn't driven through the area in years, so I was a bit taken aback. The sixty-eight-year-old who was involved in the last arraignment of the day had spoken the truth. To my right, plastered on the side of what was once Louis the Hatter, a trendy clothing store, was a six-by-six-foot billboard for Smirnoff vodka. To my left, mounted on the decaying shell of the Fine Arts, an old abandoned movie theater, was an even bigger poster of a black athlete who had been paid to glamorize cognac.

James Redmond was brought before the court on vandalism charges. He was accused of ripping down liquor advertisements. The gray-headed grandfather was upset that his eighteen-year-old granddaughter had begun selling her body to support her drug and alcohol addiction. Mr. Redmond was disgusted that black neighborhoods throughout the country continued to be targeted for alcohol campaigns. His granddaughter's plight had begun with the casual consumption of beer, and had gradually escalated to wine. Soon after, she began drinking hard liquor and smoking marijuana. Mr. Redmond went on to say that she eventually turned to cocaine, then prostitution. He told me that I might as well lock him up because he wasn't going to stop ripping down billboards that promoted alcohol.

The riots of '67 and the automotive pullouts contributed to the alcohol and drug epidemic that James Redmond was determined to address.

The boarded-up, skeletal remains of businesses that once thrived along the major thoroughfare that separates the Westside of the city from the Eastside were now being used to promote alcoholism.

On the left-hand side of the street, an abandoned bowling alley, a boarded-up cleaners, and of all places—what was once a church—were all covered with posters advertising one of the cheapest wines known to poverty, Mad Dog 20/20. Sprinkled between these vacant properties were signs of a check-cashing establishment, a hole-in-the-wall bar, and a mom-and-pop store, which offered discounts on forty-ounce Olde English malt liquor, Colt 45, and a variety of alcoholic elixirs.

Most of the residents didn't think twice about what was taking place. They completely ignored that their neighborhood was in ruins and advertisements were being used to brainwash them into drowning their sorrows.

A few more minutes into my ride, on the right of me, buildings were being demolished. The cranes churned and dust swirled, filling the warm, blistery mid-day with a thick, murky cloud of concrete residue mixed with dirt. The noise and activity were a pure indication of development, of optimism. I pushed the buttons to my power windows hoping that I could get them up before the wayward cloudy deposits found their way onto my tan interior.

Several workers dressed in bright-orange reflective vests and hardhats stood in the middle of the street—their job, to stop traffic long enough to allow two pickup rigs to back up in the cordoned-off area.

In an attempt to drown out some of the noise, I turned on my radio, then the air conditioner, because it didn't take long for the mid-day sun to turn my enclosed vehicle into a sauna on wheels.

I stopped in the turning lane on Seven Mile Road and Santa Barbara waiting patiently for the traffic to clear so that I could make a left onto Darwin's street. Santa Barbara was very well maintained. Trees lined both sides of the road. Their rich, full branches hung over the asphalt like a canopy, which stretched the entire block. This was paradise compared to the red cinderblocks that cast an intimidating shadow over the dirt paths of Herman Gardens. As a kid who grew up in the projects, I could only imagine living on a street that greeted visitors with a sign that stated the neighborhood was being watched by its residents, or on a block where children didn't have to constantly be on guard while riding their bikes on the sidewalks.

Darwin's street had shade—and plenty of it. But it was still hot, sweltering; even on a block that was protected from direct sunlight. The leaves lacked water, and the brown discoloration made it obvious there hadn't been any precipitation for some time.

I crept down the street in search of his address. The homes were very beautiful. Well-kept immaculate lawns surrounded Cape Cods, Georgian Colonials and stylish Victorians. The flowerbeds and hedges were picture perfect. Since I could remember, Darwin's area had always been known as a desirable neighborhood.

"There it is…" I said to myself as I pulled to the curb and honked.

My horn seemed to disturb an elderly neighbor who was sitting in front of her flowerbed. She held up her hand-size garden rake as if she were threatening me with it. The looked on her wrinkled face was straight out of a Stephen King novel. Her gaze was very serious indeed.

Out of my open window, I managed an apologetic response to her invasive slant. "I'm sorry."

The woman nodded pleasantly, her entire demeanor reversed. She smiled before continuing with her chore.

Dressed to impress, Darwin stepped from his home donned in a blue double-breasted suit, white shirt, and blue tie. The journalist locked the door to his modest red-brick Cotswold Cottage.

He waved to his neighbor as he made his way toward the curb. "Good morning, Ms. Ouseley."

The woman responded as she quivered, "Tell your friends not to be blowing their horns…this is a quiet neighborhood."

"Yes, Ms. Ouseley. You be careful in this heat…" Darwin said politely while getting into my vehicle.

"What's going on, Darwin?"

The journalist buckled up. "This heat is too much. Do you ever ride with your air on?"

"I've always been the type of person that preferred the natural air as a coolant… it's much more satisfying to me than the air conditioner. So I'm always in search of a good cool breeze, hoping it'll find its way through my open windows."

With the sun not yet reaching its height, I couldn't believe that the heat index had already reached scorching levels. We were on our way to record temperatures again. For several days, the city's residents had complained about the heat. If the scorching weather persisted, it would only be a matter of time before the city would declare a state of emergency and place restrictions on water.

There wasn't a lot of traffic on the John C. Lodge at ten a.m. because rush-hour congestion had already subsided. We felt extremely fortunate that one of the busiest freeways in the city wasn't jam-packed. Darwin and

I were headed toward the southern most portion of downtown Detroit—and the Lodge was the single most direct route.

We were tuned into WCHB. The morning female personality was taking calls from listeners, the topic—relationships. My passenger listened intently to the program produced by the radio station on which I was scheduled to appear.

"Okay, caller...if a woman is quick to have a sexual relationship, she is referred to as a whore—where as if a man were to do so, he'd be considered a stud?"

Stephanie Crockett baited each of her callers into revealing what should have been their most personal sexual exploits.

"How could a woman have sex with a man outside her relationship and not think that it would affect said relationship? She had sex with her boyfriend... then went out with her girls and had sex with some guy she met in the club. Unbeknownst to her, the guy happened to be someone that worked with her boyfriend. Now she's having a hard time dealing with her boyfriend's rejection. She can't figure out why her man no longer wants to be in the relationship...go figure," the caller explained.

Darwin asked, "What's your take on that?"

I hadn't really heard what was going on—my mind was on all the work that was ahead of me with opening Sheila's House. I was also thinking about Gram and Barbara Olson, and how they had destroyed my preconceived ideas of how arrogant and selfish the rich could be.

"Hear what?"

"Where are you?"

"Man, my mind is on all the work ahead."

Darwin countered, "I just want to thank you for taking the time to do this."

"Believe it or not, I don't think that I'll be able to get a good night's rest until this thing with your cousin is resolved. This thing is haunting my dreams."

"Is that right..." The man seated next to me seemed genuinely concerned.

"Yeah, but I'll be all right." I immediately changed the subject. "Tell me something, do you have someone of significance in your life?"

He knew what I was doing. The reporter smiled. "Yes, I've been dating

a wonderful woman for several months. Her name is Donna," Darwin said
as he directed his attention toward me. "We were planning on announcing
our engagement just before this thing with Sheila. Why do you ask?"

"How about you two come over to my house one day…"

"I'm sure she would like that. I've told her about you…how you're trying to help me with Sheila's case, and she can't wait to meet you."

"You gotta go in today?"

"Nah…I'm off until next week. Bereavement. Plus, I needed to take the
time to help in planning the funeral."

"You guys make up your mind when you're going to have it?"

"Saturday, but they won't release the body, so we're having a memorial
service…you'll be able to meet Donna at the services. You are coming,
aren't you?"

"We'll be there."

"I was hoping you would," Darwin whispered solemnly.

It was obvious that he was still fighting depression. I really liked him.
He was real; he wore his emotions on his sleeve. The journalist felt that
he had spent most of his childhood proving his masculinity, so he wasn't
worried that people saw him as being a compassionate, caring, and sensitive person. Most men don't want that part of them brought to light—but
the guy seated next to me felt that a man wasn't a man unless he was able
to show that side without the fear of being judged as being soft.

"Tell me something. Where did you want me to take you after we visited
the crime scene?" I asked, accelerating in hopes of getting more of the
warm breeze that found its way across my face.

"You tell me something. You don't really believe that this warm air is
soothing, do you? Turn on the damn air, man."

"All right…little baby…can't take a little heat, huh…"

"I'm not trying to get all sweaty."

"By the way, nice suit…" I said.

"Yours ain't bad, either. That shade of green looks pretty good on you.
I don't have that color. What's that, pea?"

"No. It's forest green, my friend. So, you still haven't told me where you wanted to go after we checked out where your cousin's body was found. As I said, I have a few things to do."

He turned his attention toward me. "Well, it's like this. My cousin touched a lot of people in life. I hate what her death has done to her children. But more than that, I hate what it has done to those boys that discovered her body."

My eyes veered from the road and toward my passenger. "What are you getting at?"

"One of the boys is so scared that he refuses to go out of the house. He's been having nightmares. Their father is a single parent, and he is barely making ends meet, so he doesn't have enough money to send the kid to a therapist."

"Darwin, what do you think I can do? I'm not a therapist."

"I know that they're a little young for the mentoring program, but I was thinking that you might be willing to make an exception."

"I guess we're gonna have to do something to try and help that family. How did you get involved?"

"I interviewed them after they discovered Sheila."

"Okay, my man, let's do whatever we can. But I can't be long. I have a meeting. By the way, I'll let you know when we are going to have our next town hall meeting at YAAT. I would like for you to attend."

"No problem," said Darwin.

It was like déjà vu; my mind was spiraling and my thoughts distant. The area seemed so familiar. Physically, I had never stepped foot in the neighborhood, but my mind kept trying to convince me otherwise.

"This is so weird. Why do I feel as if I've been here before?" I whispered under my breath. Confusion was tying my reality up in knots. Although my mind had placed me in the area during the hours of darkness, I was certain that I had recently visited that neighborhood—and I had done so unexpectedly. Even under the veil of a midsummer's sun, the decaying properties, and the abandoned tenements along with all the litter, seemed familiar.

The yellow Lay's potato chip bags to my right, the fruit punch pop bottles directly in front, the Kellogg's Corn Flakes cereal box that I had stepped on, the Mad Dog wine bottles and discarded beer cans that were scattered about—it was all there, in the exact spots the night I'd paid my visit.

In order to completely convince myself that I had recently been in the area, I needed to see one more thing: we had to get to the alley so I could check if there was a light hanging from a pole.

Darwin and I removed our jackets as we walked through a vacant lot that put us in direct line with the red-hot sun. The knee-high weeds camouflaged that the open space was completely littered with trash. If we wanted to get to the rotted-out wooden shell that was once a garage, we would have to maneuver through the clutter. I battled with the crass images that my mind produced. Recognizing that a brutal murder was associated with our location caused me to guardedly ingest a complete visual of the area.

While attempting to get a grip on my thoughts, strange mumblings, which seemed to be coming out of nowhere, added to the perplexity. It was as if the mumblings were the distorted sounds of a very old, incredibly weird film that I was watching in third dimension, a virtual reality. The closer we got to our destination, the more intense and distinct the voice.

"Judge, you all right? Did you hear anything I said?" Darwin asked. He seemed incredibly concerned, as if I had spaced out for a second. "Are you okay?"

"Oh yeah...I'm cool." At that moment, I realized that the mumbling was Darwin's attempt to communicate with me.

"Were you purposely ignoring everything that I was saying. What's up with that?"

Before I could answer, we were stunned to play witness to two crackheads huddled up in the very garage where Sheila's body was found. They were in the rear smoking rock cocaine. Crack is a very powerful, mind-altering drug. It can strip a user of any sense of dignity. The addict's only care in the world is how he or she will get more.

We startled the ragged duo; they obviously thought we were the police.

"Shit, Leroy, it's five-o..." one of the men said as he got to his feet and threw his hands up in surrender.

Leroy closed his eyes and continued pulling on the piece of antenna that they were using as a pipe. My guess is that he felt if he were going to jail, he might as well smoke his shit up.

"Leroy, put that shit down," his antsy partner insisted.

The shameless junkie removed the pipe from his lips, then blew out his euphoria before opening his eyelids. He looked at me—his gaze, glassy and empty; he then briefly shifted his eyes toward Darwin before glancing toward his partner who seemed ready to soil his worn dirty jeans. Without warning, that fool picked up a piece of crack that set between the milk crates they were using as chairs. Then he dropped the chunk of dope into the hot antenna; it sizzled. The junkie flicked his lighter and began to pull the fire into his homemade paraphernalia.

"Fuck... Leroy...that was my shit," the confused junkie blasted. He wasn't sure what he should do. He wanted to slap that stem from his partner, but he didn't want us to reach for our guns. Thing is, he didn't see any guns—so he grabbed the hot stem from Leroy.

"Ahhh..." he screamed as he ran past Darwin and me.

The reporter and I watched the dope addict run down the alley feverishly blowing at the pipe as he tossed it from hand to hand.

"That stem is burning the hell out of his hands," said Darwin with laughter.

Leroy got to his feet and walked toward us. As he casually approached, that idiot had the nerve to ask us for a dollar.

Darwin ignored the junkies' request and pointed toward the yellow crime-scene tape that surrounded the area where the two young boys had discovered Sheila's body.

THE MAYOR

Gram called and asked that we not meet at nine o'clock as we had agreed. He insisted it would be much better if he could stop by my house after my wife and children had turned in for the evening. I could sense panic in his voice, which was a cause for concern. There was no way that our earlier tête-à-tête could have caused the monotone with which he made his request. Although I had told him that it was imperative we speak in person, I didn't give him any reason to believe that our planned discussion had anything to do with him.

Something else was going on. The billionaire was not the type who would show signs of weakness—especially in conversation. So my first thoughts were that a copy of the tape, which featured him and Otto, had somehow ended up in the hands of his wife.

ABC Eyewitness News greeted me as my lids popped open. I rubbed my eyes in an attempt to focus because I had fallen asleep on the couch in the den while awaiting Gram's arrival. I yawned, and then stretched while viewing the news in an effort to identify the sound that had awakened me. It wasn't until the chimes of my doorbell echoed a second time that I realized I needed to get myself together, quickly—I didn't want Gram to wake my family.

The only light in the den came from the television, so I turned on the lamp that sat atop the end table. As I made my through the house and toward the front door, I straightened the blue terrycloth robe that my children had gotten me for my birthday.

"Who is it?" I asked while turning on the light in the foyer.

"Gram!" my visitor responded.

Upon opening the door, my friend stepped through the threshold and immediately extended his right hand to me. I noticed that he held a large manila envelope, similar to the one that Maggie had given me earlier, firmly gripped in his left hand.

Our customary salutation—*hello, how are you, what's going on*—took place as I led my guest through the house and into the den. Gram didn't waste any time. He opened his package, pulled out a tape, and immediately loaded it into my VCR. Before he would turn it on, Gram's eyes nervously darted around the room. It seemed as if he were trying to ensure that none of my family members would enter the den unexpectedly.

The wealthy law school dropout sat on the sofa next to me. He picked up the envelope and removed a letter from it. "Listen to this." Gram read:

"It's evident that you believe that your wife's money gives you the power to control people's lives. I've witnessed firsthand how you manipulate and buy people. Well, it's time someone turns the tables on you. Over the next few days, you're going to witness firsthand how I plan on stripping you of both your power and any right that you may feel you have to your wife's fortune. I'm also going to make life miserable for any politician that you throw your wife's money behind, starting with this one."

Gram picked up the remote. I could see the baffled expression that found its way on his face. Of course, he knew that he had people who didn't like him. He also realized that he could be a little pushy at times. But enemies—those who saw him in the vein of the letter that he had read—he didn't feel that anyone thought of him like that.

Occasionally, I would glance at the television and gaze at Carolyn Otto as she sat naked atop the sprawled-out, motionless body of the city's top man. Aaron Dennis looked as if he were in utter ecstasy as the attractive assistant district attorney grinned slowly while tenderly rubbing his hairy chest.

Seeing that black widow with the mayor blew me away. Although I had heard rumors linking the two, I looked at it as just that, a rumor. But the truth was right before me. The woman who was moving her pelvis like a hula dancer—the same vixen who had made love to the man sitting next to me—was doing the do with the second most powerful person in the city.

I shifted my eyes toward the stunned billionaire. I couldn't tell whether he was intrigued with the sexy way in which Carolyn slowly ran her tongue around the mayor's nipples, or pissed because she worked her way to his neck, before teasing the honorable civil servant with seductive French kisses. I wondered whether Gram was having flashbacks of his encounter with the sexually charged woman who seemed to be very good at putting married, wealthy, powerful men in compromising positions. She certainly looked as if she were a very competent lover—from the activities displayed on the tape. She also had an extremely high sexual appetite.

We continued to watch as the mayor suddenly took control of the encounter. He rolled her over, pinned her arms on the bed, and began moving his hips as if he were drilling for oil.

Gram didn't look comfortable; he began nibbling on his bottom lip. Without warning, he abruptly pushed the pause button on the remote just as Aaron Dennis slid his head under the bedspread and out of sight of the camera.

"I don't know who sent me this tape…and I don't know what they expect to gain by sending it to me. But I think that I had better tell Aaron what's going on," he said. Gram placed the remote on my coffee table before directing his attention toward me.

I dropped eye contact. "What's going on, Gram?"

"What do you mean?"

"With you…I mean…what's going on with you? What have you gotten yourself involved with?" I asked with concern. I wanted to get straight to the point—to tell the truth, I don't know why I didn't. I guess I wanted to give him an opportunity to come clean with me—to hear him say that he himself was layin' pipe to a woman who hated my guts.

He looked very confused—he had a habit of squinting his eyes upon introducing his bewilderment. "I'm not understanding what you're getting at."

I reached, and pulled a tape from under the couch. "Gram, this tape was delivered to me at work."

"You mean to tell me that whoever's behind this sent you the same tape? They must be aware of our relationship with Aaron," Gram babbled. He was completely clueless; he had no idea that he had the co-starring role in this particular flick.

"Listen…this particular tape isn't of Aaron."

"Oh no!"

"Tell me something," I insisted.

"What…"

"How long?"

He squinted his eyes again. By his expression, I knew what he was going to say. "What are you talking about?"

I was hoping that I already had the answers. After all, in the tape, Gram stated that he had made a mistake, the billionaire had gone to the well one time, and that one time was too many. He told Carolyn that it would never happen again—unlike the mayor, who seemed to be completely sucked in by the manipulative female, although it was he who was doing the sucking, according to the tape in my VCR.

"You and Carolyn…what's going on?"

I could tell that he realized what was on the tape. He closed his eyes and ducked his head in shame. Gram picked up, then balled up in disgust the letter that had accompanied his tape. "Damn!" He turned his attention toward me. "I blew it, Greg."

"Do you think that she's setting you guys up?" I asked.

"Why would she want to do that?"

"You mean, besides the fact that she's crazy as hell…"

Gram's eyes were locked on the tape as I laid it atop the coffee table. "So, you're suggesting that she taped us?" he asked, already knowing the answer.

"Yes," I said before grabbing the remote. I fast-forwarded the tape, and then paused it at a still shot of her bedroom. "Does this room look familiar?"

My guest got to his feet and began to slowly pace around my den. I could clearly sense his frustration, disappointment, and the nervous energy that hung over him like a dark cloud. I guess it suddenly dawned on him that Carolyn was the common denominator in the dangerous game that someone was attempting to play.

"I screwed up by involving myself with that woman." He stood in front of my television and gazed at the screen. "She's evidently after something... and she thinks that Aaron and I can provide her with whatever that something is, if it is in fact her."

"It's her... she's dangerous and very ambitious," I barked.

Gram turned his attention toward me. "Why do you two hate each other so much?"

I paused for several seconds.

Gram made his way over to the couch. He removed his brown blazer, folded it neatly, and laid it over the arm of the sofa. He loosened his dark-brown tie before making himself comfortable next to me. I guess he could tell that if I were to open up, that my story was going to be a long one.

When I noticed that he was comfortable, I began.

"I had the utmost confidence that I could win the case when I walked into the courtroom for the arraignment with my briefcase in hand. I was set to defend my first client. Judge Simon Cornelius was presiding over a racially charged, high-profile case, which involved a young teen who had been accused of murder. I had reservations about the Greek who was to hear the case because he was a known racist.

"The allegations surrounding my client's arrest stemmed from an apparent carjacking. The vehicle that was taken had a two-year-old child strapped in the backseat. While trying to escape, my client was said to have struck and killed the owner of the expensive automobile—the charges levied included kidnapping, murder and car theft, just to name a few. The kidnapping charge was a federal offense, but Otto wanted the kid for murder.

"The accusations alone had sparked civil unrest because the forty-two-year-old victim was a white woman who was adored in her upscale Bloomfield Hills community.

"I had taken on Timothy Jackson's case pro bono because both he and his mother convinced me that he had nothing to do with the carjacking. His mother was a single parent who worked two minimum-wage jobs, and she couldn't afford to secure the services of a high-profile attorney. If I hadn't stepped in, Timothy would have been assigned a public defender. And we all know that nine times out of ten, court-appointed legal representatives would have spent more time trying to convince the teen to take a plea agreement rather than trying to prove him innocent.

"After hearing his side of the story, I was convinced that Timothy needed someone to fight for him. With this being my first opportunity to seek out justice for a client, I needed to be as thorough as possible.

"I discovered that on the night of the carjacking, Timothy was on his way home from spending much of the day with his grandmother. As he made his way down Joy Road and Greenfield, somewhere around nine o'clock that evening, he noticed a Mercedes parked in the middle of the block. He admired the dark-blue vehicle, but as he passed, something about the luxury automobile caught his attention. Timothy noticed that a child was in the backseat strapped in a toddler safety restraint. According to my client, the little girl was crying her eyes out. Timothy turned, and then headed back toward the car. He peered in and saw the keys in the ignition—he also noticed that the doors were unlocked. The teen opened the back door and immediately removed the child from the seat. For several seconds, he attempted to calm the little girl, but was unsuccessful, so he carried the adorable blonde to the front passenger-side door, opened it, and made himself comfortable. Timothy sat the child in his lap and gazed around at the light-blue interior.

"With the little girl crying hysterically, the teenaged Samaritan realized that he might be able to find contact information from the glove compartment. He attempted to do so, but it was locked. Timothy went on to say that that's when he reached over and pulled the keys from the ignition.

"As he was going through the documents in search of the owner's name, the teen looked out and saw the flashing lights of several blue and white Detroit police cars, which had surrounded him. He was immediately arrested and charged.

"Getting a change of venue was a major coup for me—the dynamics of the jury pool was a major concern. If I were forced to present my case in predominantly white Bloomfield County, where the carjacking and murder took place, the jury pool would have been reflective. Having the case tried in Wayne County at least gave me a shot at a more diversified pool.

"It amazed me that the change of venue did nothing to alter the course of the selections: We ended up with eight Caucasians, a Hispanic, an Asian, and two Blacks on the jury.

"Carolyn Otto was assigned to prosecute.

"She opened with racially charged statements, which immediately created a division among the jurors. The deck was stacked against my client. And having a middle-aged racist Greek judge didn't help, seeing that he wasn't about to stop the prosecutor from her unwarranted ethnic tirades.

"Carolyn immediately charged that if the little thug had stolen a car in his own neighborhood, then maybe the loving mother and wife would still be alive. She went on to insinuate that all ghetto teens should be kept on some kind of leash, under lock and key.

"She personally attacked me in the media by insisting that my becoming an attorney was some kind of quota that had to be met; as if the bar examination was rigged in my favor.

"I eventually lost the case, although none of the evidence pointed to my client's guilt. Timothy's fingerprints were only found on the driver's side, in the exact locations that he admitted touching while being questioned. He never touched the steering wheel, and when it was first dusted, out of the four sets that were discovered, not one belonged to my client. Yet, during the trial, the technician responsible for securing the evidence testified that he, in fact, retrieved a single print, which was later identified as belonging to my client. When I cross-examined him, he insisted that he'd never told me that he hadn't discovered my client's print on the steering wheel.

"Then there was the driver's seat, which was pushed back in such a way that the person driving would have to have been at least six feet tall. My client was five-six, if he were that."

"That's a damn shame," said Gram. He sat forward on the couch and looked me dead in my eyes. "What happened to the kid?" my inquisitive guest asked.

"He's locked up to this day. I'm still looking for ways to get his case reheard. Anyway, I tried a few more cases after that, before turning my attention toward a judgeship. So you know if Carolyn Otto didn't think that I was competent enough to be a litigator, how do you think she felt about me becoming a judge, so quickly at that?"

"If she played the race card like that, then why in the hell would she fuck Aaron?"

"Believe me...she hasn't fucked him yet," I said with the utmost seriousness.

"Damn, Greg, she's gonna stick it to me, isn't she?"

I handed Gram the tape that was sent to my office. "Take this...if I were you, I would destroy it." I walked over to the VCR and removed the cassette of Otto and the mayor. "I'm meeting with the district attorney in the morning. I'll see if I can get a clue as to what's going on," I said as I handed him the second tape.

"What should I do about this one?" he questioned as he accepted the cassette from me.

"Give it to him...but don't tell him that you allowed anyone else to see it. He would be totally embarrassed."

Gram replied stressfully, "I know what you mean...because I am."

❖❖❖

Tensions were high in the district attorney's office.

With Carolyn Otto on one side of me, and Geoff Sanders on the other, I sat before the gray-headed elected official of eighteen years and watched as he seemed to be wrestling with his convictions, trying to decide whether to override his top prosecutor and gain favor with me, or back his man and take a chance on me holding a grudge.

His roaming blue eyes indicated that his unique style of diplomacy, along with his unflappable demeanor, was about to be tested.

Geoff was still determined not to extend a deal to the only lead that we had in the Morgan case. I didn't know that much about Monahan, but according to my assistant, the chief prosecutor was a fair man. Maggie said that Monahan took a liking to his two volatile assistants because they were about results. She stated that the DA knew Otto and Sanders stretched the boundaries of the law, but he didn't believe they broke the plane for questioning their ethics.

Ethics seemed to be the only angle that I could use. But in this case, I was prepared to use whatever I could to achieve my objective. If necessary, even threats of drawing more attention to what I believed to be a racist regime.

Monahan had to feel as if he were sitting on a keg of dynamite because both of his ADAs were known to have short fuses. And not knowing me from Adam made it more difficult for him to see the situation for what it was. He didn't know how I would react if my concerns weren't addressed. If his worry was that his guys would explode, then he would soon find out that I gave less than a damn. It was me who was more likely to ignite into a rage if my request wasn't taken seriously.

Sanders evidently had led Monahan to believe that Sheila Morgan's murder wasn't important enough for his office to make a deal with a known narcotics dealer. But I was certain he could tell I was none too pleased with Sanders's refusal to do what was necessary to bring Sheila's murderer to justice.

Geoff stood up. "I don't appreciate some rookie judge coming in here and trying to change my way. I don't do deals, Joe, you know that."

I interjected, "Rookie or not, you're still going to respect my position." I directed my next statement toward the DA. "I would think that your office would do anything necessary to catch this psycho."

Carolyn mumbled under her breath, "Fraud, it should've been my position."

I wasn't sure why Ms. Otto was asked to join us. I could only assume that Sanders had invited his strongest ally to help him distort the facts—thus, throwing a smoke screen over my request.

I was not at all happy with Otto's rudeness, so I quickly asked that she be excused. "I'm going to ask that you excuse Ms. Otto from this meeting. I don't see that she's needed."

"I'm a part of this team. You can't come in here dictating what goes on in this office," she said with a frown.

Monahan was not at all pleased with his assistant's demeanor. He realized that she was on the brink of misconduct.

"Carolyn, I'm going to ask you to step out of my office. I'll talk to you as soon as this meeting is concluded."

Otto quickly fired back, "But Joe…"

"Now, Carolyn…" the DA insisted.

If the disgruntled ADA were truly a black widow, her gaze indicated that she, as the most venomous spider in North America, was about to spin a web specifically for me. She was going to lay down whatever scent necessary to entice me into her silky trap before injecting me with her deadly toxin. She truly had the ability to render her prey susceptible to her lethal, hypnotic, paralyzing green eyes. Carolyn Otto kept her evil stare locked on me until she closed Monahan's door behind her.

"Judge Mathis, I want to apologize for my assistant's bad judgment." Monahan directed his next statement to both Sanders and me. "I'm very sorry for what happened. But I'm afraid that I have to allow my prosecutors to do what they get paid for. If a deal is made to gather information on the death of Sheila Morgan, that decision will be made by District Attorney Sanders."

I quickly replied, "I'm not trying to play the race card, but we all know that if it had been a white woman that was murdered in the way that Sheila Morgan was…you people would use the full force of this office to uncover her assailant. I'm very appalled that a black citizen is not afforded that same respect."

"This has nothing to do with race," Geoff Sanders insisted.

"Then you tell me why you won't make a deal?" I asked.

"Because Eugene Scott will want more than we are willing to give him."

"How do you know…just make an offer…" I insisted.

Geoff Sanders's arrogant reply was classic. "I do this every day. I don't have to make an offer, because I already know."

I was upset—and to tell the truth, I felt like grabbing that prick by his collar. The DA's office was being very standoffish. They didn't seem to have the least bit of interest in solving Sheila's murder. I had to swallow my words because I was about to curse out both Monahan and his top man. Tension was definitely in the air. Sheila meant the world to Darwin and his family, and I was ready to demand that she be respected. I was set to blow.

I took a deep breath in an effort to contain my anger. Once I felt that I was under control, I said, "I'm going over your heads. I'm going to the mayor, to the press, and to whoever will listen. This office will have a lot to answer for. First, you leak falsehoods, by stating that Sheila Morgan was a prostitute and drug addict. Then when the coroner tries to explain that a full toxicology examination wasn't performed, someone from this office told the pathologist that one wasn't necessary. And what do you think the public would say when they found out that this office would rather put all of its energy into putting away a drug dealer rather than trying to find a savage killer?"

The ADA was none too pleased with my threat to plaster his name all over the press. After all, he was a politician. Bad press isn't the end-all. But negative press about a white assistant district attorney refusing to do whatever he could to find the nut job responsible for the decapitation of a decent, hard-working black mother, in a city where eighty percent of the population is black—well, that wouldn't be a good look for a district attorney wannabe, nor for his boss.

Monahan interceded, "I don't know what you think you would accomplish with doing that, besides starting a panic. But, I really don't think that what you're suggesting is necessary, and/or prudent."

Geoff Sanders began to pace around the office as if he were trying to get a grip on his thoughts. "You are not going to force me to make a deal with Scott. You can do or say what you want. To tell you the truth, I could not care less what you do. I'll give the press everything we have…all the reasons why I shouldn't make a deal with your friend."

I was dumbfounded. "What are you talking about?"

"We're looking at Scott for several attempted murders. And we're sure that we can connect him to two homicides. That's not a good look for a newly elected judge—being friends with a murderer," the ADA said as he continued to pace.

"*Puh-leeeeeze*…you're a damn fool. Half the guys that I grew up with are in prison for murder. My life is an open book. But I'll bet that you won't like the results of going up against me," I said with confidence. "I'm sure that this office will find a way to pin something on Scott. Like I said, he's your scapegoat," I offered sarcastically.

Monahan questioned, "What are you insinuating?"

"You know damn well you dropped the ball on Sheila's case," I responded. "Now you're gonna do whatever you can to divert attention away from her murder. I'm not saying that he was a saint, but that man probably didn't do half the crap that you guys are trying to pin on him. He's a convenient scapegoat for you, dropping the ball on Ms. Morgan. No matter what you do or say, it still won't make sense to the public that you refuse to make a deal with him. How do you justify not doing so when he could possibly be the only person capable of leading law enforcement to the bastard that chopped off the head of a defenseless woman?"

Sanders quickly interceded, "I'll tell you what I will do…I'll pass this over to Carolyn… I'll allow her to deal with this."

The district attorney was aware that Sanders was playing games—he knew that Otto and I were each other's nemesis; he knew that she would do anything she could to get under my skin. Monahan stood, and in an effort to quickly put an end to Sanders's antagonistic attitude, he shouted, "This meeting is over!"

❋❋❋

Linda had taken more time than usual in the mirror, I didn't understand why; she didn't need makeup because her beauty was natural. But I couldn't argue with the end results—she was breathtaking. Her form-fitting black dress was flattering to her figure.

Her dark-brown hair fanned out in cover girl curls around her teak-wood complexion. She never overdid it with the makeup and this was no different. A little eyeliner, pinkish-brown lipstick, and touch of blush to accent her cool undertones—my wife was absolutely beautiful.

Barbara had asked that we meet her and her husband for a meal at nine. It was fifteen minutes after the hour and my queen and I were enjoying each other's company while we waited for our dinner partners, who were running a little late.

The Summit's revolving dining area was the ultimate—one minute a patron could be afforded a spectacular observation point of the city's skyline; and forty-five minutes later, a view of the shimmering waters of the Detroit River and the shoreline of Windsor, Canada.

Now, I must admit that the bright lights of the skyline made the city look appealing, even inviting. But as beautiful as that visual was, it paled in comparison to the deep hazel eyes and sexy lips that captured my heart during my second year at Eastern Michigan University.

"You look absolutely gorgeous, baby." I reached over the table and took her hand into mine.

She smiled. "You don't look bad yourself, Judge Mathis." Linda blew me a kiss before saying, "They're a little late...you think they're still coming?"

"Yes, they must've gotten caught up in traffic or something. If they don't make it...that'll be all right with me." I kissed her hand, and then gave my lips an LL Cool J once-over before throwing her the sexist glare that I could manage. "The way you're looking...I wouldn't mind getting a room in this place."

She winked at me, and then, without warning, it was as if she were having an *Exorcist* moment. "Greg, promise me that when they do show up, you won't talk business tonight. You work so hard. We haven't spent much time together since you opened Sheila's House. You work late at the office, and then you go there...you need a break. I mean it, no business," she said in her mother-knows-best tone.

"Whatever you say, cutie..."

Our backs were to the glass elevators, so we didn't see Gram and Barbara step off. They walked over to the table. Gram placed his hand on my shoulder to ensure that I couldn't stand. "Judge Greg Mathis..." I reached up and shook his hand. He then turned his attention toward my wife. "Hi,

Linda, you look absolutely stunning." Gram kissed my mate on her hand.

I, in turn, stood and hugged Barbara. "How are you, Ms. Lady?"

The heiress kissed me on the cheek. "I'm so glad that you and your wife could make it. We have to apologize for being late—the press is covering some event given by GM downstairs, and when they saw us, of course, they had questions. Then the mayor insisted that we share a drink with him and his wife."

Barbara was eye-catching in her original turquoise chiffon evening dress, which was designed and created by her godchild.

When we broke our embrace, I pulled out her chair. The queen of socialites made herself comfortable. Barbara seemed so delighted to be out with her handsome husband, she couldn't take her eyes off of him. The two held hands from the time they sat down until dinner was served. I was glad to see that Gram was into his wife; that he appeared sincere about making up for his indiscretions.

During our dinner, Gram and I attempted to keep the conversation on sports because that seemed to be the only way that we could stay off business. Evidently, his wife forbade him from talking business also. Both women were determined to make the night one of relaxation.

We were having a wonderful evening—both couples were engrossed in each other and in the beautiful views. The four of us were so caught up that we hadn't noticed the four people that approached our table. Nor could those individuals make out who my wife and I were because we had our backs to them.

"Gram...Barbara...how are you this evening?" the person behind me inquired.

I didn't bother turning because I immediately recognized the voice. Gram stood and extended his hand. "Hello, Joseph...Carolyn, how are you?"

I had to give it to her—the prosecutor was definitely an attractive and desirable woman. The white string of pearls around her neck drew attention to the cut of her red evening gown. The design was meant to expose her sexy cleavage and flattering figure. She had added blonde streaks to her long, flowing hair. Without a doubt, the girl was intoxicating.

Carolyn Otto replied, "I'm fine, Mr. Olson." She slyly winked at Gram.

I was steamed—not because of my dislike of that *bitch*, but because she was intent on hurting one of the most compassionate people I knew. Of course, Barbara would be devastated to know of her husband's infidelity, but she would be even more broken up to know that Carolyn Otto was at the center of his betrayal. Barbara was not a fan of Carolyn. I guess women have a better sense of character than men—the heiress didn't know the prosecutor personally, but had witnessed her blatant flirtatious nature at social functions.

Gram acknowledged the Assistant District Attorney Sanders. "Geoffrey... how are you?"—he then turned his attention to the lead prosecutor's wife— "and your lovely wife...Hello, Stacy..."

They in turn gave a hand gesture to Barbara and affectionately acknowledged her.

"You guys having dinner?" Gram asked.

Joseph Monahan made knowing eye contact with Linda when he spoke. "We were at a function downstairs. That GM thing...anyway, Carolyn saw you guys when you came in. We came up to say hello." He then curiously asked Linda, "Aren't you..." But before he could finish his statement, I turned. The look on their faces was priceless.

"Hello," I said with a sarcastic smile.

Monahan responded alarmingly, "Judge..."—the DA's eyes quickly shifted toward Gram—"I had no idea that you knew the Mathises..."

"Oh yes...the judge and I went to law school together. These guys are our very good friends," Gram replied.

Carolyn's beautiful smile couldn't hide her black widow mentality—her evil gaze was directed toward Gram. She was obviously none too pleased that the billionaire power couple was breaking bread with my wife and me.

Barbara was gracious as she offered, "I'm sorry...we've finished dinner; but you folks are more than welcome to join us for cocktails." Extending an invitation to share drinks with a person that she didn't particular like was who she was; Barbara was polite like that.

It was obvious to me that Carolyn wanted so badly to join us.

The prosecutor knew that Barbara didn't care for her, but she also knew that developing a relationship with the richest woman in the state could enhance her career aspirations. If she were able to befriend Ms. Olson, then she would certainly have the financial backing that she needed in her next bid for a seat on the 36th District.

Monahan quickly threw a monkey wrench in her plan when he said, "Thank you, but we're going to have to pass. We have to get back to the GM function. But thank you so much...maybe some other time."

Ten minutes after Monahan and his group stopped by our table, Gram had excused himself and gone to the restroom. Several seconds after my friend left the table, I myself stepped away. Before I could make my way to the restroom, I spotted Gram and Carolyn Otto holding a conversation in a secluded area of the hallway leading to the elevators.

YOUNG ADULTS ASSERTING THEMSELVES

The moldy, discarded, empty structures that lessened the value and beauty of the community's landscape weren't being demolished because the cost far exceeded the city's budget. One such property had been vacant for several years. Formerly a Boys and Girls Club, like so many abandoned private homes and tenements around Motown, it had been left to rot.

My two partners and I were able to purchase the rundown building for a song and dance. The three of us then worked on our new venture for weeks—painting, plumbing, remodeling, and landscaping. We dressed up the outside with lilies, roses, and an assortment of other flowers and shrubbery. Afterward, we laid new sod.

Our hope was that the homeowners in the surrounding area would take pride in our efforts and in turn, put forth a similar one in upgrading their property. Just to get them started, I offered to help with digging up yards, and repairing fences.

A lot of sweat had gone into revamping the eight-room building that at one time had served as a place of refuge for the neighborhood youth. But we believed that the hard work would be worth it, if we were able to rekindle the sense of security that the children once felt.

As far as I was concerned, the Young Adults Asserting Themselves headquarters was in the perfect location. I had started my infamous journey toward foolishness just seven blocks from our site.

When I was a child, prior to my mother moving us to Herman Gardens, we lived in the area for a couple of years. I felt blessed that I would be able to contribute positively in the area from which my criminal exploits had taken root.

My face lit up with pride the day that we hoisted the welcome sign in front of the building—*Young Adults Asserting Themselves Welcomes You: Come Grow With Us.*

Internally, my wife was responsible for the color scheme, and the corporate décor. Linda was big on putting the young people in the proper frame of mind. She believed that if the kids came into a building that represented what we were trying to prepare them for, they would have a comfort level when faced with their first real job interview.

Linda set up one area to serve in a dual capacity, corporate conference room, or a town hall discussion area. The large oak conference table that normally sat in the middle of this particular space had been moved to the far corner. Snacks, coffee, and other refreshments were placed atop it. Neatly aligned before me were forty folding chairs, twenty on either side of a buffed tile island. The bright fluorescent lights reflected off the eggshell-white glossy paint. My wife said that the terra-cotta trim represented the soil from which we plant seeds. Linda had painted, also in terra-cotta, a poignant message on the conference room wall directly behind the podium: *This House is the Soil, Our Kids are the Seeds, and We are Responsible for Filling Them with the Knowledge That Serves as Their Nourishment to Grow.*

My wife had so much on her plate, but she still found time to help me. Being the primary caretaker of our children, she also was attempting to fulfill her dream of launching the first of what would later become five non-profit preschools. Linda never ceased to amaze me.

The room was packed, standing room only. I really didn't expect such a big turnout.

Parents, special guests, and of course, my kids, all twenty-five of them, filled a space that was created to accommodate gatherings, but not one the size of which we were experiencing on this day.

The young men who were on hand couldn't seem to take their eyes off of my assistant. Maggie looked as if she were poured into her blue jeans.

As I walked around greeting people, I could hear some of the teenaged boys saying how fine Maggie was. I even heard a few wishing out loud, that if they were me, they would have her working overtime. And they didn't mean doing legal work.

Parents were only allowed to attend the monthly summits. Most of those present had periodically attended, but only one person had never missed a meeting.

Ms. Cecilia Wright, one of the more outspoken parents in the area, was seated in her familiar spot—front-row aisle. The slightly overweight mother of six, as usual, dominated a conversation between two other parents. Cecilia was a very frank person, but she needed to be. She was a single parent trying to raise five boys in a gang-infested neighborhood.

Since opening the doors of YAAT, Cecilia had become our biggest supporter. She ensured that all of her children stayed active in the organization. I personally mentored her eldest son for the three months that we were officially open. Although she worked two jobs, Cecilia always found time for her children. She ran her household with an iron fist. The woman was very nice, and had the greatest of intentions, but everyone felt that she was extremely nosy.

I stood at the podium, attempting to deal with a microphone that was giving off disturbing feedback. The guests cringed and quickly placed their hands to their ears upon hearing the annoying noise.

Cecilia's head quickly snapped from her conversation and toward me. Her copper-toned face was distorted, clutched tightly, frozen due to the squeal emanating from the two speakers that hung from the ceiling.

"Excuse me, everyone. Please bear with us." I clicked the microphone off and waited for one of my favorite young people to make his adjustments.

As I scanned the room, I noticed that there were two people whom I didn't recognize—a black woman in her mid thirties, and the Caucasian gentleman seated next to Gram in the last row closest to the door. Thing is, this was Gram's first time attending one of my summits, and the individuals present weren't used to well-dressed business types dropping by YAAT gatherings—especially white ones. We had a very casual setting.

I watched as Cecilia directed the attention of the individuals sitting around her toward whom they saw as being mysterious guests; two men who stood out like sore thumbs.

My eyes veered past Gram—who wore a blue Armani suit, with a light-blue, French-cuffed shirt and gold cufflinks—toward a young man who had recently been accepted into Georgetown University. In a secluded corner, Cecilia's son, Alvin, played with the audio equipment that we'd purchased through donations.

Although the equipment was secondhand and didn't work half the time, on most occasions it fulfilled our needs. Alvin, our resident engineer wannabe, was the only one capable of making it operational when it did work.

After several seconds, I redirected my attention toward the six very patient individuals who had accepted my invitation. Our guest speakers were engaged in conversation, and they looked to be discussing Linda's inscription, which was on the wall behind them.

James Redmond and Darwin Washington were among the group staring at my wife's statement as they sat in chairs which were positioned side by side behind me.

Mr. Redmond, the grandfather who was arraigned in my courtroom on destruction of property charges, was scheduled to speak first.

While going over his case, I took into account his situation and arranged a community service plea agreement. Then I invited him to speak at our function because I felt that my kids would benefit and appreciate hearing from him.

When I directed my attention back to the front of the room, Cecilia motioned for me to approach.

"Hello, Cecilia," I said as I stepped in front of her chair.

She slyly did a head gesture in the direction of Gram. "Who is he?"

"He's a friend of mine..." I said with a smile.

"He looks official...you boys sure that he ain't gonna snatch this place from under you?"

I took her hands into mine, and then kissed her on the cheek. "You have nothing to worry about." In the midst of my kiss, someone tapped me on the shoulder. When I turned, I noticed Alvin.

"Judge, I think we're ready."

"You're telling me that we can get this thing underway?"

"Yes, sir…"

"Excuse me, Cecilia," I said before quickly making my way back to the podium.

I flicked the switch to the microphone, turning it back on. There wasn't any feedback; my young star had done his thing.

I removed the mike from its stand before directing my attention toward the eighteen-year-old who proudly stood next to his mother's aisle seat.

"First, I'd like to thank Alvin for helping to spare our ears."

Everyone cheerfully clapped while directing his or her smiles toward the young man whom I had personally taken under my wing. Alvin bowed in acceptance of the appreciative ovation. Then his clowning nature took over—he drew laughter from the capacity crowd with a curtsy, nod, and a wide grin.

I interrupted the contingent's good-natured ribbing of my audio man.

"Okay, everyone."

The noise subsided.

"Second, please accept my apology for my tardiness. I was caught up in traffic. I drove Woodward to Warren, and then took Warren to Twelfth Street. I did this because every time I take that route, I reminisce about a Detroit that once was. I also took that route because of a guy who was arraigned in my court on my very first day as a judge. You'll get a chance to meet him as he has agreed to speak today." I quickly glanced over my shoulder and smiled at my guests. I then redirected my attention. "I have a question. How many of you have paid attention to the ads that are on billboards around the city?"

Mumbles filled the room; I could see that they had no idea where I was going.

"When was the last time you drove through Farmington or Bloomfield Hills and saw billboards promoting vodka, cognac, Mad Dog, or malt liquor?"

An inquisitive expression was on most faces as the guests whispered among one another. Several others lowered their lids, hoping that closing their eyes would create a visual of them driving through the affluent areas that I had just mentioned.

Cecilia was the only person to lock her eyes on me. She looked poised; by the smirk on her face, she knew that my statement was rhetorical.

She blurted, "You know that they don't hang no mess like that up in them neighborhoods."

Several other parents quickly chimed in, "Yeah, for real..."

The mother of six looked in the direction of the two white men before continuing, "They think that we don't care...that we haven't taught our children that they no longer have to be slaves. They can't enslave us the old-fashioned way, so they try to imprison us within ourselves, within the bottle, drugs, or poverty."

I could tell that Cecilia was about to blow; she was about to get the crowd riled up, so I intervened.

"Hold on, everybody. It's not about them; this is about us. We don't create ordinances to prevent that. We don't demand that these advertisements be banned. Let's stop blaming others. This is our community; let's take it back. Let's take it back from the drug dealers. Let's take it back from the crooks, rapists, and murderers. Let's stop corporations that produce alcohol from using our community as a giant billboard."

"Look here...I'm very upset that my city is once again being depicted as the murder capital...that alcoholism and drug usage are on the rise. We are responsible for enslaving ourselves. Only *we* can break the chains that bind us." I began to pace. "At one time, Detroit, Michigan was the place to be. People flocked to this city. They came here not only for the jobs—they came because this was a good place to raise families. When I was in that bumper-to-bumper traffic on my way here, I sat right in front of the Fox. Now, anyone who knows me knows that I have a very vivid imagination."

Every single time I see the Fox, my mind envisions a time when this city was excited. In 1928, when the theater was built, our city was the talk of the nation. In the early sixties, the Fox continued to bring people together by teaming up with Motown, and we continued to be the envy of the nation. Now...when I read the papers, I'm embarrassed. We're no longer the envy of the nation; we're considered the epitome of poverty, unemployment, and crime. Not just in America, but all around the world.

"It's amazing how concrete and steel can contribute to the mindset of a city—the Fox did that. If we want to get back to being the envy of this nation, if we want to break the chains that bind us, then we have a lot of work to do. We all have imagined having affordable housing, no crime, and good jobs. These are things that any good parents would want for their kids. Not having these things makes one feel like a failure, and feeling like a failure makes one want to escape from his reality."

I positioned myself next to a man whose darkest outlook was undiminished. The city that he had struggled to bring his family to was no longer the land of milk and honey. His wrinkled, worn, caramel complexion and the crow's-feet blended with the puffed-up baggage under his defeated hazel eyes and nearly hid traces of a once handsome, optimistic man.

I placed a hand on Mr. Redmond's shoulder.

"This man had the right idea. He just executed it in the wrong way. Ladies and gentlemen, this man was brought before me because he's tired. I'm going to give him the opportunity to explain to you why. This is Mr. James Redmond. Please give him your undivided attention."

As he got to his feet, I handed the microphone to the retired factory worker. Mr. Redmond moved toward the podium with the grace of Fred G. Sanford, the character created by Redd Foxx on the hit show *Sanford and Son*. Redmond rested both forearms atop the podium as if he were completely exhausted. While peering around the room, he managed to place the microphone into its holder. The man was truly attempting to make eye contact with everyone.

I made myself comfortable in his chair and listened as he cleared his throat.

"First, I'd like to thank the judge for allowing me a chance to speak with the young people." He glanced at me. "I'm really happy that we have people like Judge Mathis."

Everyone began to clap. Redmond erected himself and joined in the ovation.

"He deserves this—and a whole lot more. Keep on supporting him; he's a good man."

The concerned grandfather gave it up for me for several seconds before taking control of the room.

"I was really about to lose hope. I felt that we as a society had given up on our young people. But your group has given me back my hope. It's really good to see that all parents aren't falling asleep on the job. All it takes is one second."

He choked up, his voice cracked. He lowered his head and then whispered solemnly, "You close your eyes for one second and you can lose sight of the children."

For a split second, Redmond looked as if he had lost his way in commemoration. But his wayward statement vanished just as fast at it had appeared. He lifted his head and said, "I think that you should all give yourselves a hand for keeping your eyes open, for not falling asleep on your children. Being here is proof positive that none of you are going to fall asleep on them."

Reluctantly, the audience applauded lightly.

"I listened to the judge talk about the Detroit of yesteryear. I wanna speak on that with the young people. You Ole Gs know what I'm talkin' 'bout so just be patient with me."

James Redmond stood proudly while saying, "I moved here from Mississippi because I needed a job. I had three children who were being brought up in the late fifties in the racist South. As a parent I wanted better for my babies, so I talked my wife into packing up and moving north. Detroit was the obvious choice—the automotive industry was starting to boom. So, my wife, three children, and I packed up my old '52 pickup and headed for the city in 1960.

"We didn't have much money when we arrived. We stayed in a motel, two dollars and sixty-four cents a night."

The children laughed at Redmond's last statement. The adults who were old enough to remember smiled while shaking their heads in agreement.

Redmond smiled. "That's right...two bucks."

Several in attendance shouted, "Those were the days…"

"Yes, they were. Anyway, an hour after we checked into the motel, after having driven for hours, I immediately went out to search for a job. I put in applications at Ford, Chrysler, and several restaurants. I had to find a job quickly because the money we had for food and lodging would only cover a couple months, if we were careful. Every day I would get up and search for work because I didn't know if I would be blessed with my dream job—a factory position.

"I was very optimistic about landing a job when we arrived, but for several weeks, it looked bleak. No one was hiring. The atmosphere around the motel between my wife and me was quickly bordering on disaster. We seemed to fight every evening after I came in from searching all day. I was tired when I got in, and I didn't want to hear her nagging at me…constantly telling me that we were running out of money. I didn't understand how she thought that I didn't realize that.

"Well, one day after spending all day pounding the pavement, I stood outside for a couple of hours because I was too scared to go into the room after another unsuccessful day. I just didn't want to hear her mouth again. Don't get me wrong. My Mattie had every reason to be irate with me; I'd taken her and our children away from their comfort zone.

"While trying to build enough courage to face her, I gazed at the truck and decided that I would ensure that we at least had enough money for a few more months. I was going to sell the truck. I really didn't want to do it, but this guy at the gas station that I frequented had inquired about it. He was willing to take it off my hands for a hundred dollars. Once I made the decision to sell the truck, I also made another decision. During the time that I was out searching for work, I had visited and applied for a position at the Fox Theatre. I remember when I first walked into that place. Although it was empty, the feeling I had as I stood in the middle of the theater and gazed at the decor was magical. I immediately promised myself that I had to bring my wife to the Fox. The entire area of Woodward was absolutely the place to be. It just made you feel that you were a part of something special.

"I knew what I had to do...I sold the truck. When I got back to the motel, I was in a good mood. The kids noticed the smile first. My sixteen-year-old daughter, Helen, ran up to me. She asked if I had gotten a job.

"Douglas, my seven-year-old son, and Debra, my youngest daughter, who was five at the time, believed that the arguing would end that day—because they thought that Daddy had gotten a job. Mattie didn't realize that I was home because she was in the bathroom washing clothes in the tub.

"I sat the children down and told them what I had done. I told them that I needed Helen to baby-sit because I was going to try and convince their mother to go out, to break some of the tension around the room.

"Mattie came out of the bathroom with a hand full of wet clothes, after washing them in the tub. She noticed that we were sitting on one of the two beds in the room. She asked what was going on. The kids smiled and blurted, 'You gotta go.'

"Of course, my inquisitive wife, while hanging the wet clothing all around the room, asked them what they were talking about. When we told her, she said that we didn't need to waste money on going out. The kids and I eventually convinced her otherwise."

James snatched the microphone from its holder and stepped in front of the podium before he continued.

"Freddie Gorman and the Originals were playing at the Fox Theatre that night. For you young cats, I know that ya'll don't know who they are—but baby, they were *for real* that night. And Mattie...she was beautiful; she had on her best dress. That black chiffon material with white polka dots clung to her like skin on a fried chicken leg. Helen had helped her press her hair and she had on just enough makeup. She didn't like wearing makeup, and I didn't think she needed any—but on that night, she could pass for one of them cover girls."

The smile on James Redmond's face was priceless. Everyone in attendance was mesmerized by his story. I crossed my legs, and just like everyone else, waited to hear more.

"After the show, we had a romantic walk along Woodward Avenue. The stores and restaurants that lined the avenue were booming with business.

People were moving about—some with their children, others obviously out on dates. The commonality of all who strolled the streets was their extremely jovial demeanor. Everyone seemed to be so happy. We stopped at one of them fancy restaurants for dinner. Back in Mississippi, we would have never been allowed in a place like the Fox, or in the restaurant that we had supper in that night. So to me, the hope of a better life had already begun. Let me tell you guys, there was something really special about this place, about the Fox, and Woodward Avenue, because two days after that magical evening, I was offered a job at Chrysler—where I worked for twenty-five years.

"We rented a house on Chene off Mack on the city's Eastside. Mattie and the kids were extremely happy. Our first Christmas was truly a blessing. Seeing the kids excited as they unwrapped their gifts. Man, ain't nothing like that. A man really feels a sense of accomplishment when he hears his children say that he's the best daddy in the world. I'll tell you…ain't nothing like it.

"Well, anyways, in the summer of 1966, we moved our family to the Clairmount and Twelfth Street area. I had purchased Mattie's dream home."

James Redmond's smile was that of remembrance.

"Every single day that woman was doing something to that place. She took so much pride in that house. Mattie felt as if she were a Rockefeller living in one of them big mansions. She was so grateful to me for steppin' out on faith with making the decision to move to Detroit that she would bring me a warm dinner every night. You see, I worked the night shift at the factory. My woman would get on a bus with a big brown paper bag filled with pipin' hot food. She would get her transfer and sit right behind the bus driver. She used to kid that the driver would tell her that if she gave him the food, she could ride for free.

"She asked, 'If I give this to you, then what would my husband eat?'

"Mattie said, 'Boy, would they laugh.'

"I remember my wife saying that she couldn't believe that she was allowed to ride in the front of the bus, because, ya'll all know that in Mississippi, back in them days, you could've been lynched.

"That bus driver really made an impression on my Mattie. When she liked you, you knew it. She felt that that white bus driver was good people, so she began fixing him a plate. She told me that every time she got on that bus, he would smile a smile bigger than the Mississippi River, 'cause he ain't never had no cookin' like Mattie's."

Without warning, our speaker's face became solemn. For several seconds, everyone watched as his eyes began to water.

"The night that the riots broke out on July 23, 1967, Mattie didn't come to the job until midnight. I usually worked from three in the afternoon to eleven, Monday though Friday, but I was called in to work on that Sunday. Mattie would normally bring me dinner at about seven every day. I called her about five and told her that I was going to work a double and that she didn't have to bring me dinner. But she surprised me by coming to the job with a basket at midnight. She said that she missed me and that she wanted us to have dinner together.

"After we ate the meatloaf, mashed potatoes, and cream-style corn, she took a cab because it was late. The cab driver dropped my wife off a couple blocks away. The police had blocked of the street due to a raid they were conducting at a popular after-hours spot—a blind pig is what they were called. According to witness statements, the big four—a specialized police unit, which consisted of hardnosed cops, four to a patrol car—was responding to a distress call of shots being fired at the blind pig. Mattie had walked right into the epicenter of the dispute. When she tried to run to the other side of the street and away from the ruckus, she was struck and killed by another unit, which had been dispatched."

A dark cloud hung over the room. The sorrowful expressions plastered on faces spoke volumes as the entire assembly watched a tear find its way down James Redmond's tired face.

"Helen was away at Howard University, so I raised Doug and Debbie myself." He hesitated for a second. "Please bear with me. I'm almost done."

Everyone whispered, "Take your time."

"I did pretty good with the kids, thanks to Mattie's efforts. My wife had already instilled the necessary values in my children that are essential for success. Douglas is a lawyer; he's raising two beautiful children with his wife of seven years. They live in Texas. Helen, her husband, and three children live in Maine; she's a very successful novelist."

An avalanche of tears erupted from Redmond's eyes when someone asked, "What about Debbie?"

Redmond sniffed, and then whipped at his eyes with his fingers. I got up and handed him my handkerchief. As I made my way back to my seat, I watched as Cecilia placed her hand to her mouth, as if she knew what was coming.

"Five years ago, Debbie and her husband were on their way home from Christmas shopping. They stopped at a light at Seven Mile and Livernois—two armed thugs brazenly ran into the street and attempted to carjack them. I guess that Debbie and Eric didn't move fast enough because they were both shot in the head."

A horrified murmur filled the room.

"Both kids died at the scene, leaving me to raise their thirteen-year-old daughter."

He wiped his face with the cloth I had provided. "This leads up to what I came here for. Doug and Helen felt that I needed someone around me, so I took in my granddaughter. She suffered a few emotional scars because of the loss, as you might imagine. She turned to alcohol, drugs, and now prostitution. I think that she began to experiment with alcohol, in large part due to the advertisements plastered around our city. For a long time she would ask me, does alcohol make you feel as good as advertised? No matter how much I would tell her that she shouldn't believe the hype, and that the people responsible for putting up those signs were just interested in making money...she didn't listen. Nothing got through."

His eyes turned bloodshot red as the floodgates opened. "She's been trying to find an escape. I felt that I let down my daughter. For some reason, I can't convince my grandbaby that I'm here for her."

His tears triggered an onslaught of emotion from the group. Even the men found it hard to mask their sentiment.

"I was brought before Judge Mathis because I attempted to tear down all the billboards I could that advertised alcohol."

He cleared his throat, and then dabbed the handkerchief on his eyes.

"I want to tell you children that for parents and grandparents, whom you will eventually become...that it's not easy. Enjoy your opportunity to be children; don't be in such a hurry to grow up. Don't throw your lives away with drugs and alcohol. Place the ultimate value on life. Remember, no matter what anyone says, drinking will eventually ruin you one way or another. Whether it's leading you to drugs...or to the gutter...or even death, so, just say *no*. Get high on life."

He lifted his hand. "Thank you for taking the time to listen to an old man."

Cecilia initiated the standing ovation as Redmond placed the microphone into its proper place while continuing his hand gesture toward the audience. He turned, and was greeted by myself and the other guest speakers as he returned to his seat.

I said to him, "thank you," and patted my emotionally charged guest on his shoulder as we passed.

Every guest speaker is given five to eight minutes to address the group, but I could tell that no one would have minded if James Redmond had more to say. Many were still trying to hide their emotions.

Cecilia waved her hands in the air as if she were giving her approval to a Sunday morning sermon. She directed her comment toward James Redmond. "Lawd, God bless you, baby..."

"Okay, everyone. We still have several other people who have to speak." I quickly diverted my attention toward our opening speaker. "Thank you so much, James. My prayers are with you and your family."

Everyone settled down, at which time I leaned toward the microphone. "Mr. Redmond has agreed to give of his time in our mentoring program."

Once again, the group expressed their appreciation by clapping.

"I'm sure that he will be an asset to the organization. The next person whom I would like to introduce...is a young man that I've taken a real liking to. This young man is a reporter for the *Michigan Chronicle*. He is also a new volunteer—one willing to do whatever is necessary to help our young people achieve success. I met Mr. Darwin Washington under very unusual circumstances. I'll let him elaborate."

I turned toward my new friend. "Come speak to the people, Darwin."

His mustache was neatly trimmed. He wore a brown tailored suit, which was accented with a maize silk tie. Both complemented his milk-chocolate natural color. His perfectly shaven bald head glistened.

The single mothers weren't the least bit interested in being discreet about their attraction toward the tall, handsome, athletically built journalist. I saw several of the ladies sit forward on the edge of their seats— their flirting eyes locked on him as if he were a magician and they were patiently awaiting his next illusion. It wasn't a secret that they were vying for Darwin's attention as he stepped to the podium.

My attention was suddenly diverted.

I watched as Linda eased her head through the door's opening. Her bubbly smile was known for lighting up a room. Thus, when those rosy cheeks expanded, exposing her pearly whites, I wasn't at all surprised at the reaction of the man in the expensive suit. His baby blues lit up when he noticed my wife's beaming grin. He immediately motioned for my better half to enter.

When Linda slipped into the meeting, her eyes immediately locked on Maggie. Of all the people whom she could have noticed when she entered, it was my assistant who caught her attention. I saw her smile turn into a grin. I didn't understand why that happened.

Darwin completed telling the story of how his aunt had raised him— and how he and his cousin were brought up as if they were brother and sister. He then described how he felt when he discovered that his cousin Sheila was murdered.

After Darwin had retaken his seat, my other guests, which included the four gentlemen remaining on my panel; Gram, and the white man (Gram's attorney) who accompanied him, were all introduced. I brought them in so that everyone could show their appreciation to those responsible for helping me open Sheila's House in record time.

After the meeting, while guests were enjoying refreshments, my wife pulled me to the side. For some reason, she wasn't in a very good mood. Linda never really showed signs of distrust in our marriage—I never felt that she had a jealous bone in her body. Although she attempted not to come across as being insecure, to me, she couldn't disguise it. "Baby, why is Maggie here...you work that girl too hard. You have her staying after work a lot lately...and now here."

"She wants to help out here...and at the rehab center," I said while scanning the crowded town meeting hall in search of Gram. I wanted to speak with him about his secret rendezvous in a secluded area of the restaurant where we had dined the previous night.

ADDRESSING FAMILY

L oud crackling streaks of lightning blazed a trail across the early-morning sky, its perilous erratic paths changing on each two-second burst. The storm was abrupt and due to the hurricane-type winds, the downpour was vicious. The hostile winds hurled splotches of water against the windows with such force I felt there was a distinct possibility that the glass panes could shatter.

I had given up on any chance of falling back to sleep long before the clouds opened—long before getting caught up in the white and blue flashes created by the electrical bolts of energy that introduced the fierce rain. It was four in the morning when I began trying to figure out why I was so fidgety—but the digital clock on my nightstand read 4:28 a.m.

I know that I hadn't fallen back to sleep.

So *what happened to the twenty-eight minutes?* I continued my thought, *I must've lost time.*

I had read about how a person could be doing something, and then suddenly, find that he or she couldn't account for several minutes. Was this actually lost time, or the early stages of Alzheimer's?

I was on my back with my hands under my head staring at the sharp blue flashes of light that entered my bedroom, courtesy of my large picture window. Add that with listening to the violent pounding of rain against the house, which was soothing, and I concluded I had been so immersed in the hypnotic storm that I had lost time.

Okay, I had figured out the lost time thing, but I still couldn't account for the restlessness. I should have been able to sleep. Thunderstorms have always been able to relax me. Plus, everything was going so well. I had solidified my position within the 36th District; my radio show was a hit. Barbara Olson had joined us at Young Adults Asserting Themselves and her influence with the members was profound.

Then there was Gram.

He hired three of our young people to work for his company. In addition, Sheila's House had been open for a little over a month, and we were at eighty-five percent capacity.

Our objective was to commit seventy-five percent of our beds to drug users who carried insurance, and another twenty-five percent to those who lacked coverage. We were well on our way to achieving that.

Barbara and Gram Olson poured extra money into the center to ensure that we were able to fully staff our facility. Sheila's House even had two psychiatrists at our disposal 24/7. We were in good shape—in a good position to begin our attempts at combating a serious issue within the community.

I just had one problem: The psychotic butcher responsible for the brutal slaying of the person for whom the rehabilitation center was named—he was still out there.

Every time I was on the air at WCHB, I started and ended my show with a passionate plea for anyone with information concerning Sheila's death to call in. I assured my listeners that any information given was, of course, on the condition of anonymity.

It hit me suddenly, but I had finally realized why I was restless.

Sheila was on my mind—but before I could sort through my thoughts about her, I heard my doorbell ring, which was followed by aggressive pounding.

Groggily, Linda lifted her head and turned it toward me. My wife peppered me with random babbling. "Hey, baby...did you hear that...what time is it...who could be at our door knocking like that at this ungodly hour...go see who it is before they wake the kids."

I got out of bed and walked over to my window, which gave a perfect view of the front of the house. Slightly pulling the curtains back, just enough to peek, I attempted to peer through the heavy rains but the rushing waters sliding down the window disrupted my focus. I couldn't make out the two shadowy silhouettes due to the downpour. I could barely distinguish that one was trying to shield the other from the storm with a coat.

The ringing of my doorbell, followed by the pounding, continued.

Linda sat up in bed. "Who is it, baby?"

"I don't know."

She reached for the lamp.

I quickly uttered, "Don't turn on the lights." As if not doing so would make our uninvited guests leave. But as I continued to stare out of the window, I realized that they weren't going anywhere.

A car, which sat at the curb in front of my house, caught my attention when its headlights were suddenly turned on. The pounding on the door and the pushing of my doorbell became more persistent when that mysterious vehicle pulled off.

I grabbed my robe from the end of the bed. While putting it on, my bedroom door was forced open. Standing in his pajamas was my son Amir.

"Daddy...somebody's at the door," he said while attempting to remove Mr. Sandman from his eyes.

"I know, little man." I rubbed him atop the head as I passed. "Go back to bed."

While standing at the landing, I flicked on the light to the foyer to alert the individuals making a ruckus at my door that they were successful in their attempt to wake my entire family.

I tied my robe as I headed down the stairs.

"Just a minute," I yelled as the knocking continued. "All right...just a second."

I turned on the porch light from the foyer and peeked out of the small glass pane on the front door. The coats they were wearing to protect them from the rain camouflaged them.

"Who is it?" I questioned.

Someone said, "It's me, Greg."

I thought I recognized the voice. "Darryl, is that you?"

"Yeah, man, open up…"

Linda called down from the landing. "Who is it, Greg?"

"Darryl," I replied while opening the front door.

My cousin and his seven-year-old daughter dripped water all over my wife's marble foyer as they entered—both were completely soaked.

"Darryl…why in the hell are you out this late with Gail?" Linda said as she hustled down the stairs.

I took the raincoat from my older cousin and hung it on the brass coat rack next to the door, before asking, "What's going on, man? What's wrong?"

My cousin's eyes were red and glassy. He stood in a puddle of water attempting to shake himself dry while Linda began to strip his adorable daughter of her damp clothing.

Out of the corner of her eye, Linda saw our eldest daughter standing at the landing.

"Camara, baby, get Momma a towel."

Several minutes later, Darryl and I were seated at the kitchen table sipping coffee.

"Linda and Camara are putting Gail to bed. You and I need to talk." I put my cup to my lips. "Who dropped you off?" I asked, before sipping.

"A friend…"

"Where's your car?"

"I don't have it anymore. I'll get into that a little later."

It was late and I wasn't in the mood to continue with the small talk. "So…what's this all about?"

Darryl gripped his cup with both hands, then hung his head solemnly before whispering, "I can't do it anymore. Greg…for years, I've been living a lie." My cousin stared into his coffee cup.

"What are you talking about?"

I tried to pick up a hint from his body language, or his eyes. But he didn't make eye contact. I could tell that he was extremely tense as he went completely silent for several seconds.

"Hey, man, you're not gonna come over here and wake my family and not tell me what's up."

He looked up, took a deep breath, and then said, "Evelyn and I have been smoking dope for years."

"What...?" I asked while trying not to look disappointed. "How long?"

"For six years."

"So, for six years you both have been functional addicts?"

"Yes..."

"Where is Evelyn?"

"At the house with several other people..."

I checked the wall clock. After realizing that it was 4:52 a.m., I asked, "Folks are at your house right now?"

"Yeah, getting high...they've been there off and on for at least two days."

"You've been missing work?"

"Both of us called in for the last couple days. But we used up our vacation time a long time ago. I've been put on notice."

"And you came to me...for?"

"Honestly, I was supposed to come here and borrow money from you. But before I left home, I decided that I would ask for a favor. I want you to look after my daughter while I try to figure out my life. Gail doesn't deserve this." His eyes began to water.

I stared at the man seated before me with an intense curiosity. I wonder how the eldest son of my father's sister had gotten caught up. He was someone whom I had great admiration for. He had always done the right thing. My respect for Darryl went to an all-time high when he dropped out of college while in his third year after getting his then girlfriend pregnant. He took on a job at GM and was planning to marry the mother of his expected child. Unfortunately, his girlfriend had a miscarriage. The tragedy caused her to go into a deep depression. The couple began fighting and the relationship soured. Darryl suggested that they go through counseling, but his girlfriend wasn't interested. They ended their relationship.

Darryl was planning on going back to school until he met Evelyn at GM. She wasn't a very likable person—pushy, demanding, and extremely spoiled. But she was able to get his mind off of his previous relationship. Darryl really didn't like her as a long-term companion because to him, she was too snobby. He once told me that she made him angry a lot because of that attitude of hers, but he really liked how she was always able to get his mind off of things. She was a fun person, which was hard for me to believe. In my opinion, she always seemed to have a stick up her ass.

Darryl said that she turned him off because of her plans for their future. She had it all mapped out. They would accumulate a lot of money working at GM, then have this big Hollywood-type wedding, have three children, and live in Southfield, Michigan.

Darryl told her that he didn't want any children until he finished school. And he definitely wasn't ready for marriage, especially to her.

But lo and behold, Evelyn ended up pregnant.

My cousin, although he felt that she had trapped him, married Evelyn. He didn't allow her to have the big extravagant ceremony that she was demanding. But from my vantage point, that was the only thing that she didn't get upon demand. Although no one in the family liked her, we accepted her and brought her into the fold after their union. Several months later, they had a beautiful little daughter, and named her Gail.

Everyone was under the impression that everything was going great for the couple. They bought a new house, two brand-new cars, and the two were always shopping for clothes. I even heard that they were planning to have another child. From the outside looking in, they had a solid relationship, and I was very proud of him. I had always been proud of him. I never saw this coming.

"So, she sent you over here to borrow money from me?"

"Yes. Our accounts are depleted; they have been for several months. We've been living from paycheck to paycheck for a while now. I expect an income tax check soon. I really don't want to blow that on drugs. She got her check a couple of weeks ago, and now it's gone." A tear rolled down his cheek.

"This ain't the time to start feeling sorry for yourself."

He wiped his eyes. "I know…but I'm not really feeling 'sorry' for myself. I'm feeling bad about what my daughter has gone through. Greg, I need you to take care of Gail."

"How do you think Evelyn is going to feel about that?"

"I'm going to do what's best for my daughter. If I have to, I can prove that Evelyn is unfit, so don't worry about that. Promise me you'll look out for Gail."

"I can do that. But are you sure that you want to seek help?"

"If I don't, I'll lose everything else...including my life."

"That's for sure..."

"I lost my car. I hadn't paid my car note because I was spending everything on crack. And we're about to lose the house. We ran out of cash after a two-day drug binge, so I haven't paid the mortgage. To tell the truth...I haven't paid the mortgage for nearly three months."

"Man..." I could no longer hide my disappointment; it was all over my face. I wanted to express my displeasure in words, but I held up. "Does she still have her car?"

"Her car is with the dope man. He's holding it until we can give him his money. We owe him for dope that we got on credit."

❁❁❁

Linda and I were sitting up in bed discussing my cousin's situation when a crackle of thunder, followed by a distinct flash of lightning, caused my wife to take refuge under my arm.

"That one scared you, huh...?" I kissed Linda on her forehead before saying, "Thank you, baby."

She peeked up at me. "What are you thanking me for?"

"For being the source of my strength...I could have easily been caught up in the madness, but you wouldn't stand for my nonsense back then. When I met you at Eastern, I still had game in me. I was all about the hustle. A different type of determination came over me when we started dating. I wanted to be the right person for you—because I knew you were the right one for me."

She kissed me. "Greg, when I first met you I knew you were a survivor. You showed character. I mean, you wanted to be at Eastern, and you were willing to do whatever you had to do to stay."

She saw the wayward look in my eyes. My wife could always tell when I was deep in thought, even if I were trying to disguise that fact.

Linda asked, "What's on your mind?"

"Evelyn sent Darryl over here to borrow money."

"For what...they both have good jobs." She sat up—it hit her suddenly. "The only reason that they would need to borrow money, especially at this time of morning..." —Linda stared at me knowingly—"they're on drugs..."

I nodded slowly in agreement.

"I can't believe this. Darryl was so responsible. How long have they had this problem?"

"For a while...thing is...he's tired. He wants help. I'm going to give him a bed at Sheila's House."

"What about her?"

"She's not ready."

"My God... What's going to happen with Gail?"

"He asked if we could take care of her until he gets himself together."

"You think that Evelyn's gonna go for that?"

"He said that he would handle her."

The telephone interrupted our conversation.

Linda answered.

My wife listened as Evelyn attempted to sound as if she hadn't been up for forty-eight straight hours smoking dope. Darryl's wife tried to lie to Linda about why my cousin had shown up at our front door. Apparently, Evelyn had no idea that Gail was with her husband. I felt bad for my seven-year-old baby cousin. It was a shame that such a sweet child had to get caught up in her parents' problems.

Evelyn tried for several minutes to convince Linda that everything was just fine and that her husband needed to borrow money because he had to get his car out of the shop that morning. She went on to say that she would ensure that we had our money back on Friday, which was just two days away.

My wife asked her how much she wanted to borrow from us. Evelyn wanted us to give Darryl five-hundred dollars.

I wondered why my wife was having a conversation with this woman— why she continued listening to the lies. My curious glare was greeted with that look. Linda had a look that was like none I'd ever seen before. She rarely got upset, but when she did, the tight lips, puffy cheeks, and the little slits in her eyes meant that she had reached her boiling point.

All I could do was shake my head, because I knew what was coming.

"Evelyn, why the hell are you lying to me?" Linda blurted in anger.

I could clearly hear my cousin's wife's response. "Girl, what are you talking about?"

"Don't you 'girl' me. You have a beautiful little daughter that you should be thinking about—" My wife was interrupted before she could really tear Evelyn a new one.

"Where is my husband?"

"He's in the shower."

"Well, you tell him to bring my daughter home. I didn't even know he had taken her. I don't know what he's been telling ya'll, but he better bring my baby home."

"We'll be watching after Gail until you two get your acts together."

"You ain't keepin' my baby...I don't know who ya'll think ya'll are..."

Linda interrupted, "Greg is going to give Darryl a bed at the rehab center. I would suggest that you check yourself in. If you don't, that's up to you. But if you try to take Gail from here...if you try to disrupt her life any more than you already have, I'll report you to Child Protective Services. Now, if you wanna try me, you're more than welcome to. But I wouldn't suggest that you do..."

Suddenly, Linda took the phone from her ear and stared at it. I could hear the dial tone.

"I can't believe she hung up on me," my wife said as she rested the receiver on its cradle.

Before we could get our thoughts together, the phone rang again. Linda picked up the receiver before I could. "Hello..."

"Put my damn husband on the phone," I could hear the caller scream.

I reached for the phone—my wife handed it to me. "Evelyn... your husband is going into rehab. You can speak to him when he gets out. Don't call my house again until you're ready to get some help. If you call here again, I'll have you arrested for child endangerment and/or possession."

POLITICAL ENTRAPMENT

"Judge Mathis...Judge..." Maggie screamed from clear across the crowded hallway. I stopped and watched as my assistant maneuvered briskly through the chaos, her beauty turning heads as she made her way toward me.

I was running thirty minutes late.

My usual time of arrival was nine a.m., an hour before my court was to convene. But on this day, I didn't step into the courthouse until half past the hour because I had taken Darryl over to Sheila's House and gotten him settled in.

His situation was so unbelievable to me.

It was really hard for me to see my cousin in such a depressed state. He was really remorseful that he had taken the plunge into a world that he fought so hard to stay away from—a world that he saw every single day as a kid in the drug-infested jungles of Herman Gardens.

I could clearly remember how as a teen he tried to steer me in the right direction—always on my back about one thing or another. Always preaching how making the right choices were going to be crucial in our efforts to escape ghetto imprisonment.

Darryl was so straight-laced and all about the books. He used to always say that ghetto is a mentality more so than where you lived—that once educated about the differences, one could easily escape being a product of his or her environment. At the time he was telling me these things, I didn't have one clue what the hell he was talking about—it was all psychobabble to me.

Whatever the case, I never expected that he would allow himself to get trapped in what he described as "ghetto mentality." He never meant that everyone who was on drugs was from the ghetto—just that most from our environment try to escape their reality with dope because they've been programmed to settle.

Looking for a rational explanation for his bad decision, I truly didn't believe that he had ever recovered from his girlfriend's miscarriage. People give so many excuses for turning to drugs. But whatever the reasoning, it doesn't justify the hell that they put themselves through. Nor do they seem to understand or care how their selfishness affects others. Because that's what it is—selfishness. These people look for an escape from their reality, but what about their loved ones' reality? I had to watch someone I admired so much reduced to tears because he felt that he couldn't control his own mind, and he didn't know why.

It was easy to see the sense of urgency in Maggie's eyes, as she got closer. "Judge, I need to speak with you now."

"What's wrong?"

She ushered me into a secluded corner before whispering, "They're about to try..." My assistant needed to catch her breath.

"Try what?"

She huffed and puffed several times before saying, "Judge, they're going to be sending people to you... city councilmen or women, building inspectors, and others. They're going to offer bribes to you. As a matter of fact, a building inspector is waiting to speak with you now. He's one of the people involved."

I was blown away. "Who's behind this?"

"The chief judge, Carolyn Otto and Geoff Sanders..."

"How did you come across this?"

"How else...snooping..."

She scanned the hallway as if she were a part of some sort of espionage movie, where she was performing a cloak-and-dagger scene.

"I had to catch you before you got to your chambers." She opened her eyes as wide as she could; I'd never seen her so uneasy. My clerk was one of the coolest people I had run across in a long time, and to see her pushed off of her square was something new to me. "Judge Mathis, I know I didn't have to warn you because you would never involve yourself in what they're trying to trap you in, but I felt you should know just the same." Her demeanor didn't indicate to me that she really believed what she had said about my integrity. I guess she had been around long enough to see others get sucked into corruption.

"And you're positive that the chief judge is behind this?"

"Yes, sir…but it was Otto who convinced him that you were already taking bribes."

"I bet she didn't have to do much convincing," I said as I headed for my chambers.

❂❂❂

Maggie escorted a short, heavyset, half-bald white man by the name of Ronald Frazier into my chambers. I'd met this middle-aged building inspector just before we opened Sheila's House. Mr. Frazier was responsible for checking the center for code violations. He had given us the all-clear sign to open just a month prior, so if it hadn't been for Maggie's warning, I would have been totally surprised to see him. There was absolutely no reason for him to be visiting me.

When he entered, I was sitting at my desk going over my docket.

Because of my tardiness, I only had a few minutes to prepare. I really didn't have time for the bullshit that was about to take place—but I needed to get a gauge on how far the chief judge and his co-conspirators were willing to go in their efforts to discredit me.

I listened to this man pussyfoot around for six minutes about future inspections and how easily code violations creak up. He told me how he had inspected other properties and found that they were up to par—then he would conduct a surprise inspection in a matter of months and find numerous infringements. He never outright asked for a payment or favors, but he certainly was headed in that direction.

I interrupted his clumsy, meaningless conversation because I just had too much to go over before heading to my courtroom. Plus, I had to figure out a way to protect myself from the chief judge and his foolishness before allowing his flunkies to play their hand. But whom would I take this to? I couldn't go to the prosecutor; for all I knew, he was probably involved. I wasn't going to attempt to fight this fight by myself.

❂❂❂

"All stand...court's in session...the Honorable Judge Greg Mathis presiding." My bailiff's familiar voice echoed throughout the hollow walls.

Once again the faces in my courtroom seemed familiar. I made myself comfortable, picked up my gavel, and started court with a swift tap. My bailiff stood center stage and announced, "Case 64333A; the State versus Lisa Jennings, prostitution, and possession of drugs. Edgar Martinez for the defense and Terrence Simmons for the People..."

"Your Honor...Edgar Martinez, public defender... My client is here because she refused to help law enforcement entrap a drug dealer, a man who also happens to be her pimp," stated the short, chunky Hispanic with the spot in the middle of his head.

ADA Simmons intervened, "I hope you have more than hearsay..." The prosecutor was tall and gangly; he wore his long brown hair in a ponytail.

"Judge Mathis, my client was not on the stroll nor did she have drugs in her possession at the time of her arrest." The public defender stood, and gazed at the ADA. "Your Honor, the police had no reason whatsoever to stop, let alone search the defendant. This is not a probable cause issue. This was strictly a case of the police trying to gain leverage on a criminal that they've been unable to mount any evidence against."

The prosecutor immediately got to his feet. "Judge Mathis, Ms. Jennings is a known hooker and drug user. That in itself gave police probable cause. She was pulled over in an area known for drugs and prostitution."

"Judge, she lived in that area," the public defender countered matter-of-factly.

My question was directed to the prosecutor. "Explain to me, if you will…where does it say in the statute that a citizen spends the rest of his or her life being profiled due to his or her history?"

During the first arraignment of the day, I allowed both sides to squabble for eight minutes before I took control. I was in total agreement with the public defender. There was absolutely no legal reason for the police to have stopped that woman, no matter what they knew about her past. I dismissed that case and had a few words for the prosecutor. He asked if he could approach—I granted his request.

I covered my microphone.

The ADA whispered to me, "Judge Mathis, I think that you're doing an outstanding job."

"Thank you," I responded to his compliment.

He continued in a hush, "I'd like to apologize for wasting the court's time with this case, but when my bosses discovered that you were scheduled to preside, they insisted that we go through with this farce. I had argued that the police didn't have probable cause with my superiors. But once again, they knew you were scheduled to hear this case so they pushed for me to proceed."

Again, I was hit with what could have been construed as a conspiracy to undermine my seat. It seemed to me that the individuals behind trying to discredit me would stop at nothing. I saw this latest move as a ploy to test my knowledge of the law. I was very grateful to the man standing before me. Allies were what I needed because the people who were out to get me had formed a strong allegiance.

"I'd like to see you in my chambers after I adjourn for lunch."

Terrence Simmons was definitely someone whom I wanted to get to know. But I had to be careful—his cozying up to me could've been a scheme. I wasn't sure whether he was really trying to blow the whistle on his colleagues or simply make me believe that he was.

"I can do that. I'll be here most of the day anyway. I have six cases on your docket, including the next one," Simmons stated before he stepped away from my bench.

My next case dealt with domestic violence. I read the incident report prior to entering my courtroom, so I was well aware of the circumstances surrounding the case.

John and Silva Adams had gotten into an argument after consuming alcohol for nearly eight hours. John apparently snatched a bottle of Jim Beam from his wife, went into the kitchen, sat down, and attempted to guzzle what was left of the whisky. Silva crept up behind her husband and crushed his skull with a skillet, busting his head open and knocking him flat on his ass.

After seeing her husband of twenty-eight years lying unconscious and bleeding from his injury, she apparently realized what she had done.

Silva frantically picked up the phone and dialed 911.

When the paramedics arrived on the scene, they found it difficult to pull Silva away from her outstretched husband. She fought them off as they attempted to tend to John, so the medics called for the police.

According to the officers, when they arrived, their first thoughts were attempted robbery. Her actions were not those of someone who had committed assault but of someone very concerned. Silva was attempting to be protective of her husband. The officers also stated that both John and Silva reeked of alcohol, and she was unable to provide details surrounding the incident because of her intoxicated state.

One officer pointed out that when he finally saw the wound, he began looking for a possible weapon. That's when he discovered the skillet and saw blood on the back of it. He said he approached the wife and again asked what had happened.

He again emphasized that she wasn't coherent enough to answer.

The paramedics brought John around before he was rushed to the hospital. Upon his arrival, it was determined that he needed thirty stitches and a boatload of Tylenol. The CAT scan revealed that he sustained a concussion, but the blow to the head hadn't caused any other problems to the brain. The tricky part came when the doctor told the police that although the victim needed to sleep off the effects of his alcohol consumption, it would be a mistake to allow him to do so. The doctor recommended that

John be admitted for observation and that the police hold off from questioning him until the following morning.

The bony, sixty-eight-year-old man who stood before me was wearing a shabby gray suit that looked as if it had been pulled from a laundry bag. His dingy attire was as wrinkled as his tired face. Years of aggravation and frustration were clearly decipherable. The crow's-feet and the thick bags he carried under his dark-brown eyes spoke of his depressing life's journey. His halfhearted grin revealed that dental hygiene was definitely not his forte; years of alcohol abuse and neglect had taken a toll on what was left of his teeth.

The big gauze patch, which covered a hole in the back of his nappy Afro, was reflective of his wife's brutality. John looked to be in pain. However, this man was determined to speak in defense of his wife as she was being charged with domestic violence.

Silva was several years his elder but looked to be far younger. At first glance, her appearance gave the impression of a church-going grandmother. Truthfully, she was a person with a problem. If left unchecked, she could likely lose not only her freedom, but quite possibly her life.

John was asked to describe the circumstances that had led to him being clobbered. The question, as it was posed, ignited a few chuckles from the gallery; even the corners of my mouth turned up.

He danced around the question, but kept insisting that his loving wife was not at fault.

John carefully attempted to enunciate each word—a deliberate attempt to display that he had a formal education. His raspy monotone was undoubtedly caused by years of abuse to his throat. "I stole from her."

"What did you steal?" I asked.

He looked bewildered and jittery. "She had every right to hit me. We shouldn't be here." His eyes darted around the courtroom. "Can we go home, Judge?"

"Mr. Adams, we have to go through with these proceedings. So tell me, what did you steal from her?"

They both looked embarrassed as they made eye contact with each other.

"I felt that she would've insisted on another bottle if she were allowed to drink what was left," John said.

Silva interrupted her husband with a sincere plea to the court that she be allowed to seek help for her alcohol problem. While addressing the remorseful woman, I noticed the young man whom I mentor enter my courtroom. A tall, frail gentleman with a dark complexion accompanied Alvin. Cecilia Wright's son had his eyes locked on me as he sat in the back of the courtroom. His friend appeared to be as nervous as a devil worshipper walking into a church; it was as if he expected lightning to strike him at any time. The young man's eyes rapidly veered around my nearly packed venue while he made himself comfortable next to my biggest supporter's eldest child.

I ordered both John and Silva Adams to AA and gave Mrs. Adams probation because she had never been in trouble with the law.

The next case on my docket presented me with another prostitution and drug case, but this one was a bit troubling. When I was in my chambers reviewing my docket, I felt that I recognized the name of the person being charged. But because of that damn building inspector, I ignored the possibility. It wasn't until she stood before me that I realized who she was.

"Case number 832939B, the State versus Gerri Ward…one count prostitution, one count possession with the intent to distribute… Once again… Edgar Martinez for the defense and Terrence Simmons for the State…"

She was once a high school homecoming queen, head cheerleader, and all-around beauty. Gerri had the eye of every overactive testosterone-laden male that was on the campus of her high school. The stories that my wife would tell of her younger cousin were filled with promise. Everyone expected her to achieve great things because her intellect matched her beauty.

If a flower has been deprived of water and sunlight, it will surely wilt and die. Once an exquisite blossom filled with everything necessary for growth, Gerri had the potential that most only dream of. I didn't recognize the woman who stood before me as that once beautiful flower—she wasn't the same little girl whose potential seemed unlimited.

Her once full head of silky black hair was cut really low; it looked nappy, uncared for. In three short years, that once gorgeous redbone had deteriorated. Her face was covered with splotches of acne. Her once respectable appearance was now that of a full-fledged streetwalker.

For three years, no one in the family knew where Gerri was—she disappeared a year after graduating from high school. She left with a boy the family knew was nothing but trouble. He was a dropout who had a criminal record before his seventeenth birthday. Charges of firearms and drug possession were why the family attempted to steer Gerri clear of the young thug. But the disrespectful idiot managed to convince my wife's little cousin that he was the only one who loved her.

I couldn't honestly say that I didn't see this coming.

But nevertheless, seeing her hurt my heart—and I knew how devastated Linda would be if she had seen Gerri chewing gum like a cow as she stood with her hands on her hips. The girl blew a bubble or two as she swayed her hips from side to side.

She didn't recognize me.

"Would counsel please approach," I ordered.

The two gentlemen stepped to my bench. I covered my microphone and whispered to the lawyers. "I'm going to adjourn for about twenty minutes." I directed my attention toward the public defender. "I would like to see your client in my chambers …just your client."

To my surprise, when I entered my chambers, Maggie was standing at my desk with a package in hand. Although I hadn't received any surprise mail since the package containing the tape of Gram and Otto, my gut told me that my assistant was holding another such surprise.

"Judge, I was about to leave this on your desk." She placed the package down. I was mentally exhausted already, having had to deal with my wife's cousin entering my courtroom; the last thing that I needed was another tape of someone's infidelities to add to that psychological fatigue. Maggie could see that I was drained. I guess it was the way in which I lifelessly planted my ass in the soft leather and allowed my body to surrender to the comfort of my seat. "Thanks. Is there anything else?" My monotone was dry and defeated.

"No, sir." Maggie's gaze was caring. "You look stressed," she conveyed as she made her way around my desk.

I glanced at the package and saw that the mayor had sent it, so I didn't bother picking it up. Before I could say a word, my clerk began to massage my shoulders. I realized that I should have stopped her, but it felt so good. I exhaled, and closed my eyes.

"You're really tense...your muscles are so tight," she said while she gripped, rubbed, and manipulated the tension. That girl knew what she was doing.

"That feels good..." I whispered. It was euphoria that I should not have allowed myself to experience, because just as she hit the spot, just as she began to relieve the tension, my door flung open, and in stepped unexpected trouble. I tensed up immediately.

"What the hell is going on in here...I knew it!"

Maggie snatched her hands back as quickly as a child caught with his or her hands in a cookie jar. "Nothing, Mrs. Mathis..."

I sat up in my chair and gazed at my wife with my mouth hung open. Although my relationship with Maggie was strictly a business one, I knew that my wife was bordering on jealousy. She had never really come out and said anything, but I could tell that the long hours I had been putting in recently were causing her to be a little suspicious. Linda had expressed that she felt my assistant had a crush on me, but I laughed it off.

"Hey, baby...what a surprise," I said. In those awkward seconds, never once did I allow my eyes to stray from hers.

Maggie quickly excused herself and headed toward the door. Everything seemed to be happening in slow motion. When the attractive clerk got to the point where she had to pass my wife in order to exit, boy, if eyes could punch. My wife peered at that woman like Tommy Hearns readying himself for a championship bout.

"Hello, Mrs. Mathis," Maggie managed to say.

My wife's reply was cold, hard, and threatening. "Maggie."

It took me several minutes after my assistant left my chambers to break through the barrier that Linda had built around her.

"So…what brings you to these parts?"

"I met with Barbara around the corner…she was a little distraught."

"What's wrong with her?"

"You're not going to believe this…but she thinks that Gram is cheating on her."

"Are you serious?"

"Yes."

"Wow!" I responded. I thought to myself, *damn, that's all I need—my wife is going to be on edge—that damn "boys will be boys" shit that she always talks about is directed at me now.*

Linda and Barbara had become extremely close, and Linda felt that Gram was a very special person. My wife was usually good in judging one's character. This thing had her losing sight of mind.

I could tell she was terribly disappointed that there was even the slightest possibility that Gram could have been having an affair. She knew how Barbara felt about her husband. The socialite was a hard-nosed business-woman, but she was a pushover when it came to Gram.

"Does she have any idea who he's seeing?"

"She's hired a private investigator. I hope she's wrong. Greg…"

"Yeah."

"What's going on with you and Maggie?"

"Linda, we've talked about this. You know that I'm not cheating on you. Why are you acting so insecure?"

"I don't want to fight with you. But you have to admit—" She looked sad.

I quickly changed the subject. "Baby…you're never gonna believe who was in court seconds ago."

"Who?"

"Gerri…"

Linda's hunched shoulders and scrunched-up face clearly indicated that she had no idea who I was referring to.

"Your cousin…Little Gerri."

My wife's hands quickly covered her mouth in an attempt to stop her anxiety from escaping. "Where has she been? Why was she in your courtroom?"

"Relax, she'll be here in a second." I got up, and then sat on the end of my desk. "I took a recess so that I could speak with her. I'm hoping to get the answers to all your questions."

Linda sat up in her seat—shock was still evident. "Oh my God… It's been three years since anyone's heard from her."

"I really didn't get a chance to get into her case. When I noticed who she was, I immediately suspended proceedings and asked that her public defender send her in here. I don't think she realized who I was."

Maggie tapped twice, then opened the door and stuck her head in. "Judge, someone is here to see you."

"Send her in."

Linda stood and immediately directed her attention toward the door behind her.

I couldn't tell whether she was shaking her head in disbelief upon seeing her little cousin as she entered, or whether she was in shock of how Gerri looked. The sassy hooker, still popping gum, immediately recognized her older cousin.

"Heyyy!" Gerri said.

Linda extended her arms, but her cousin acted hard and uncaring as she walked past my wife and planted her ass in one of my chairs.

She asked in between snapping her gum. "You Cousin Greg, ain't you?"

My wife was stunned—she sat next to her cousin and placed her hand atop Gerri's. "Are you okay? Do you realize that the entire family has been looking for you for three years?"

"Whatever…" the wayward prostitute said as she slouched in her seat.

I was getting a little perturbed. "Sit yo ass up in that chair… And don't you think for one second that I won't have a bailiff come in here and car yo ass to jail…"

Gerri reluctantly sat up, but she continued to smack on her gum, which had become very annoying. I handed her a piece of paper. "Put that gum in here." The seriousness of my order made her comply instantly.

"Why ya'll trippin'? That's why I took off—'cause all ya'll do is trip," she said as she slowly wrapped her Bubblicious.

Over the next several minutes, Linda prodded and pried in an attempt to get her little cousin to loosen up enough to disclose some information about her life other than the obvious. But Gerri wasn't ready to share herself with anyone, especially the wife of a judge. She was now a product of the streets and wasn't at all interested in changing her life, or leaving her man. Linda wasn't able to get much out of her so she tried a different strategy; my wife started talking about the family—the kids, and how they were growing up. Three new children were born into the clan in the three years that she had been gone. One of the new additions was courtesy of Gerri's older sister, Pamela.

Lori Nicole was seven months old and was as cute as they come.

Linda reached for her purse, which sat at the side of my desk. She removed her wallet, opened it, and showed Gerri a picture of her new niece. Finally, I could see that the girl wasn't completely gone—she had a gleam in her eyes as she viewed little Lori. Gerri's once stone-cold demeanor was thawed, if only for a second.

I excused myself. I had a plan, and in order to execute it, I would have to enlist the help of the prosecutor and public defender handling Gerri's case. When I stepped from my chambers, I immediately noticed my bailiff standing in the reception area talking with Maggie as she sat behind her desk.

I interrupted their conversation and told them that I needed to speak with ADA Terrence Simmons and Public Defender Edgar Martinez. Maggie knew where to find the ADA and my bailiff had just left Martinez. As the two left my office, Alvin and his friend entered.

"You look real good in that robe, Judge," Alvin said with a smile. He closed the door behind him. "Judge Mathis...I need to speak with you for a second."

I sat on the edge of Maggie's desk and crossed my arms. "I don't have much time. What's on your mind?"

"This is my cousin Buster. We need your help, Judge."

"What's going on, Alvin?"

"Buster is on crack and he wants help."

"Have you spoken with your mother? She knows what to do to get him in."

"My mother won't help him."

"Why?"

"Because he's stolen from her... My mother doesn't believe that he can be helped."

"That doesn't sound like Cecilia Wright." I directed my next statement to Alvin's cousin. "Buster is it?"

"Yes, sir," he answered.

"How old are you?"

"I'm twenty-nine, sir..."

"How long have you been using?"

"Since I was seventeen..."

"Why now?"

"What do you mean, Judge?"

"Why...after so many years of living that life do you want to seek help?"

A tear escaped his weary eyes. "I'm tired." He sniffed several times, then wiped his eyes before continuing, "I'm so tired."

"Do you have a job? Do you carry insurance of any kind?"

"I don't have a job, or insurance."

For some reason I felt for him—I couldn't exactly figure out why. I didn't make it a habit to feel sorry for people because that emotion won't help them; it only hinders.

"If I give you a bed, you're gonna have to work around the center to pay for your stay."

Alvin smiled at me and whispered, "Thank you."

"You guys step into my chambers for a second. I have something that I want to give to Buster," I said as I walked toward the door that led to my chambers.

Cecilia's son and nephew both followed me into my workspace. When we entered, I noticed that Linda and Gerri were still seated—the two seemed to be communicating. They both briefly directed their attention toward Buster, Alvin, and me.

"Excuse us for one second," I said while heading toward my desk.

Buster roamed around. He picked up pictures, looked at plaques. He even pulled a book from my shelf, while Alvin followed me to my desk.

MY WIFE WON'T UNDERSTAND

Here I am again, on the eleventh floor of city hall, I said to myself as I sat in front of his desk. It wasn't the same mahogany executive desk that at one time engulfed a portion of the spacious office. This one was modern glass. On my very first visit, I remembered seeing plaques, what seemed like hundreds, which acknowledged nearly two decades of accomplishments. There were still commemorative inscriptions, but far fewer, and they hung on the opposite wall. The only thing that looked the same was the large picture window, which offered a splendid view of the Detroit River, and the skyline of Windsor, Canada.

When I first entered that office several years prior, the most powerful mayor in the country had summoned me. At that time I couldn't believe that this man was about to offer me a position on his staff. As the first black mayor of Detroit, Coleman Young was a force; he was the only mayor in these United States that presidents feared. The men who occupied the office of the presidency while Young reigned as mayor knew that when he came to town, he didn't come to hear the bullshit—he came to get results. Neither before, nor since, has there ever been an elected official who had the balls to curse out the top man in the country. No one was too good to be called a *muthafucker* as far as Coleman Alexander Young was concerned, not even the president. Hell, he called himself, Mr. Motherfucker!

My reminiscing had to be put on hold as Mayor Aaron Dennis entered his office. I didn't bother looking over my shoulder as he approached. I simply waited for him to step to his desk before I would get to my feet and extend a hand to him.

Dennis was on his second term and was looking to push for a third. But he was beginning to develop an annoying arrogance—one which had become apparent to his supporters and political opponents alike. Once a prudent and extremely likable politician, his newfound egotism had caused him to be reckless both politically and privately.

The media knew that they could get under his skin by simply referring to him as the second-most powerful man in the city. When the papers were fed up with his rants or his strong-arming, they would immediately put him in his place by stating fact: His biggest supporter was the most powerful man in the city. The press would insist that if Gram Olson wanted the mayor out of office, he would be out.

"Hello, Mayor," I said as we firmly gripped each other's hand.

"Judge, I'm sorry that we're meeting under these circumstances. Did you get a chance to view the tape that I forwarded to your office?" he asked as we both made ourselves comfortable.

"Yes…" was my disgruntled reply.

"I had no idea what it was until I looked at it," the mayor whispered. "Why would it be sent to me?" he questioned as if he expected that I would have a logical answer. But I was as clueless as he was—for nearly a month, I hadn't heard a peep from the individual or individuals responsible for sending the package containing the tape. Once I told Gram about it, I kinda let it go. I hadn't thought about it until I got the package from the mayor. I was truly stunned when I saw what had been recorded.

"It's not what it looks like," I said defensively.

"I'm not here to stand in judgment. I'm glad that I got that tape, and I'm hoping for your sake that there aren't any more. Whether it's innocent or not, it's not a good look." The mayor's tone was a little belittling.

He's got nerve, I thought to myself. Without thinking, I blurted, "So, how did you handle the tape of you and Otto?"

His face lit up like the Christmas tree at Rockefeller Center. He curiously tilted his head slightly to the right; the man was obviously freaked out. It was as if he were completely oblivious to our entire conversation. "What tape…?"

"Gram didn't tell you?"

"Tell me what?"

"Gram has a tape of you and Otto engaging in sex."

The mayor got to his feet—he stared intently at me without saying a word. It was at that moment I realized, for whatever reason, Gram had failed to inform Aaron Dennis that he was an unwitting participant in some sort of pornographic tryst.

"How could that be?" the truly stunned mayor murmured as he casually strolled over to his picture window and peered out. The top elected official in the city seemed to go into contemplation.

I wanted to say something, but I didn't think that he would answer; he was trance-like. Political controversy had to be the least of his concerns. If I were to wager a bet, it was his wife and children that he was most worried about.

"How did he get a tape?" the mayor whispered under his breath. I wasn't sure if he were posing the question to me, or to himself.

I got to my feet and slowly made my way toward the window. "Someone is playing a very dangerous game. You received a tape, Gram got one, and so did I."

My declaration got his attention. He directed his wayward gawk toward me before saying, "What! Who's on the third tape?"

For the next ten minutes, I bombarded the honorable Aaron Dennis with inquiries of my own. I didn't want to leave any room for him to ask me questions about the tape that I had at one time in my possession, because I wasn't about to reveal that the third tape was of Carolyn Otto and Gram.

The most important question I posed was, why would he jeopardize his name for a fling, especially with someone as spiteful and vindictive as Carolyn Otto? Plus, that bitch had racist tendencies. Her sleeping with a black man, no matter how powerful, immediately led me to believe that she was up to something.

I also wondered if Aaron's newly discovered self-importance had finally gotten the best of him. The only thing that I could get out of him was that he and Gram were going at it. Apparently, the billionaire had been using his power with the city council in an effort to block several land development proposals that the mayor was throwing his weight behind. And, to top it off, Aaron Dennis wasn't too pleased that Gram would be running for mayor in the upcoming election. When the mayor divulged that information, it made perfect sense to me why Gram didn't share that he had received the tape of his honor and Otto.

I ended up leaving the mayor's office in the midst of a cat-and-mouse game. I avoided going into details about the third tape, and he avoided answering my questions concerning him and the ADA.

I began to think, *the land deal that he was referring to, could someone associated with that deal be behind the tapes. That building inspector who stopped by my office unexpectedly, could he be tied in with this somehow?*

If it hadn't been for me receiving that tape from the mayor, the drama concerning the recordings would have continued to a footnote.

The brutal slaying of Sheila Morgan had become my top priority. I was so caught up with trying to get the district attorney's office to work with the police, and make a deal with Eugene Scott, that I had completely forgotten about Gram's situation.

Carolyn had been assigned Eugene's case—but that heifer refused to budge.

My leverage was a little different now (not talking blackmail), but with her connection to the two tapes, she was a person of interest to me in more ways than one. If she were unaware that she was being filmed, then maybe she would be grateful that I would've given her a heads-up. A visit to her office could prove to be beneficial. Either way, I needed to determine who it was, and what possible reason they had in bringing me into the middle of the shit storm that was brewing. So, I headed to the prosecutor's office.

I despised the woman, but I had to admit, she was extremely attractive. She wore a pin-striped, powder-blue power suit like she was poured into it. Carolyn sat on the end of her desk and crossed her shapely legs. "I told you where I stand with the Scott case."

"I'm not here about Eugene Scott," I said as I stood before her.

"Well, what's this about?"

"I'm here to talk about Gram Olson and Mayor Aaron Dennis."

The prosecutor's tone was laid-back. "What about them?"

"You're going to ruin them…" was my claim.

"Look, I don't have time for games, so either tell me what this is about… or get out so that I can get back to work."

"Attitude is not something that I'm prepared to deal with. I'm sure that what I have to say to you is worth three or four minutes of your precious time." My sarcasm was noteworthy, but since I went straight into putting her on Front Street, she didn't have time to respond to it. "Now, you can either take the time to listen, or wait until the press gets hold of the information that I'm trying to share with you."

She suddenly got interested in what I was saying. The prosecutor uncrossed her long, sexy legs, got to her feet, and positioned her five-foot three-inch frame directly in front of me. "What's this really about?"

"What are you up to?" I asked.

"Again, I don't have time for games…"

"You're screwing both Gram and Aaron."

She turned her back to me. I had clearly struck a nerve; the woman's stride was strong and deliberate as she made her way over to her desk. The ADA then made herself comfortable in her chair. The sassy, controlling, prosecutorial witch, like all cats preparing to fight, hunched her back, and the fangs came out—she was ready to attack. "What do you think you know about me!" She tightened her beady green eyes, and then said with a snarl, "Whatever it is that you're trying to do…I want you to know that it won't work. And, if I were you…I would be extremely careful with throwing out accusations…"

"As much I would love to see your ass bite the dust, I figure even you should have an opportunity to defend yourself." I made myself comfortable in a chair that was positioned in front of her desk. "There are videotapes circulating around. These sexually explicate recordings show you, the mayor, and Gram in compromising positions."

"Oh my God…you've got to be kidding."

Based on her response, I was sure that the prosecutor was unaware that her privacy had been invaded. And, I think that she was more flabber-gasted to learn that I had actually witnessed her naked, than whether I had developed an opinion of her promiscuity. In order to clear up any mis-conceptions that she may have had, I was ready to tell her what I thought of her. I was ready to call it like it was—the fact of the matter: I knew that she was a power-hungry whore long before viewing the tapes.

I talked to her for several minutes. Of course, I never went into discussing the various possibilities surrounding the tapes. And, I never tried to hold what I knew over her head in order that she would work with me on Sheila's case; I didn't operate that way.

My own thoughts were clearly on who could have been behind the tapes—someone had gotten into Otto's home, and into my office. When I thought about someone gaining access to my office, a thousand things ran through my mind. *Why didn't Gram talk to Otto about being filmed in her house? Why didn't he talk to the mayor about the tape? Who the hell was trying to set me up? And most of all, what would my wife think if the tape that was sent to the mayor ended up in her hands?*

While on my way to appear as a guest on a colleague's radio program, I thought about Linda. My wife was a bit upset when she left my chambers earlier. No one would blame her. After all, she had been informed that her little cousin was working as a prostitute for over three years. Atop that, she walked in as my assistant was giving me a massage, though it was innocent. Linda had been hinting that she suspected my recent long hours were due to my having an affair with Maggie, so the tape that the mayor provided to me would surely go a long way in confirming her suspicions.

When I put the tape into my VCR earlier that day, and sat on the end of my desk with remote in hand, I wasn't prepared for what I saw when I clicked the start button. There I was, sitting behind my desk going over paperwork. As I continued watching the tape, my first thought was why someone would bother breaking into my office to rig up a video recording device. I couldn't figure out what they expected to accomplish.

Then she came in.

My eyes were locked on the screen. I watched with intense curiosity as my depiction looked up from the documents and gazed at her. She stood before my desk, her perfect Coke-bottle figure draped in a chiffon pullover sundress. The audio on the tape had been purposely removed.

When I walked around my desk, Maggie and I embraced, but because there was no sound, I was sure that the innocent hug would be looked at differently.

I was simply congratulating my assistant for her decision to take the bar, but without the sound, what was being portrayed on the screen could be construed as misconduct.

My thoughts were all over the place. I figured that I would speak with both David and Maggie the following morning. Someone had gotten into my office, planted, and then removed a video recording device; and apparently, they did so undetected. But for now, I had to think about the radio program—because I was turning into the parking lot of WCHB.

INNER CITY JUDGE

"**H**ello, Detroit... Welcome to 'Keepin' It Real.' I'm your host, Moe D. Today we will be talking with someone that I consider to be a *very* special guest. He comes to us from the streets of Detroit. His story is one of inspiration. This man pulled himself away from the clutches of gang affiliation. As a one-time member of those dapper bandits, the Errol Flynns, this man was surely on his way to a life of crime...but he woke up.

"Our guest was recently elected the youngest judge ever to hold a seat on the 36th District Court. This electrifying political powerhouse has also recently joined the WCHB family as the host of his very own show."

The man, whose voice was bigger than his six-and-a-half-foot frame, directed his attention toward me, before I was welcomed to his show.

"Judge Greg Mathis! I wanna welcome you to 'Keepin' It Real.'...How are you today, Judge?"

I scooted my chair closer to the table, shifted my eyes toward my host, and smiled before answering, "I'm just fine, Moe... Thank you for having me on today."

My host continued with his smooth baritone setup voice, a monotone known for taking his guests into a sense of comfort. Maurice Daniels was a hard-nosed deejay, with a cutting-edge style when it came to interviewing.

"It's not every day we get to have a Black judge on our show. So we thank you for dropping in."

"No problem..." I replied.

"Judge Mathis, you were considered to be a longshot for the seat for which you were elected. Why do you think that you overcame the negative press and prevailed?"

"Well, Moe, I think that the people had a clear understanding of what I bring to the table." I lightheartedly asked, "How many judges do you know that have a true working knowledge of the criminal element...I mean, from the inside?"

The DJ chuckled. His sparkling white teeth were clearly noticeable because of his dark-skin tone. The disc jockey of ten years sported a neatly trimmed, faded haircut and his face looked to be as smooth as a baby's bottom, no facial hair whatsoever. The hip-hop attire that he was wearing—a designer high-yellow Tommy Hilfiger hoody, baggy jeans, and Air Jordans—made homeboy look like a high school senior, although he was a thirty-two-year-old grown man. If I had seen him on the street, I never would have imagined that voice coming from him.

Out of nowhere, his hard-hitting voice took over. "I heard that you were involved with a stickup at Cobo Hall during a concert when you were running with the Flynns street gang. Can you tell us about that?"

"The Flynns, as far as I was concerned, were like no other assemblage. We were over two hundred strong, and although we were hoods, we certainly didn't dress the part.

"Our motif was that of old-school gangsters—our double-breasted suits and Borsalino Como fedoras contributed to our debonair personas. We had the mentality that we were untouchable, and that the city belonged to us. Whatever we wanted, we took. And no one—I do mean no one—would dare try and stop us.

"We named ourselves after Hollywood's greatest swashbuckler and enigma, because we saw ourselves as being dangerous, confident, and yet mysterious."

With Maurice bringing up my gang affiliation, I knew that he was about ready to pounce. I gave a slight nod to acknowledge that I was expecting him to go there, then I said, "Yes...that's true. The Average White Band was playing that night. My boys and I took over the stage and held up the place."

The DJ was harsh in his counter. "You sound like you're proud of that…"

I could feel him trying to bait me—but I had a little something waiting on him. I've been around long enough to know that if you put all your cards out on the table, it's hard for someone to use one of them against you.

"I'm not proud of the fact that I was a malicious child, nor am I ashamed to talk about my past. You see, Maurice, what I did as a kid will help me to understand the individuals that stand before my court every day. I have a better chance of identifying those who will take full advantage of a second opportunity, the way I did. If I'm able to steer one in the right direction, then my past, and everything that I did wrong, would be worth it…because I could then honestly say that I was intended to walk the path that I've walked. God knew that I would be strong enough to handle the trials and tribulations of being a teenaged gangster. Remember one thing, Maurice, God truly watches over fools and babies. Back then, I was a fool… but, I was still His baby."

I could see in his eyes that he was not going to try and ambush me again, because he knew that he couldn't. I think he realized at that moment that there was absolutely nothing he could dig up from my past that would shame me. The hard-hitting Maurice Daniels had a newfound respect for me. He immediately went back to his setup voice and didn't divert for the rest of the interview.

"Judge, I hear that you have a mentoring program."

"Yes, a couple of friends and I started the program to give young people, ages sixteen to twenty-six, a chance at a better life." I looked at the radio personality before saying, "Moe, do you mind if I say a little something to a few people?"

"Not at all…"

"I want to say to the parents of the younger individuals in our program… I thank you so much for helping to make the program what it is. I would especially like to say thank you to one particular mother. Although we have an age limit, Ms. Cecilia Wright has underaged children that participate in the program. But because she has become such an inspirational force, who am I to say that they are too young. Thank you, Cecilia."

"Judge Mathis, I hear that you've also opened a drug rehabilitation center?"

"Because of a very generous donation, we were able to open the center—it's something that I'm very proud of."

"May I inquire about your benefactor?"

"I haven't discussed releasing that information with my financier yet... so I would rather keep that close to the vest until they give me permission to do otherwise."

"What prompted your desire to open a rehab center?"

"Well, for a long time, I watched drugs drain the life out of people. I have family and friends who have fallen prey to drugs. Let me tell you something, Moe. The young people in our community need to see that we as adults are willing to do what we can to create a better environment for them. We have to begin to really look out for our community because those that don't live within it, don't care. A little more than a month ago, a body was discovered in an alley on the Eastside—a young, beautiful woman had been decapitated."

My host said, "I heard about that. That's crazy..."

"Yes, it is. What's really crazy is when people of authority won't do everything that they can to protect the citizens of this community."

"You sayin' that the police aren't looking into it—and if not, could it be because they don't look at drug addicts and prostitutes as being people?"

"No. I'm not trying to say that the police aren't looking into it, because they are. But their hands are tied. What I am saying is that there is a possible lead that is not fully being explored by the prosecutor's office. And let's get one thing straight, Sheila Morgan was not addicted to drugs, nor was she a prostitute. She was a hard-working mother of three who has family and friends that loved and cherished her. Even if she were on drugs or selling her body...she was still a human being, deserving of justice."

I was well aware that my comments would ignite a political firestorm. I could expect backlash from the prosecutor's office, the chief judge, and even the mayor. But I knew that there would be repercussions for speaking my mind going into the interview. I also knew that I had an obligation to say what I said. I made a promise to Darwin that I would do everything in my power to seek justice for his cousin—and I had every intention of doing so. I prepared myself to deal with the consequences of my decision to speak up.

The rest of the interview went well. Maurice turned out to be a cool dude; he ended up volunteering to participate in the rehab center and the mentoring program. Turns out, he had a brother who was using crack and he didn't know what to do to help him. I told him that if his brother were ready to undergo treatment, Sheila's House would welcome him with open arms.

After doing Maurice's show, I had to run down the hall and prepare to host my own program.

I spent several minutes prepping my guests on the various subjects that we would cover. I ensured each of them that they would have an opportunity to give their opinions about the Morgan investigation, the rehabilitation center, and what the hiring of several members of Young Adults Asserting Themselves would mean to the community.

All three would give their views on what we needed to do as individuals to uplift the community. I would ask each what citizens needed to do to prevent Detroit from being turned into a ghost town. But first, of course, I would give a little background on each guest.

Everyone in the studio complimented Gram Olson on his expensive titanium Movado and black onyx cufflinks which came to view when he removed his black blazer and draped it over the back of his chair. The businessman nodded in acceptance of the flattering remarks that were directed toward him. He tucked the end of his gray silk tie between the last two buttons of his white shirt before making himself comfortable.

Darwin Washington rolled the sleeves to his light-brown shirt over his elbows. He then flung his dark-brown tie over his left shoulder before relaxing in the chair next to Gram.

Ronald Daly didn't bother removing the blazer to his gray suit. He reached into his inside jacket pocket and pulled out his reading glasses. The police commander put on his glasses and then took a seat.

As soon as they were all seated, two of my assistants fitted my three guests with headsets. My interns adjusted our visitors' microphones. They then placed glasses of ice water before the gentlemen whom I had invited to participate in a call-in session on my community affairs program.

My producer held up his right index finger, poised and ready.

My attention was drawn toward him. I then split my focus between watching my producer readying to give his cue—and the flickering "ON THE AIR" sign mounted over the door. We had seconds before our theme music would end, and the sign, which indicated we were broadcasting across the metro area, would beam a steady white and red illumination.

He pointed his finger in my direction. I leaned closer to the microphone. My eyes once again veered toward the "ON THE AIR" sign; its bright light was my final cue.

"Welcome to 'Street Judge.' I'm your host...Judge Greg Mathis."

As usual I opened the show with a passionate plea for anyone to step up with information concerning the brutal slaying of Sheila Morgan. Although a month had passed since she was murdered, I felt that it was imperative that I kept the crime fresh on everyone's minds.

"Ladies and gentlemen, I once again ask that anyone who thinks that they might be able to shed light on the brutal slaying of Ms. Sheila Morgan, please step forward. As a community, we must do whatever is necessary to work toward keeping our city safe. Sheila was a young, loving mother...a woman dedicated to doing whatever she could to care for her children. So, please, there has to be someone out there who knows something. We've had several leads that haven't panned out. The police need your help. Dial 343-3333 and leave any information that you think might be of help."

I took a sip of water before I continued, "I have seated next to me three individuals who are very interested in the plight of the city. They will be fielding questions for the next hour. These gentlemen represent a smorgasbord of personal goals. They all have dedicated themselves to the pursuit of achievement...and they are just as determined to give back. I have with me, to my left, Mister Darwin Washington, journalist from the *Michigan Chronicle*; and Mister Gram Olson, president and CEO of a Fortune 500 company, and board member of several others. To my right, a very dear friend; this man had a hand in my achievements, the head of Special Crimes for the Detroit Police Department, Commander Ronald Daly." I made eye contact with each before saying, "Welcome to 'Street Judge,' gentlemen."

All three replied in unison, "Thank you for having us."

"Let me start with Mister Washington. Ladies and gentlemen, I've come to know this man due to my interest in the Sheila Morgan investigation. Darwin and Sheila are family. Sheila was his cousin… The two were extremely close. Once again, welcome to the show, Darwin."

The journalist and I made eye contact before he replied, "My pleasure. I'd like to thank you, Judge Mathis, for everything you've done in trying to help my family bring closure to this terrible tragedy. Since I've come to know you, you have been extremely helpful and supportive. And for that, Sheila's children and I thank you from the bottom of our hearts."

"You coming to the aid of our mentoring program is thanks enough, and is greatly appreciated. You've made a significant difference since you've been involved. I've also seen the effects of your thoughtfulness toward the two young men who discovered your cousin's body."

"Judge, it's all about the kids. We adults have screwed up this world so much that if we don't take the time to give the children insight on our mistakes, that would be a sin."

"Darwin, I've heard that you had a really rough childhood."

"Yes, I did. I was teased each and every day because my mother was, and still is, a drug addict. When the kids discovered that the homeless woman they encountered every day was my mother…of course, you know the old adage, children can be cruel. Well, they ripped me to no end."

I asked, "What do you think stopped you from going down the same path that your mother took? I mean, it wasn't as if you had a father to help mold and guide you."

"I went to live with Sheila and her mother when I was ten. The two of them wouldn't allow me to feel sorry for myself. They instilled pride, determination, and self-respect in me. I was constantly told that if I were not going to love myself, then I couldn't expect that anyone else would respect me, let alone love me."

"If you could say something to the person that took the life of your cousin, what would it be?"

"Well, Judge Mathis, I would ask that that person understand that he took the life of a very special person. She was a very forgiving person. I can guarantee that the person responsible for her death has already been forgiven. Sheila was like that. So I ask that you turn yourself in and take responsibility. Children have been affected by your actions—not just Sheila's children, but the two teens that discovered her body."

I directed my next statement toward the law enforcement officer. "Commander Daly, could you tell my listeners what, if any, progress the police have made in the Morgan case?"

"We've run across several leads, but we haven't had anything solid. Our investigation has been stalled. But I continue to work the leads that come in. Everyone expects that the police can solve any crime, but that's not the case. The majority of crimes committed would not be solved if it weren't for the public."

My producer cued me. It was time for the station to break for commercial spots, so I interjected, "Excuse me, Ron, but we have to pay some bills." I leaned closer to the microphone and spoke to my listeners, "Stay tuned for more of 'Street Judge'...right here on WCHB-FM, 96-point-7 on your radio dial."

When we cut to our commercials, I allowed my eyes to veer in the direction of Gram. I gave him a hand gesture before saying, "Gram, I need to speak with you in private after the show."

"I was going to ask that we speak. I got a call before I got to the station. We do have some things that we need to discuss, so I'll stay around," Gram stated.

Upon the conclusion of our forty-five-second spot, I introduced Gram and told my audience of his and his wife's support, and how one of his many companies, Olson's Technologies, had designated itself the official sponsor of YAAT.

Gram made it a point to express his feeling of how our organization made it easy for his company to open the doors to the bright minds of the community. He expressed that he was truly impressed with the way in which the young people of my organization had been prepared for the work force. Gram surprised me when he announced that Olson's Technologies was prepared to commit over one million dollars to YAAT's scholarship program.

I expressed my appreciation for his and his wife's generous donations all across the board. He and Barbara allowed me to inform my audience of their many contributions, so it was with great pleasure that I revealed that the Olsons were responsible for funding Sheila's House. That's when the phones lit up.

I introduced our first caller. "Lilly Thompson, you're on the air."

"Judge Mathis, I love your show," the elderly woman expressed.

"Thank you, Lilly. Did you have a question or comment?"

"First, I'd like to extend my condolences to Mister Washington and his family. I don't know what's gotten into our young people."

Darwin responded to the caller's sentiments, "We thank you for your thoughts and prayers."

Lilly went on to say, "I read your column all the time, Mister Washington. I'm proud that you are always willing to put it like it is. You've touched on everything that this city needs to address. I especially love your hard-hitting exposés on the drug epidemic and how our own people have become modern-day plantation owners—and how the pushers don't care that they have reduced our people to thieves and murderers. I'm praying that one day your words will enlighten these young folk. Mister Washington, I hope that the tragedy that you have experienced doesn't prevent you from exposing the truth."

"I can assure you, Ms. Thompson, I have no intention of altering my approach," Darwin said with a smile.

Lilly Thompson continued, "Judge Mathis, I didn't vote for you, and for that I am ashamed. I was like so many others that believed that you were not the right person for the job. I am so happy that you've proven me wrong. Keep up the good work. I know that others would like to call in so I'll be quick. I just have a few more things to say."

I insisted, "Take your time, Lilly."

"Mister Olson, I would like to thank you and your wife for your contributions to the community. You are truly a rare breed."

Gram smiled and said with all sincerity, "This is my community also… there is absolutely no reason whatsoever why you should be thanking me. My wife and I believe that Detroit is a fantastic place. We would like to do our part in bringing this city back. Barbara and I both believe that teaming up with Judge Mathis is the first step."

"I have a question for the police commander. Mister Daly, I don't want to sound as if I'm playing the race card. But why is it that a crime such as the Morgan case doesn't receive the same priority from the police as it would have if, say, the woman was from Dearborn Heights?" the caller asked.

Ron was kind of perturbed. He had to field that same question for over a month, and to him, it was getting old. "Ms. Thompson, I can assure you that we have given this case top priority. But the police…regardless of what the citizens of this or any other community might think, can do but so much. We need the public's help in solving most crimes. When no one steps up, that makes our jobs more difficult."

Ms. Thompson thanked everyone and we ended the call.

Most callers expressed their sympathy to Darwin and his family. However, a few suggested that since the crime was committed in the city, it had to be a black-on-black offense. The Caucasian participants were unsympathetic and wanted to make it clear that Detroit, as long as it remained eighty percent black, would never recover. These callous individuals expressed a real resentment toward Gram and Barbara for attempting to help uplift the black community. They hated Mayor Dennis and called him a black arrogant ass.

Gram held his own with exposing their racist remarks. He blasted them for insinuating that Blacks were barbarians. He gave statistics reflecting that, unlike what one caller claimed, Blacks were not the ones burdening the state when it came to welfare recipients. Gram's numbers revealed that an overwhelming amount of whites made up the state's public aid commitment.

I was truly impressed with Gram's convictions, which made it even harder for me to swallow that he had cheated on his wife with someone whom I couldn't stand.

Ron was not just sitting idly while Gram was being bombarded. The commander made it clear to the racist callers that they were contributing to the problems of our society. He also gave a few statistics of his own, making it clear that overall, heinous crimes like the one perpetrated against Sheila Morgan were more likely to be committed by a Caucasian. The law enforcement officer ignited the ire of those callers with his claim that his own race had produced the likes of Bundy, Gacy, Berkowitz and Dahmer, just to name a few. Both Gram and Ron made it clear to my audience that they were about helping people regardless of skin color. Ron even offered to help some of the ignorant callers by passing along the names of a few psychiatrists that could help them work through their issues.

But it was our final caller of the day that shook both Gram and me to our foundations.

The voice was distorted, obviously disguised behind some sort of altering device. I couldn't believe that the person behind the tapes that were distributed to Gram, the mayor, and me had the nerve to call in to my show.

"Mister Olson, Judge Mathis, I hope that you two, and your friend—the mayor—can appreciate my gift. As I said in my letters to you both, I would be reaching out when it was time. As you may have guessed, it's time."

"Who is this?" I asked. My demeanor was of a very serious nature. The person on the other end of the phone had pissed me off with his games.

"Mister Olson, I hear that you have aspirations of becoming mayor..."

Gram didn't seem at all bothered by the caller, even though the person on the other end had gathered information that could ruin his life. I was more perturbed than the billionaire. I wanted my producer to cut the caller short—the show was approaching its conclusion, but it didn't seem that the signal for the end was coming fast enough.

"Yes, I'm very interested in running for office. Tell me something, why is it that you disguise your voice?"

"Because...I'm not ready to reveal myself. When it's time for me to announce to the city how I'm going to destroy you and your friends, then—and only then—will I come forward. But, for now, I'm going to make sure that you don't get a chance to use your financial power to buy an election.

My plan is to ruin you, the current mayor, and the man that is the host of this show." The voice distortion equipment that he used didn't camouflage the malicious intent of the caller.

That was it for the caller—my producer was not going to stand by and listen anymore. The call was disconnected, and I was given the signal to end the show, which I did without hesitation.

"First, I'd like to thank my guests for stopping by. This has been a very productive hour. I'd like to say to the last caller, you're playing a very dangerous game, my friend. Whatever it is that you hope to accomplish, your methods are a bit extreme."

As I prepared to end the show with my usual parting words, Darwin interrupted me.

"Excuse me, Judge Mathis...would you mind if I said something before the show goes off the air?"

"Not at all," I replied.

Darwin leaned closer to his microphone. He gave a quick glance to everyone in the room before saying, "Donna, I know that you're listening to the show." He took a deep breath, and then blurted, "You have meant so much to me over the years. You've supported me in any and everything that I have tried to do since we've been together. Most of all, I appreciate you supporting me in my decision to raise my cousin's children. I will always love you for that." He paused. He seemed to be attempting to gather himself.

The journalist's and his girlfriend's lives had been interrupted by unforeseen circumstances. Through it all, both he and his longtime girlfriend realized how special their love truly was for each other. And Darwin understood that he was blessed with an extremely selfless, loving woman.

I watched as he tried to maintain his composure; I could tell that Sheila was on his mind. He and I had talked about how he regretted that his cousin wouldn't be around to share in his special day.

He wiped his watering eyes. Darwin peeked at everyone once again before stumbling over his words. "Well...you know. Anyway, if you still want to marry me, I'm ready. I think that we should get married as soon as possible; that is, if you're still willing."

I nodded my head in approval of the journalist's proposal. My wife and I had come to really like Donna, and we both felt that the two of them would make a wonderful couple. Both were so altruistic and caring. I winked at my guest as he sat back in his chair. He seemed relieved that he had gotten that proposal off his mind. Darwin directed his next question to me. But, before he could say a word, my producer pointed toward us.

My producer hit the speaker. "Donna is on the line...she says...yes! She'll marry you."

Everyone in the studio clapped and cheered.

Darwin smiled and turned his attention toward me. "Judge Mathis... would you do the honor of marrying us?" the journalist asked.

I was completely caught off guard by his request, but I was also honored. I smiled. "I'd be honored."

We all laughed.

After signing off, the guys and I congratulated the journalist on his upcoming nuptials. We sat around for a few minutes giving him an old-fashioned ribbing. He thought it was crazy that three happily married men would try to give him the business about the pitfalls of marriage. But it was all in fun. During our exchange of adolescent banter, I couldn't help but wonder what was going on in Gram's head. I wondered why anyone would even consider cheating on a woman like Barbara. But someone else knew—someone who seemed to be interested in using what he or she knew as a weapon in an effort to destroy the billionaire.

It seemed as if Darwin's proposal had taken Gram's mind off what had taken place prior to the journalist asking for his girlfriend's hand in marriage.

It was Ron Daly who reminded us of the call, and the tone in which the person behind it had delivered his message.

The police commander directed his question to both Gram and me. "The person on that last call sounded as if he wanted blood...what's that all about?"

Before either of us could respond, one of my assistants entered the booth and handed me a note. "Thank you, Sandy," I said as I unfolded the piece of paper.

The message stunned me. Everyone could see that my focus was distorted.

They were all aware that the piece of paper I held was responsible for my sudden loss of concentration.

"What's wrong?" Darwin asked.

I stood. "The rehabilitation center...two gunmen shot up the place. I gotta get over there."

SHEILA'S HOUSE

W
e could see the red and blue flashing lights as we came within a block of the center; hordes of people were rushing toward the scene. When we turned onto the street, Darwin, Ron and I were all very nervous—several marked and unmarked squad cars surrounded an emergency medical vehicle. Detectives and uniformed officers walked the perimeter around the cordoned-off rehabilitation center. What was before us had the makings of a serious tragedy.

When we pulled to the curb opposite the red-brick, forty-six-hundred-square-foot structure, which once served as a Kroger grocery store, I noticed the panic-stricken faces of area residents as they stood around discussing the drama that had just unfolded.

My friends and I rushed from the car and through the maze of spectators.

We attempted to head toward the commotion, but two uniformed officers, whose jobs were to prevent anyone from walking onto the perimeter, impeded our progress. Ron flashed his badge, and just like that, we were allowed access to the walkway, which led to the entrance some twenty-five yards away.

The lead detective stepped from the building as we approached the door.

"Excuse me, gentlemen. This is a crime scene," the law enforcement officer stated.

Ron flashed his shield once again. "I'm Commander Daly...Special Crimes. These gentlemen are with me." Ron pointed to me before he continued, "This is Judge Greg Mathis... he's responsible for this facility. Who might you be?"

"I'm Lieutenant Myers. I'm the lead detective."

I quickly asked, "What happened?"

The thin-framed Columbo wannabe stated, "Apparently, two armed men entered the facility in search of a patient, intent on murdering this individual. All hell broke loose. A second patient foolishly risked his life to prevent further chaos."

"Was anyone hurt?" I countered with concern.

The detective smiled. "One of the gunmen, but the other escaped without injury."

Ron quickly intervened, "Who were they after?"

"It seems as if they were after..." He paused. The detective couldn't remember the names of the people involved so he reached into his jacket pocket and removed his pad. The officer opened his notepad and began flipping through the pages. "Seems as if everyone thinks that Darryl Greene was the person that they were after, but that's still unclear. Buster Wright is the individual that hit one of the gunmen over the head with a fire extinguisher and held him until we arrived." His eyes veered from his pad and toward me. The detective asked me, "Do you know these individuals?"

"Yes, Darryl Greene is my cousin...and I gave Buster Wright a bed earlier today."

"I guess admitting this Buster Wright was probably a blessing, huh!" the detective stated as he escorted us in.

The four decorative fountains in each corner produced the tranquil sound of a bubbling brook. The arboricola and cat palm floor plants along with several varieties of floral arrangements were scattered throughout the lobby to help us create our own Garden of Eden. The décor was intended to produce a feeling of serenity, to welcome back home those that attempted to escape life. The road to recovery for the residents of Sheila's House began upon their entering the lobby.

Because we believed that one of the first things that the user loses when succumbing to the life is their oneness with nature, our first mandate was to help the patient develop a healthy respect for God's creations. The drug user needs to find his or her way back to the living; he or she needs to understand what they surrendered upon attempting to escape reality. Taking for granted something as simple as fresh air—or how beautiful and relaxing greenery can be, or even water—there is nothing more surreal than listening to the freedom water has as it flows from the falls. All of this could be rediscovered by simply visiting our lobby.

Sheila's House was supposed to be a sanctuary, yet for a few horrifying moments, its sanctity had been compromised. The fear etched on the faces of those seeking treatment for their affliction was that of realization. Drug treatment was just that—a way to understand and deal with narcotics abuse, not a cure for the evils of the world. Individuals who are successful with treatment maximize their chances of not being involved with the violence associated with drugs. It seemed as if our residents finally understood our motto: *If the drugs don't kill you, the violence associated surely will.*

Several people were huddled up—protectively sheltering and attempting to console one another as the police questioned them. Neither Ron nor Darwin knew who I was looking for, so they stood next to me and waited. My eyes veered around the room in search of two people out of the forty or so that congregated. I needed to find out what was going on with my cousin—and I also wanted to thank Buster for his courageous act.

I spotted Darryl.

My cousin had his head resting atop the full-length, L-shaped receptionist counter. A female resident was rubbing on his back in an effort to soothe him. I made my way through the maze of humanity and toward Darryl. My friends followed.

"Darryl...you okay?"

My cousin lifted his head; he was scared, truly frightened. "Greg, man... what the hell is going on? I came here so that I could avoid going through anything like what just happened."

"Man, I was told that those people came in here after you. What kind of shit are you involved in?" I asked.

Darryl went into denial. "I don't know. Everyone is saying it was me that they were after because of Evelyn."

I was stunned. "What the hell does she have to do with this?"

"She came by here. We got into an argument. She was screaming something about our dealer being after her. Evidently, she called the police and told them that her car was stolen. The police spotted the car on Woodward. They pulled it over and arrested her dealer for driving a stolen vehicle. Apparently, she told her dealer that I called the police, then she told him that he could find me here. Several people heard Evelyn and me arguing, so they told the police that the gunmen came in here looking for me."

I placed my hands on my face in disgust. It was hard for me to believe that Evelyn would be willing to jeopardize the life of her husband, and others, for a damn car.

"Did you recognize either of the gunmen?" Ron asked.

"No..."

I excused myself, after spotting Buster standing alone next to one of the waterfalls on the opposite side of the room. I could see that he noticed me heading his way. Buster seemed mighty calm.

"Hey, Buster, are you okay?" I asked while extending a hand to him.

He took my hand into his. "I'm fine, Judge. Thank you for asking."

"You took a real chance, young man. I don't recommend that you go around playing hero."

He smiled. "Judge Mathis...all I wanna do is get this monkey off my back. If I'm able to do that, then I'll feel like something of a hero." Without warning, he broke into laughter.

"What's funny?"

"I don't think I would have done what I did today if I weren't using. You know...people that have my problem don't feel we have anything to lose, so we do stupid things like hitting people over the head with fire extinguishers."

I heard laughter behind me. When I turned, I saw Darwin grinning. He'd left Ron with Darryl and made his way over to meet the man who had risked his life for others. The reporter found Buster's statement funny.

Still with a smile on his face, the journalist extended his hand to the courageous resident of Sheila's House. "Hi, I'm Darwin."

While the two shook hands, I completed the introduction by telling the reporter that Buster was Cecilia Wright's nephew. I went on to explain to

Darwin how Alvin had brought him to the courthouse earlier that day with the hope that I would try and help his cousin kick his addiction to cocaine.

Suddenly, I noticed that every person in the lobby had gone silent.

Everyone gasped as they directed their undivided attention toward the paramedics who were pushing a gurney toward the front door. I quickly realized that the gunman was being wheeled out, and three uniformed officers were escorting him.

I headed toward the exit.

From where I stood, I felt that I could make it to the door before they would, although shocked patients obstructed my path. A trail was being made for the gurney, which caused more people to impede my attempt to speak with the person brazen enough to walk, with guns blazing, into a facility run by a 36th District judge.

It was paramount that I speak with the gunman because I needed to know whether my cousin's wife was responsible.

"Hey..." I barked while weaving through the people. I had to excuse myself because I forced my way past some folk that, simply put, didn't move out of the way fast enough.

I couldn't make it to the door before the paramedics pushed the gurney out of the building, so I followed them out. When I exited, I saw several news trucks—the media was in full force. My top priority was catching up with the group before they reached the ambulance and before they got within earshot of the news crews, so I ran after them.

"Hey...you people, hold on for a second," I yelled.

One of the officers recognized me—he had everyone stop halfway down the walkway. I rushed up to them. "Excuse me, gentlemen, but I need to ask the suspect a question, if you don't mind."

Uniformed officers were holding the contingent of reporters back. I could hear several yelling, including one who said, "Judge Mathis...seems as if your past has followed you."

Another screamed, while holding a microphone, "What do you have to say about the violence that seems to follow you?" His cameraman seemed primed to pick up my reaction.

I ignored the heckling reporters and directed my question toward the gold-toothed, young hoodlum who lay stretched out before me. His high-top faded haircut was braided, making it look as if worms were crawling from the top of his head. His haircut allowed me to see the bump that he had sustained from the blow to the skull.

"You took a pretty nasty shot to the head," I said as I examined it.

He looked at me with sinister intention. "Who the hell are you?"

"I have one question for you. Were you coming after Darryl Greene?"

He struggled, but his hands were cuffed to the gurney.

"I came to check into the center...then somebody hit me in the head." The suspect continued with a grimace, "Who the fuck hit me with that fire extinguisher?"

❂❂❂

Darwin and I stopped by Darryl and Evelyn's place after leaving Sheila's House. I had to confront her personally. She needed to know that she had put lives in danger with her reckless behavior. I was also willing to give her a bed, if she felt that she was ready to deal with her problems.

When we arrived at the house, I saw her blue Chevy Camaro in the driveway. There were two other cars parked in front of the house, one of them blocking the driveway. Although she didn't come to the door, I knew she was home, and that she had company.

Darwin and I stood on the porch and looked on in silence at the affluent cul-de-sac. It was nearly five in the evening and we both were tired. I'd been in court all morning, had several runs that I had to make during the afternoon, then spent an hour and a half at WCHB. From the radio station I had to rush over to Sheila's House, and finally, here. To tell the truth, I was exhausted.

While gazing at the sky, I noticed the only blemish in the blue and fiery-red picture-perfect horizon. A group of dirty gray clouds was moving in fast from the east.

After breaking the seductive hold that the evening allure had on me, I pressed the doorbell several times as I had when we had first arrived. We waited for several seconds. When no one came to the door, I opened the screen door and knocked.

"Evelyn, I know that you're in there. I'm trying to give you a chance to open this door. I have Darryl's key. I will let myself in. Just to let you know, if I have to use the key, I'll be coming in with the police."

Finally, Evelyn spoke from behind the door. "You can't come into my house. I don't care if you're a judge or not. You still need a warrant."

We could hear one of her guests say in a panic, "He's a judge...shit, I'm outta here."

When I heard the panic in her visitor's voice, I said, "Foolish girl... guess who signs off on warrants? All I need is probable cause...I have that. I'll have everyone in there arrested on drug charges."

Before I could get the next statement out of my mouth, two men and three women scurried down the driveway from the side of the house. They evidently had exited the ranch-style dwelling from the side door. I never saw five people move so fast.

Darwin noticed the white vertical blinds at the large picture window being pulled back—Evelyn peeked out. She watched as her friends got into their cars. The reporter tapped me on my shoulder and pointed toward the window.

"Evelyn, open the door," I insisted, upon seeing her.

She quickly disappeared from view. It took a few minutes but I could finally hear her unlocking the door.

My cousin's wife stood at the entrance wrapped in a green robe. She looked nothing like the fashion-minded shopaholic who spent much of her free time in the mirror. It was obvious to me that Evelyn had surrendered her soul to the life. She no longer cared about her appearance—or about how people perceived her.

"Can we come in?" I asked.

She stepped to the side and allowed us to enter.

Evelyn attempted to gussy up. She ran her fingers through her hair, then pulled her robe snug to her body. She closed the door before turning her attention to Darwin and me.

It was dark, the blinds were drawn, and the lights were out. When Evelyn turned on a lamp, I noticed that their thirty-two-inch television, which used to sit in front of the large picture window in the living room, was missing. Although the house had a stale, musty stench of dope, cigarette smoke, and alcohol, it was still neat.

I got straight to business without hesitation. "I'm not here to pass judgment on you, but I'll be damned if I'll have you sending people over to my rehab center to bring grief to my cousin and the residents that are trying to turn their lives around."

"Look here, Greg…" She walked over to her sofa and sat. "I'm not going to get into any of my business in front of your friend. I really don't appreciate that you would bring a stranger over to my house and speak on something so private."

"Aren't you the little hypocrite…you go over to the center and dump your business in front of a building full of strangers. Now you got the nerve to catch an attitude. Get some help, Evelyn. If you're not willing to check yourself into Sheila's House, then I'll help you find another facility."

Evelyn crossed her legs. She shifted her eyes toward Darwin, who was standing in front of the fireplace looking at several photographs that sat atop the mantle.

"Greg, I don't need any help. What I do is recreational."

Of course, I'd heard every excuse in the book.

Being educated on the streets—and in the courtroom, I'd had the misfortune to have witnessed firsthand the tendencies of all kinds of drug addicts. The two most common, as far as I'm concerned, are the Hustling Addict and the Functional Addict.

The Hustling Addict is the one that doesn't try to hide the fact that he or she uses. This individual does whatever is required to feed his or her habit. Then there are the ones who go to work every day—the functional ones. In the beginning, the functional ones do anything they can to hide the fact that they use. They will go so far as to denounce the Hustler, calling them anything from junkie to crackhead.

When the functional ones start to really lose themselves, they begin to borrow money and take off from work. Then comes the neglect. They begin to neglect themselves, their families, and responsibilities. When they are uncovered, they claim that they're recreational users, they'll be fast to remind you that they go to work every day, and that they don't have to steal. But what both the hustling and functional addicts have in common is that they'll both swear that they can stop whenever they want to.

"Evelyn, you know that I've seen and heard it all. You're a functioning addict headed in the direction of a hustling addict. It will be more difficult for you to recover if you allow yourself to become a hustling addict. Get help now, while you still have the desire to maintain some dignity. Gail needs her mother."

I'M AS GOOD AS DEAD

I had just gotten comfortable. It was also six p.m.—thing was, I hadn't planned on showing back up at the office after all that I had done during the day. But, I felt that it was the best place for me to be. I had to get my thoughts together. Contemplation was in order. Should I, or shouldn't I, show Linda the tape? For several days, we had been having some heated discussions about our relationship.

My dilemma was, do I show her the tape and add fuel to the fire, or do I not mention it and take the chance that she be given the recording by someone else? My decision was a difficult one, because we had never had the types of arguments we were having concerning fidelity. What started out as my wife inquiring about my relationship with my law clerk, had festered into periodic bouts of jealousy.

I decided that it was best that I sit my wife down and tell her of the tape with the hope that we would be able to talk through our problems. The only other way to solve our issues would be for me to let Maggie go—and I wasn't willing to do that. Not because we had anything going on, but I felt that that particular move wouldn't have solved our problem, it would have just put a Band-Aid on it. Plus, it wouldn't be long before Maggie left anyway; she was smart enough to pass the bar on her first go at it. Whatever was going on was deeper than me having an attractive assistant—who, by the way, went the extra mile to ensure my success.

I reached for my briefcase, which was on the floor next to my feet. After sitting it on top of my desk, I opened it. I then got to my feet, walked over to my bookcase, and removed the tape from the exact spot where I believed that the camera used to capture my assistant and me had been positioned. I put it there because I believed that if the person responsible for the recording returned, he wouldn't put his camera there a second time.

When I returned to my desk and sat, I stared at the cassette. Talking to my wife wasn't going to be easy. She thought that I had lied about Maggie's looks. She also felt that my assistant and I were up to no good on the occasions that we worked late. It didn't help that Linda had walked in on my law clerk trying to ease my tensions with a massage. Now, the tape that I was holding—in a way, I could see where she was coming from; but then again, she's supposed to know me better.

A tap at my door disrupted my train of thought. I immediately placed the tape into my briefcase and turned my attention toward the door. Before I could say a word, Maggie let herself in. She seemed a bit flustered.

"What's wrong?" I asked.

"Judge Mathis...the chief judge is on the rampage," she timidly announced as she approached my desk.

"So, what's his problem, young lady?"

"I was listening to you on the radio and he happened by," she said as she leaned on my desk. "He listened for a while. All along he was mumbling that you should not have been doing any radio interviews. Then he said— she mocked—'*That's not what judges do.*' The man went ballistic when he heard you talking about the DA's office's lack of interest in Sheila Morgan's homicide."

When Maggie got excited, her big, beautiful blue eyes opened as wide as the ocean. My assistant was usually so cool under fire. But I noticed that when it came to any so-called pressure situations that involved me, she wasn't so calm. I think she felt that she needed to protect me, but at the same time, couldn't figure out how to do so fast enough. I could understand why she felt the chief judge's rants would be of concern, but I also got the impression that something else was bothering her.

"Don't worry, young lady. I'll handle him." I winked at her, then asked, "I want you to tell me what's really bothering you..."

She hesitated. I knew that she was going to avoid telling me the real reason that she was so uncomfortable. I was right. She said, "Your docket has been completely cancelled until Monday because the air conditioning unit went out. Maintenance is already working on the problem, but they don't think that they'll have the issues addressed until Saturday. So I guess you can start your weekend a day early," she whispered with a smile. "Also, I sent flowers to Darwin Washington as you requested. I put on the card, 'congratulations on your upcoming nuptials.'"

"Thanks for sending the flowers." I didn't take my eyes off of her.

Her next statement was filled with sentiment. "Judge, those kids…who's going to take care of Sheila's children?" Her empathy was sincere, and I was touched by it.

"Darwin is going to look after them." I wasn't about to let her get out of my office without getting to the root of her dismay. "Maggie, take a seat."

She lowered her eyes before she sat.

"Tell me…what's going on with you?" My inquiry was caring, and I think she sensed that.

"Judge, I really like you—I really like working for you. I know that after I take the bar, I'm going to be fielding offers—"

I interrupted her before she could finish. "Maggie, this isn't about you taking the bar, or about you being made a job offer. What's going on?"

She managed to make eye contact. The young woman who had always managed to smile seemed so sad. "The chief judge is coming on to me. He makes me feel so uncomfortable. Look, Judge…I thought that I could handle him, but I can't."

Speak of the devil—and he shall appear.

Without warning, the door flew open. Maggie peered over her shoulder just in time to see the chief judge enter. Her eyes made it obvious she was tense.

My attention shifted in the direction of my supervisor. I could tell by the way that the little big man stormed in that he was none too pleased. The chief judge walked straight up to me. His eyes briefly veered toward Maggie as he approached.

"Mathis, we need to talk," the chief judge said in anger.

My supervisor's stare was sharp and piercing, but he had to know that I wasn't at all intimidated because I didn't budge from my position. I held my stare. I was angry as hell that he had been coming on to Maggie. We were like two kids from kindergarten, fighting over a toy, neither willing to give ground.

He was the first to break. The angry little man directed his next statement toward my clerk. "Would you give us a moment..."

Maggie seemed unable to move, so I whispered, "You can go for the day. I'll speak with you later about the matter we were discussing. I'll handle it. Don't worry about coming in tomorrow. Tell David that you both can start your weekends right now. You two have worked your asses off, and you both have put in a lot of overtime, so enjoy your weekend. We'll talk on Monday."

When she stood, her expression seemed to plead that I not address the chief judge about what we had discussed. "It'll be all right," I whispered.

Maggie turned, and without ever making eye contact with my supervisor, she headed toward the exit. When she closed the door, the irate chief judge blasted, "Judge...I don't like the fact that you're doing radio programs."

I closed my briefcase, and then crossed my legs before saying, "So, I take it that you don't like my show."

"Hell no...what were they thinking when they offered you a show?"

"That, unlike you...I can make a difference."

"You're a judge, and you should be carrying yourself as such. Hosting radio shows, simply put...it's just not what judges do. But to make matters worse, you go and say that the prosecutor's office is sleeping on the job. Do you realize what kind of heat I'm getting from the mayor? The DA went to the mayor and told him that you came into his office running rough shod, trying to dictate to them how to do their jobs. You are to drop your involvement in the Morgan case. You will let the prosecutors and law enforcement do their jobs. Do you understand me?"

I said as calmly as I could, "Look, there is nothing in my job description that says I can't attempt to rectify incompetence. And quite frankly, even if there was, I would still do what I'm trying to do. Keyword being, *trying*...

At least I'm trying… Those arrogant bastards in the DA's office aren't the least bit interested in pursuing—with everything they have—the animal brazen enough to chop a woman's head off. I'm my own man…being a judge is what I was elected to do. Being a person, with a desire to make my family and friends feel safe, is what I am compelled to do."

"You sure you want to battle with me?" His snarl was that of a miniature chihuahua.

"I'm not the least bit interested in battling with you. I want you and everyone else around here to do what the people pay us to do. Now, if that means that you and I have to go toe to toe…then so be it. I'm not backing down on this. Murder is bad enough without a mother of three having to have suffered through a decapitation. The prosecutors are slandering this woman's reputation because they're so damn worried about their conviction rate rather than the three children left without their mother. My wish is that we…that's you and I…would be able to do the right thing. Make these people act as if this were a white woman that was murdered."

"Oh no you're not…I'm not about to let you turn this into a black and white thing. What are you trying to do?" His anger was evident. "You better watch yourself…you're skating on very thin ice." The chief judge turned and stormed out of my office.

Before he could get out the door, I yelled, "It is a black and white thing…whether you choose to accept that or not!"

❁❁❁

When I sat Linda down, with the intent of explaining the videotape, it was an awkward moment because she already had preconceived opinions of my relationship with Maggie.

I put on the tape and we watched together. As I expected, my wife was none too happy. I attempted to explain that me embracing Maggie was totally innocent; that the hug was in response to her announcing that she was going to finally take the bar exam.

Either way I looked at it, I stood a much better chance that Linda would be receptive to my explanation if I told her rather than allowing someone else to bring that tape to her attention.

Since I hired my assistant, three days a week we had worked late in efforts to put the office, and my docket, in the best possible position for a successful transition. Although our relationship was strictly a professional one, my wife said that she could clearly see that my very attractive law clerk had a lustful eye for me. She accused me of purposely turning a blind eye to Maggie's advances, and that our working late was just an excuse to cover the fact that we were having an affair.

The biggest problem she had with me was that I had told her that Maggie was a nerdish librarian type. She couldn't believe that Maggie changed from the ugly duckling that I had described into the beauty that was on the tape, in just twenty-four hours.

My being honest only added fuel to the proverbial fire, because my explanation of the transformation, and of the hug that had gotten her so steamed, didn't seem to matter; she was on edge.

Even though she was bound to make my life a living hell for several days, I didn't have any regrets telling her about the tape.

I went on to inform my wife that what she saw as lust, was just appreciation. Maggie was grateful that I had spent time edifying her on various points of law. I assured my wife that my assistant was a very dedicated and respectful individual, whose sole purpose was to work as hard as she could. I also explained to Linda that I felt Maggie's only objective was to prove that she was more than a pretty face—and that she was out to prove that I made a great decision when I added her to my staff.

I could see my wife picking that tape apart—studying the way in which we hugged, trying her best to read something in the embrace. At that time, I wasn't really sure whether it would have made a difference if the audio had been available.

I was unable to convince her that nothing was going on between Maggie and me. I didn't want to fight with her, so I told her to take a day for herself. To take that time to reflect on our relationship and the things that we'd gone through. She needed to remember who I was—my character, my dedication to our marriage. I told her that I would keep the kids while she went out and pampered herself, then I grabbed a pillow and a blanket and camped out in the den for the night.

As I watched the news while lying on the couch, all I could do was hope that reflection would bring my Linda out of her funk.

There had to be a reason why she suddenly believed I was being unfaithful. My first thought was that her spending so much time with Barbara might have had something to do with it. Linda had always looked at Gram and Barbara's nuptials as being picture-perfect. I felt that the heiress' belief that her husband was cheating, contributed to my wife's sudden insecurities. I guess Linda figured, if a marriage that she felt was picture-perfect was filled with lies and deceit, then what chance did she have?

I had always shown my wife the appreciation and respect that she was due. I never once thought about being unfaithful.

I shared with my wife how important Maggie was to the success of my office. I told Linda that in the short time that we had known each other, I found my assistant to be not just a dedicated employee, but also a very sincere friend.

The following morning, I took the kids to the movies because Linda was to spend the day trying to sort through her anger.

When the kids and I turned onto our block on our return trip home, we noticed a red Monte Carlo backing out of our driveway. We couldn't identify who was driving because the vehicle headed away from us. I don't remember having ever seen that car before—and I couldn't recall any of Linda's friends owning a brand-new automobile.

As we entered the house through the unlocked side door, I screamed, "Hey baby, we're back!"

She didn't answer. I was certain that if she were home, she would have responded to the screaming kids as they ran through the house. My wife would have reacted to the kids' madness by screaming at me for getting them hyped up on sugar. And of course, she would have had every right; it was my fault. While we watched *Batman Forever*, they devoured popcorn, hotdogs, and an assortment of adrenaline-filled junk. In addition, after the movie, we stopped off at the park where they consumed ice cream and drank pop. Hell, they were on summer vacation, and they were spending a Saturday with their usually consumed father.

Since Linda didn't come into the kitchen screaming, I assumed that the Monte Carlo that was pulling out of our driveway belonged to one of her girlfriends, who had stopped by to take my wife for a ride in her brand-new car. I also figured that they would be right back, since she left the side door unlocked.

The pitcher filled with water looked thirst-quenching, but the apple juice had a slight frost, so I pulled it from the refrigerator. I took the cap off of the bottle and began to guzzle from it as I headed for the den. *Boy, if my wife had caught me doing that.* Linda hated when I drank directly from containers.

Upon entering the den, something caught my eye. I slowly lowered the bottle from my lips and stood in shock—my eyes were locked on my cocktail table. I allowed my eyes to scan the room before easing my way toward the package.

❁❁❁

The tinted windows of the spacious limousine were completely fogged up.

There was enough room in the vehicle for the couple to make themselves comfortable on the floor, yet they were on the seat. He sat with his pants down by his ankles, and she straddled herself over him. The scandalous seductress wrapped her arms around his neck. At one time, I saw her sensually stick the tip of her tongue in his ear.

She then threw her head back and took a deep breath. Her eyes would roll up before she would exhale passionately while feverishly grinding her plump ass. Several seconds later, she began to nibble on his earlobe.

He held his hands on her waist and slightly lifted her, after which, he lowered her gently down on his rigid manhood. From the look on their faces, they were both headed for a climactic end to the ecstasy they shared. Gram and Carolyn clasped in each other's arms, and then lay down on the backseat. They continued to hold each other tightly while rolling around, until finally they took their escapade to the floor of the roomy vehicle.

I'd had enough. Their heated exchange of sexual passion was nauseating, especially after Gram insisted that he wouldn't give in to the temptation again.

After removing that tape, I replaced it with the second one that I had received. But before I would play it, I opened my bedroom door and shouted for the kids to stop running through the house. I then reminded Camara to holler upstairs when her mother pulled into the driveway.

"Okay, Daddy!" my eldest daughter yelled up the stairs.

I closed my door, made my way back over to the bed, and sat before aiming the remote at the television.

The office on the screen was all too familiar—and the man leaning at the front of his desk, with his eyes closed and his head tilted back, was the city's top elected official. I could tell that he was being serviced. This was a tape that was bound to ruin him—I couldn't believe that the mayor would allow himself to be caught with his pants down. Once I saw Carolyn come up for air, I heard my daughter scream up the stairs that her mother was coming. I quickly removed the tape. I put both of them in my briefcase, locked it, and slid it under my bed. I then folded the letter that accompanied the tape and stuck it in my pants pocket.

As I headed down the stairs with the juice bottle in hand, the first thing I noticed was Linda had gotten her hair styled. Like any woman would, she loved it when I recognized that she had gone that extra mile, so I made sure that I acknowledged it. "Hey, baby, your hair looks really nice..."

As if doing a commercial, she pushed up on her fresh hairdo. "Why, thank you, sir..."

I hugged her. "Have you been enjoying yourself so far?"

"I must say...yes, I have." She kissed me before asking, "What about you and the kids?"

"We had a great time." As I escorted her into the kitchen, I asked, "Who's driving the new Monte Carlo?" I guzzled more of the apple juice while waiting for her to respond.

"What new Monte Carlo...what are you talking about?"

"We saw a brand-new Monte Carlo backing out of the driveway when we came home. I thought that one of your girls had come by."

"No, I've been at the beauty shop. None of my friends drive a Monte Carlo," she said as she walked over to the refrigerator.

"Did you leave the side door unlocked?"

"No, I made sure I checked it. I left out of the front door because my car was in the driveway. You're saying that the door was unlocked when you came home?"

"Yeah..."

We both looked at each other curiously for several seconds. "Did you leave anything for me before you left?"

"Like what?"

"Nothing," I said.

I needed to change the subject. But my mind was on the fact that someone had broken into my house and left that package in my den. The note stated that it was going to be revealed that my bid for the property with which I opened Sheila's House should not have been the winning one. It went on to state that undue influence was behind me securing the property, and that my position as judge was going to be brought into question once the information surrounding the purchase was made public.

"What's wrong?" she asked as we entered the kitchen.

"Nothing, baby..."

For the next several minutes, we talked about how Gail was getting along with the kids, and what we expected from both Darryl and or Evelyn if they wanted their daughter to come home. In the middle of our discussion, my wife remembered that she was supposed to deliver a message.

"Hey, baby, I almost forgot...Darwin called. He told me to tell you that he was going to be with the Johnson twins until six thirty. He said that he wouldn't be able to meet with you and Ron until about eight o'clock."

Her curious expression prompted me to explain.

"Since my original plan to handle Gerri actually backfired, he, Ron and I are going to try another approach. It's my fault that your cousin is really pounding the pavement these days... She's trying to raise bail for her foolish boyfriend."

When Gerri was released from custody after appearing in my courtroom, Ron and I followed her because we were sure that she would lead us to her boyfriend. We felt that if we watched him long enough, we would eventually catch him holding, or selling drugs. Our hope was that if Gerri's boyfriend were incarcerated, that would increase our chances of getting through to her.

It didn't take long.

On the commander's first night, he actually picked the boyfriend up on drug and possession of firearms charges.

"Don't blame yourself. That girl loves that man. None of us understands why, but she does. He doesn't give a rat's ass about her. And if she doesn't see that for herself, I don't know how you or Ron can get her to see it," my wife said with concern.

In the midst of our conversation, the phone rang, but my wife and I ignored it because we knew that the kids would answer.

"We're gonna try something that Ron has in mind. He's gonna arrest your cousin. She doesn't have anyone that'll put up bail for her now that her boyfriend is locked up. I'm going to ask whatever judge she goes before to give her a choice of going through rehab and my mentoring program as a condition for release, or go to jail."

My cousin's daughter ran into the kitchen. "Cousin Greg, you have a phone call."

"Thank you, baby."

I walked over to the wall phone and picked up, then whispered into the receiver, "I got it, guys." When the kids hung up, I said, "Hello..."

"Hey, Judge, this is Ron. Can you meet me at 1300 in about twenty minutes?"

I was a bit curious about why he wanted to see me so soon before our scheduled get together. "What's going on, Ron?"

"We picked up the second shooter. The guy that shot up the center the other day... He wants to talk...to you."

I checked the wall clock. "Okay...but give me at least thirty minutes."

After hanging up, I walked back over to the table, stood behind my wife, then kissed her atop her head. "I gotta meet Ron downtown."

Usually when I got home, I would immediately pull into the garage—especially on hot days, because leather seats hold heat. I didn't bother seeking shade for my car; I left it parked in front of the garage with the windows down since I expected to leave right away. I had planned on taking the kids over to my brother's house, at least until I saw the package.

I walked out of the side door and headed for my Explorer.

Before I could start the engine, I saw Linda through my rearview mirror as she exited the side door. I thought that she was going to move her car, until I saw her face as she approached the rear. The look on her face had me a bit concerned.

She walked up to the driver's side window. "You're not going to believe this."

"What's up?" I asked while turning the ignition.

She shook her head in disgust.

"Linda...what's wrong?"

"Darryl left the rehab center. Evelyn went there with his income tax check."

I was outdone. "What..."

"The two of them left the center no more than five minutes ago. He's screwing up, Greg."

"Shit." I couldn't believe what I was hearing. "Do me a favor. Call Ron and tell him that I'll have to meet him later."

"What are you gonna do?" my wife asked.

I put my foot on the brake, put the car in reverse, and then said, "I'm going over to Darryl's house."

HELP FROM THE PROSECUTOR'S OFFICE

My cousin's fake sincerity was upsetting to me, but I had to give credit where it was due—Darryl was convincing. He could have won an Academy Award for his performance on the rainy morning when he pounded on my door seeking help. So I needed to tell him face to face what I felt about his little charade.

I wanted to catch my cousin by surprise, and my very own stakeout was how I would do it. For twenty-five minutes, I sat in my Explorer, which was parked several houses down from my cousin's, and waited for his return. It's kind of hard to stay unnoticed in a cul-de-sac, but I was almost positive that Darryl and Evelyn were preparing to binge on crack and cognac. I figured that they would be suffering from crack anxiety, and would be too keyed up to notice my car when they arrived.

I was hoping that the adults who were staring at me from their windows wouldn't approach me in fear that I was stalking one of their little people as they played on this Saturday afternoon. Then, I would be forced to tell them that I was playing amateur detective. And of course, that would blow my cover.

Four little children rode bikes up and down the sidewalk, two others played tag, and another played hopscotch. Watching the boys and girls triggered thoughts of my past; my mind briefly drifted to when Darryl and I were young. Back then my cousin had a knack of identifying and steering clear of trouble. Darryl was always the voice of reason.

But now, the guy whom I was waiting on was a stranger to me. The more I thought about him leaving the center, the more upset I became.

Sorting through my feelings was something that I needed to do—quickly. I didn't want to confront Darryl and Evelyn out of anger, because doing so meant that I would lose sight on why I was there in the first place. This whole thing was not about Darryl's inability or unwillingness to fight for his life. It wasn't about his wife luring him back into that world. This was about the little girl who should have been with her friends—playing tag, riding her bike, or even playing hopscotch in front of her own home. This was about Gail.

Just as I was able to gather what I felt was the proper perspective of the entire situation, I noticed their Camaro through my rearview mirror as it turned onto the street.

Evelyn was driving.

As I suspected, they drove right past my car without as much as a glance. She quickly pulled into their driveway and cut off the engine. Darryl exited from the passenger side and pulled out several bags from the backseat.

The two of them went into the house through the side door.

I wanted to give them a few minutes to get started. If I were correct, they would be getting high in the basement. The door was ajar. I figured I would be able to enter undetected.

I checked my watch—it was 4:15.

"Twenty minutes should be long enough," I whispered to myself of how long I would wait before making my move.

As soon as I took my eyes off my watch, I glanced into my rearview mirror once again. Turning onto the street were the same two cars that were at their house when I confronted Evelyn a couple days ago.

Both vehicles pulled to the curb in front of my cousin's house.

There they were—the same five individuals that scurried from the house the day that Darwin and I paid Evelyn that unexpected visit. With bags in hand, the three women and two men rushed to the side door. It took all of ten seconds before they were able to gain access.

Some kid screamed, which drew my attention. "I got you...you're it," she said as she ran in front of my car in an effort to catch another girl. The little girl doing the chasing looked to be about ten. She stopped directly in front of my bumper, placed her hands her on her hips, and declared, "You know that I got you. I'm not playing anymore, if you're gonna cheat."

Caught up in watching the kids chase after one another nearly caused me to lose sight of my objective. I removed the key to Darryl's house from the pocket of my Pistons warm-up suit, got out of the car, and headed down the street.

It was time for me to crash a party.

Easing the door open, I stepped in and carefully closed it behind me. Standing in the foyer for several seconds, I listened, trying to ensure that I had an unimpeded path to where everyone had assembled.

I could hear talking and laughter. As my eyes carefully scanned my surroundings, I noticed that the blinds were drawn. That was a sign they had gotten started.

Without warning, loud music blared from the basement—that was my cue. When I got to the basement stairs, I once again listened to ensure no one was coming.

The coast was clear, so I descended. The aroma of cigarettes, dope, and alcohol got thicker with each step I took. The laughter that filled my cousin's finished basement seemed to be infectious. When one of Darryl's guests would chuckle, everyone seemed to join in. The extra noise helped to camouflage my approach.

One of Evelyn's female friends noticed me first. She had a crack pipe to her lips. The woman blew out the smoke that she had previously inhaled, then said, "Hey guys, you didn't tell us that you had another guest." As she spoke she realized that she had seen me before. The woman attempted to hide her pipe. No one caught on until she said, "Aren't you the 'Street Judge'?"

Everyone then turned and saw me standing before them, shaking my head in disgust. Darryl put down his pipe, stood, and looked as shocked as everyone else. "What are you doing here?" he asked.

Evelyn, who was standing behind the wet bar with a drink in hand, shouted, "You can't keep coming over here uninvited."

The couple's guests got to their feet as if they were about to leave, but

Evelyn wasn't about to let that happen. "Ya'll ain't gotta go nowhere. He's gotta get the fuck out."

"Shut the fuck up, Evelyn," Darryl yelled before he turned his attention toward me.

"What's up, cuz... Is this about me leaving Sheila's House? I appreciate you trying to help me...but I do this for recreation."

Evelyn barked, "Be a man...you ain't gotta explain nothin' to him." She mumbled ghetto-fabulously, "He gets on my damn nerves."

For ten minutes, I listened to Darryl babble and his wife hurl insults. She was mighty close to crossing the line with me, but I let it go because I had promised myself that I wouldn't get angry. I was confronting them for one reason and one reason only.

I was the voice of their daughter, Gail.

When the both of them took a breath and waited for my response, I gave it to them. "I listened to the dumb shit that both of you had to say... but now, you're gonna listen to me."

I walked toward the bar because I wanted Evelyn to see the seriousness in my eyes; she needed to see me up close and personal. I glared at her and curled my bottom lip as tightly as I could. "Evelyn, you have one more time to show your ignorance toward me. Understand this, I don't like you, and I never have. If it weren't for Darryl, you would already be locked up. But he no longer has any cards to play. I want you to test me, so open your damn mouth one more time."

I paused, to see if she would respond. She sipped on her drink and didn't say another word. "I don't give a fuck about you." I pointed to Darryl. "Or for that matter, that stupid son-of-a-bitch husband of yours. If you two want to screw up your life, that's fine... This is about one person. Don't come for Gail...If you do, I'll have both of your asses thrown in jail. If you think that I'm going to stand idly by and allow her to be a part of this shit, you're sadly mistaken."

I then turned my attention toward Darryl. "Now you...I can't believe you came over to my house asking for my help, then turned around and shat in my face. I went out of my way to help yo ass. Stay the fuck away from me, Darryl. When your income tax check is gone, don't come cryin' to me. I'd rather help one of these people turn their life around than be screwed by you again." I didn't mean what I had said, but I needed him to think I did, at that time. It was all about *tough love*.

I didn't give either a chance to respond—my dramatic exit through the side door was meant to give Darryl a cause for concern. I wanted him to think I was so fed up that there was a possibility I could bring law enforcement into play.

As I headed down the street toward my car, I had to first sidestep one cyclist and then the two children who were playing tag because they ran directly across my path. I almost stumbled, attempting to avoid them.

"Judge...can I speak with you for a second?" someone yelled from behind.

I turned and waited as the woman who first noticed me enter the basement trotted toward me. "Judge, please. I need to speak to you."

The woman looked panicked.

When she approached, I asked, "What can I do for you?"

Her eyes darted around the cul-de-sac, and she whispered, "Can you help me...Evelyn told us about you."

"Oh really...How do you think I can help?"

I noticed that her eyes were glassy, about to water. She moved closer. "I don't have any insurance to go into rehab. Judge...I don't want to do this anymore. I don't know how to stop without help of some kind."

I whispered, "I'm not too happy with some of the people that I've reached out to lately. Let me start by saying, crying crocodile tears doesn't faze me any more. If you want my help, then you're gonna have to prove you deserve it."

"How can I do that?"

I headed for my car. "You'll figure it out."

The Explorer was hot as hell when I entered.

Before I could put the key into the ignition, the woman ran up to my open passenger window and stuck her head in.

"My name is Gwen." She extended her hand to me.

I reached over and took her hand into mine. "I wish you the best, Gwen."

"Judge, can you take me away from here?" Her eyes veered toward Darryl's house. "I came with those guys. If I go back in the house and ask them to take me home, they'll tell me to wait. I don't wanna wait...I wanna leave."

I smiled. "Gwen, you got family?"

"Yes, but they don't want anything to do with me."

"You've been hooked long?"

"Yeah... Judge, please... Can you give me a ride?"

"Where would you suggest I drop you?"

"At Sheila's House..." The look in her eyes spoke volumes.

"Get in. My cousin's departure means that we have a bed. Don't let me down. Better yet, don't let yourself down." Gwen hopped in my car.

Darryl was a real disappointment to me.

The tears and guilt that were on display the morning he insisted he wanted to do what was best for Gail was fresh in my mind. I had to dissolve any notion that if I couldn't help Darryl, I wouldn't be able to help anyone. That feeling would eat me up, if I allowed it.

That boy meant so much to me, and knowing the kind of person he was is why I felt like a failure in my efforts to help him. To me, it should have been easy to help someone like him, but I had to remind myself that the Darryl of the present was nothing like the person I had grown up with.

❁❁❁

Feeling unworthy of my calling didn't last long, thanks to my mother.

As I checked Gwen Ellison into Sheila's House, I could hear my mother saying, *"Baby, I've always told you...you can lead a horse to water, but you can't make him drink. And that goes for your family as well."*

I was determined to keep the promise that I had made to Alice Lee Mathis. I wasn't about to allow my cousin, or anyone for that matter, to get in the way of my keeping that pledge. I had told my mother that I would try to help as many people as I could—so I had to ensure that any failed efforts didn't drain my spirit.

Gwen Ellison smiled at me as she stood at the receptionist's desk. I was convinced that she was really going to give her all in the program. It's impossible to tell whether someone is genuine when it comes to seeking sobriety, but I had a good feeling about Gwen. I don't know why I felt the way I did about her, but it started with her determination to leave Darryl's.

Maybe God's intention was that I go through what I did with Darryl, so that I could meet the young lady before me—the one who couldn't seem to stop smiling and the woman who kept putting her hands together as if she were praising The Father and thanking Him for what she perceived to be her blessing.

At that moment, Gwen looked as if she were ready to take on the world.

The sincerity depicted in her body language was validation as far as I was concerned. This woman was going to make it—I could feel it in my bones.

"Gwen, if you should need anything while you're here, just let me know. I come by every day," I said with a smile.

She stepped up to me, returned my smile, and threw in a hug before whispering in my ear, "God bless you. Thank you so much."

I could feel her shivering—not from fear, but from delight.

The man who was hired to run Sheila's House entered the reception area from the door behind the desk. "Judge" —he called as he put some paperwork atop the counter—"I need Gwen to sign these documents."

"Jordan, you keepin' this place afloat?" I asked my manager.

He pointed to the signature lines on the documentation, and instructed Gwen, "Sign and date here."

His eyes shifted to me before he responded to my half-hearted inquiry. "Buster has been a blessing around here. I also want you to know he's doing great in group...and he volunteers to help out every day. He's only been here for a few days, but I can tell you right now that he has the makings of a counselor."

My manager's words brought about a smile. "That's great. Keep your eye on this one." I put my hand on Gwen's shoulder. "I have a feeling that she's going to be just as good."

Gwen added a smile to her puppy-dog expression as she glanced up at me from her paperwork.

❁❁❁

Once again, I found myself on the Lodge Expressway headed for down-town Detroit. I traveled the same route every weekday morning. But this time it was Saturday evening, and quite frankly, I would have rather been home. My day had been exhausting thus far. From physical fatigue to total mental drainage, I was beat.

For the second consecutive day, I spent most of the morning, and the early afternoon with the kids, which was the best part of my day. Running around with them in the park, seeing the smiles on their faces—I didn't have a reason whatsoever to complain about the physical exhaustion, because I truly enjoyed myself. I had fun.

It was the mental part of my day that had taken a toll on me, and that part was only getting started. I was on my way to confront someone who felt it necessary to shoot up a place I had created to help bring inner peace to those escaping the violence, which accompanied their drug addictions. I was supposed to visit with him the previous day, but I ran into a few problems. So I called Ron and asked that he set up a meet with the second shooter who was behind the incident at Sheila's House.

Whenever I found myself being inundated with thoughts of how violent the city had become, I got frustrated. Sitting behind the bench and lis-tening to the stupidity that people got themselves caught up in, was what flustered me the most. My guess is that I was disturbed because I was once one of those people.

When I actually needed to be void of thoughts that the city was going to hell in a hand basket, I found myself reflecting on the young people of YAAT. These youngsters made me believe that through their leadership, the city would reach prominence, and the nation would achieve wondrous and miraculous things. Young Adults Asserting Themselves was my saving grace—the program helped me to maintain my belief in the youth. I had a lot of confidence about the future success of YAAT.

But Sheila's House was a different story.

My cousin was the third person to unexpectedly leave the center—and we'd only been open for a little over thirty days. I can't lie—I was a little annoyed. Linda warned me that I was going to be disappointed for a stretch of time. She reminded me that most of the individuals who would seek the help of Sheila's House would not be walking through our doors. They were ready to change their lives, but would be doing so due to pressure from family. My very intuitive wife stated that we would have to first weed through and find the ones who were genuinely seeking help before we would play witness to our desired results.

Once again, something that my wife had said managed to put my mind at peace. Then I started thinking about her jealousy—once again, I got a little aggravated.

I realized that my true frustrations were largely because how easy it was for my cousin to forget the condition that he was in when he arrived on my doorstep with his seven-year-old daughter in tow. He evidently forgot how he felt that rainy morning; he forgot about the tears, the regret.

The reality is that he was apparently hit with drug-addict remorse that morning.

Darryl failed to allow himself to understand that after his income tax check was gone, he was going to once again be hit with that same feeling of remorse. But this time, it would hit him even harder, because he would have to deal with the fact that he'd screwed up with me.

I thought about what Linda had said about users coming to the center because they felt pressured by family. It made me feel that much better about Gwen. She hadn't talked to her parents in four years. And her sister wasn't willing to help her, either. That girl wanted help because she was tired of crashing on the floors of dope addicts. She wanted to change her life because that's what she felt she needed to do to gain respect for life.

❁❁❁

It seemed that I had spent more time in the drab, dreary interrogation room since I was sworn in as a judge than I did being a street thug and lawyer combined. This time I sat across the table from a young man who had wreaked havoc on Sheila's House. A place run by a judge; how damn stupid can you get?

For over thirty minutes, Ron and I prodded Marcus Hill. The nineteen-year-old was scared, too frightened to tell us who ordered him and his partner to run roughshod over the rehab center.

I made it clear to the young criminal, "I'm gonna need a little more than what you've provided, if you want me to go to the DA. I can't go to the prosecutor with vague information, asking for a deal."

He gazed at Ron, then at me. We could tell that he was contemplating whether he should be a little more forthcoming. After several seconds of soul searching, he said, "Okay …it's like this. Gene told us that we needed to take that cat out."

We later found that Darryl was not their target—quite frankly, that surprised me. After his little disappearing act from the center, I felt that it was possible that my cousin could have been hiding out from a vengeful dealer. I was even more surprised to learn that the two gunmen were sent to Sheila's House to seek out and murder Cecilia Wright's nephew, Buster.

After the alleged gunman confessed who it was that he was paid to hit, one thing crossed my mind. *Did Alvin, the young man whom I mentored, use me and the rehabilitation center? Did Cecilia Wright's son knowingly pick Sheila's House to hide his cousin from distraught drug dealers?* I was more inclined to believe that Alvin Wright had no idea what his cousin had gotten involved in.

But, if that was what Alvin had done, I wasn't going to be happy with his decision.

I wondered, *did Buster bravely risk his life to save others in the center—or was that whole thing nothing more than him trying to save his own ass?*

I couldn't get Marcus Hill to tell me why he and his partner were hired to kill Buster. However, he did insist that he could provide us with vital information if I would speak on his behalf with the district attorney's office.

"Who is Gene, and why did he want you clowns to kill Buster Wright?" Ron Daly asked.

Marcus shook his head several times; he was determined not to answer the commander's question. "I'ma need witness protection. If you want the answers, I need guaranteed witness protection. Because, if I say anything without protection, I'm as good as dead…"

"How do we know that what you have is worthy of witness protection?" the police commander asked.

"You ever heard of anyone by the name of Eugene Scott?" the young man questioned.

Ron Daly and I locked eyes.

Marcus continued, "He was released because no one would testify. They were all scared after it was discovered that even if he had been convicted, his conviction would have been overturned because the police screwed up with the warrant."

I was aware of what had been going on regarding Eugene's case, but I didn't realize he had been released. "Ron, I didn't know that Eugene had been released. I heard about all the problems they were having with his case. When did they let him go?"

"His attorney picked him up this morning," the commander replied.

My thoughts were on why Eugene Scott would send shooters after Buster Wright. I was also curious how he knew where to find Cecilia's nephew. But Marcus wasn't ready to answer those questions—not until we could assure him that he would be placed in witness protection.

"So...you're telling us that Eugene Scott ordered you to take out Wright?" Commander Daly asked.

"I ain't tellin you nothin'...I was only askin' if you knew him."

I chimed in, "Look, if you want our help, you're gonna have to help us. I didn't come down here for nothing. Remember, you asked to see me."

Marcus tightened his lips, as if to tell us that they were sealed.

I glanced at the police officer. "That thing with my cousin-in-law is going to have to be put on hold. I have a couple stops to make."

I trusted no one in the prosecutor's office, but I did remember an encouraging conversation I'd had with ADA Terrence Simmons. So I decided to see if I could enlist his help in sorting through this mess.

I got to my feet, and as I headed out, I said to Ron Daly, "I'll get with you later."

Marcus yelled, "What about me? He's gonna kill me...you have to do something."

I could hear the trigger-happy wannabe gangster's pleas as I closed the door to the interrogation room behind me.

❋❋❋

Eugene Scott's release had to be a big blow to ADA Geoffrey Sanders's ego. That meant that his decision not to make a deal would look bad for the entire office. Monahan couldn't feel good about that. I was really angry that neither Sanders nor Otto had offered Eugene a deal. They let their arrogance cloud their judgment.

Although it was Saturday, I was certain that Geoffrey Sanders would be at the district attorney's office. If I were correct about Sanders, then I needed to be there also.

I imagined him walking around infuriated over Eugene's release. If the man had done the right thing in the first place, both Eugene and the person responsible for Sheila's death would have been behind bars.

My purpose for going to the DA's Office was not to gloat—not to rub Sanders's egotistical nose in the dirt—to do so could easily have been construed as juvenile. I wasn't even going to remind him of how he had insisted that Eugene Scott's case was a slam-dunk and that he didn't need, nor would he ever consider, a plea. I knew that Sanders would have insisted that the other prosecutors be at work, so that they could mount some kind of retaliatory strike against Eugene Scott's defense team. If I were correct, that meant that Terrence Simmons would also have been called in.

ADA Simmons had assured me that he would provide me any assistance he could if I ever needed. If there were any chance of getting Eugene Scott to provide me with the information surrounding Sheila's murder, then I needed the assistant prosecutor's help.

I was confident that the young criminal that Ron had in custody could provide us with evidence connecting Eugene to the assault on the rehab center. So, if I could convince Terrence Simmons to circumvent Sanders and seek an indictment, then turn around and offer Eugene a deal, we might finally discover who murdered Sheila.

I realized that my plan wasn't going to be easy.

Sanders would want another shot at Eugene, and he would not look too kindly on any of his colleagues doing an end run when it came to the drug dealer. Atop that, I couldn't be sure if I could trust Terrence. But I had to try, because if Sanders got word that Ron had a witness who could tie Eugene to a crime, there was no telling what that man would do. Either way, I wasn't going to give him a second opportunity to blow my chances of finding Sheila's murderer.

When I entered the hallowed halls of the Frank Murphy Building, it was so quiet that one could literally hear a pin drop on the well-buffed marble floors. I stopped at the security desk so that I could sign in.

The guard informed me that just about everyone from the prosecutor's office was in. I glanced at the sign-in sheet and noticed that the chief judge was also upstairs.

According to the logs, he was meeting with DA Monahan.

When I stepped off the elevator, I saw several of Sanders's underlings scurrying about the hallway. Some carried what looked to be law books, while others had boxes filled with files.

They looked so frazzled that I could virtually walk past them unnoticed.

I headed for Monahan's office.

When I arrived at his door, I noticed that it was partially cracked. I could hear him talking with the chief judge, so I stood outside the door and eavesdropped.

"This thing is getting out of hand...I'm not sure that you should try to do anything to discredit him. I'm not going to be involved. Whatever your personal vendetta, keep me out of it. I happen to think that Mathis is a good judge," I heard the district attorney say.

Then the chief judge declared, "I'm sure he's taking bribes. But now I hear that he's trying to set me up. I don't know how he found out that I was on to him. I know that you don't believe that he's dirty...but he is. You have to help me prove it."

"I don't have to help you do anything—not unless you have proof of his guilt."

ARE YOU CHEATING?

Terrence Simmons quickly ushered me from the building and into the parking lot. He didn't want us to be seen together, which was understandable considering the way that Sanders and Carolyn Otto felt about me. The guy standing before me left no doubt that he was totally intimidated by his two colleagues.

"Listen, Judge Mathis, you're asking me to commit career suicide. Geoff Sanders is unforgiving. As we speak, he's upstairs threatening to bring down the cops that he claims compromised his case. He's also devising legal strategies to retry Scott. The man is obsessed, and his sidekick is a vengeful black widow. I'm not ashamed to say that she scares the hell out of me."

Even though we stood alone in the parking lot, I could sense the fear he had of being spotted with me. His eyes searched around as if he expected, at any second, someone to pop out from behind a car and scold him for being in my presence.

While surveying his surroundings, he babbled, "If I go behind his back and do what you've asked, he'll crucify me. He wants Scott on his terms; he's vindictive like that... Look, Judge, it won't make any sense trying to make a deal with Eugene Scott anyway—Sanders would just have it rescinded. Then he would turn his full attention to coming after me. If he's got the balls to try and come after you, then you know that I don't stand a chance if he decides to come after me."

I needed to calm him, to give him confidence in what I was trying to do. The indictment was the objective—anything else was a worry for another time.

"I understand what you're saying, but if we put everything in order and you take it to Monahan, then what can Sanders do?"

"Plenty, that's what I'm saying... He's got Monahan's ear."

"If you can help me secure the indictment against Eugene, I'll find a way to take the hit for you with Sanders and Otto."

His hesitation made it clear that he was reluctant—his eyes continued wandering wildly around the parking structure. The assistant prosecutor took a deep breath, exhaled, then made eye contact with me. "Okay, all right. What the hell, this ain't the only job in the metro area. Whatcha got so far?"

I smiled. "I've got a witness who's willing to testify that Scott ordered him to murder someone at my rehab center. The shooter wants witness protection for his testimony. I'm about to go to the center and speak with the guy who was the target. Evidently, this guy has something on Eugene Scott."

"When you get everything together, call me. We'll set up a meet and I'll go over what you've collected." Terrence Simmons extended his hand. "I gotta go back in before he sends someone to look for me."

"Thanks." I took his hand into mine, and then assured him. "It'll be okay."

❀❀❀

For several consecutive years, my schedule had been hectic.

Attending law school, heading political campaigns, running for public office, coordinating Young Adults Asserting Themselves, and working a regular nine-to-five had all contributed to taking me away from my family for long stretches of time. Sure, I no longer attended law school, nor was I spearheading anyone's campaign. I had already been elected to public office, so you would think that I would have had more time to dedicate toward family. But adding the rehabilitation center had already begun to take its toll on depriving my family of quality time. My children complained so much that I had to finally put my foot down and pledge my Saturdays and Sundays to them. Since I had spent Friday and Saturday with them, I felt that I could use this Sunday as a workday.

Darwin and his little cousins had come to be accepted into my family. My goal was to seek punishment for those who brought harm to my extended relatives. I told myself that my pursuit of the individual who murdered Sheila superseded any personal directive as far as promised weekends to the kids. Plus, it wasn't as if I hadn't spent most of the weekend with them.

Before I pulled into the parking lot of Sheila's House, I noticed a brand-new, customized, shiny, black Ford Bronco parked at the curb in front of the building, its music blaring. Two thug types were sitting in the front seat keeping an eye on the center. Seeing those individuals immediately sparked fear and concern. The smell of gunpowder still lingered in the lobby, and the two suspects bore a resemblance to those sitting in the Bronco. Just like the gunmen responsible for spraying bullets around the center, these two also had do-rags tied around their heads and hid their eyes behind dark shades.

When entering the center from the parking lot, I would usually use the back door. After seeing the vehicle in front of the building, I made it a point to walk around to the front entrance.

As I approached the vehicle, the driver lowered the music. When the passenger rolled his window down, the cool breeze generated by their air conditioner brushed across my face. It was refreshing, considering the temperature had reached the low nineties.

In an attempt to present himself as being hard, the passenger mumbled to me with a thuggish arrogance, "Whatcha need?"

From behind a sarcastic grin, I countered, "That's just what I was about to ask you. You waitin' on anyone from this building?"

"I don't think that you should be concerned with that, Pops..."

That boy lost his damn mind—"Pops." The fool had the nerve to call me "Pops," at thirty-six years old. No one should be calling me "Pops" except my children.

I couldn't believe that fool. I think I was more upset with him for that statement than I was about them sitting in front of the building with their music blasting.

They couldn't have been more than twenty. No matter what their ages, I still couldn't get past the passenger referring to me as "Pops."

"Gentlemen, first let's start with this 'Pops' thing… I'm a little too young for that label," I said calmly. "Anyway, I'd appreciate it if you two would move on. You can't loiter in front of this building."

Both of the young thug types seemed a bit perturbed over my request to move their vehicle from in front of the center. The passenger tilted his head slightly to his right, then lowered his shapes just enough so that he could peek over them. The hooligan said with attitude, "We ain't goin' nowhere. I'd advise you to step."

"You sure you wanna mix it up with me?" I asked with just as much attitude.

The driver quickly got out of the car and began to make his way around the front of the vehicle. As the heavyset knucklehead, who looked to be a French fry away from needing a new jogging suit, stepped to the curb, his slender passenger eased his door open, got out of the car, and slowly approached me from the rear. I wanted to laugh because the two of them looked like a black Abbott and Costello trying to play thug.

I quickly divided my attention between the two as they closed in.

Without warning, I heard someone yell, "Get ya'll stupid asses back in the truck. I can't believe that ya'll fools 'bout to try and go up against a judge. That man is hard…"

My eyes followed the path of the voice.

To my surprise, headed down the walkway, which led from the entrance of Sheila's House, was Eugene Scott—his short lethargic stride reminiscent of a lion carefully stalking its prey.

"Hey, Scoey, don't worry 'bout them fools…I'ma tighten they asses up."

His roar ignited fear.

In the blink of an eye, the two young characters who were readying themselves to be physically confrontational hustled their asses back into the Bronco. They seemed terrified.

I've always been amazed at how a person who heads a crew creates such fear in his followers. I could clearly remember when Andre started out, and how he had gathered, and then was able to instantly get his group under control. To watch a guy as intimidating as Eugene immediately fall in line upon securing a position as enforcer was indicative of Dre's leadership skills.

Dre was a master manipulator who brought fear through psychological wit rather than brawn. When Dre got convicted, his enforcer took over the crew and immediately established himself as being more ruthless than his predecessor. A well-blended mixture of strong-arm tactics and organizational savvy, which he obtained from working side by side with Andre, made him even more dangerous than his boss ever was.

"What up, *baby*... Nice little joint you got goin' here," he said as he approached.

I wasn't really surprised to see him.

Since taking over the organization, Eugene Scott made it a point to dole out bodies just as examples of what would happen to anyone who even thought about betraying him. Knowing how he worked made it imperative that I be extremely careful with the way I handled our conversation. I couldn't let him know that I was aware of his intentions of eliminating Buster, nor that I was going to do whatever I could to get Buster to turn on him.

"What are you doing here?" I asked.

He stood directly in front of me and smiled. "I came by to see what you were up to. Scoey, you look like you surprised. What, you didn't expect me to get out, did you? I'm like the Teflon Don, baby..."

"To tell you the truth...I didn't. I was told that they had you dead to right." I changed the subject. "Enough of that. How did you know that I ran this place?"

"Come on now, Scoey...you know damn well that there ain't much that goes on in this city that I don't know about..."

He used my nickname as if he really knew me. I wondered if Andre had explained to him why I was called Scoey. I bet that he didn't know that I was given that nickname because I had introduced disco to Eastern Michigan's student body, and that "Scoey" is a derivative of "disco."

"So, you're tellin' me that you came down here especially for me. You don't even know me like that. How much did Dre tell you about me?"

"He told me enough... He said that you didn't wanna run with him when he started hustlin' powder. He said that you bailed because you didn't wanna break yo promise to yo momma. But I didn't come here to reflect on none of that."

"Then let me assume that you came to tell me what you know about the death of Sheila Morgan..."

"Who..." His twisted facial expression slowly straightened itself. "Oh... the woman who lost her head," he said with an uncaring grin. "I think that I'll hold on to that bit of information. It might come in handy somewhere down the line."

"Eugene, that information couldn't possibly do you any good now."

"You never know, Scoey...you just never know."

Once again, I changed the subject. I pointed toward his two stupid henchmen. "You need to teach your little wannabes that they should respect their elders."

"Yeah, I'll handle that," he said. Eugene gazed at his two employees, but then turned to me. "What you tryin' to do with this center? Take away my livelihood?" Eugene extended his bald fist; he obviously wanted some dap for what he felt was witty banter.

I didn't find his statement worthy of acknowledgment so I refused his soulful gesture and quickly stepped around him. "I got things to do right now. Take care," I said while heading toward the entrance.

"So it's like that...you just gonna leave a brotha hangin' like that, Scoey," he insisted while watching closely as I opened the door. "This ain't over, partna. Remember, judges can be got, too."

I ignored him; just because he knew my nickname didn't mean he knew me. Evidently, Andre never told him that I wasn't the type of person he could threaten—directly or indirectly.

When I entered the center, I walked straight up to the receptionist's desk. Our security guard was sitting behind it.

"Larry, that guy that just left here. Who was he looking for?"

"He was looking for Buster Wright."

"What did that guy say?"

"He told me that he was a relative and that it was a family emergency."

"So I take it you got Buster out of the group. Did they talk?"

"No…I went to get Wright. Thing is, he never showed up. When I went back to see what was taking him so long, he was gone."

I was startled. "What do you mean he was gone?"

"No one knows where he is. I was told he left out of the group several seconds after I did. He should have literally been right behind me, but he never showed up."

I was curious to know if someone had accompanied Eugene. "Did that guy come in by himself?"

"Yes…"

"Look, I want you to lock up the entrances, grab a couple others, and check around the building. I'm gonna go check the security tapes."

We had monitors behind the receptionist's desk, but in order to check what had been recorded, I needed to go into my office.

The guard had recruited three others to help him search around the building for our missing resident. They searched up and down and were unable to locate any sign that Buster Wright was ever on the premises. When they reported to me that they were unable to locate him, I was already going through the tapes.

It had taken me a while to figure out how to call up each camera's recording, but finally, I was able to watch the guard enter the group meeting. He pulled the facilitator to the side. There was no volume so, of course, I couldn't hear what was being said. It was like watching a silent movie.

The guard exited. At that time the facilitator's eyes veered toward the fourteen people who sat in a circle before him. He mouthed something, and Buster stood and headed for the door.

I had to switch to the recording from the hallway camera to see what Buster did after he left the group meeting. On that recording, I watched Buster walk to the door leading to the lobby and peek out. Without warning, Buster turned and broke into a full sprint. I pulled up another camera angle, which showed Cecilia's nephew entering into the men's open bay area. There were only two people in the area, and they were sleeping. Buster hurriedly stuffed his gym bag with the little things that he had with him upon checking in. His face clearly depicted fear.

The next time I was able to locate Buster on the cameras, he was running out of the back door, which was kind of strange because that door has an alarm on it that didn't go off. I turned my attention toward the guard.

"As you saw, he left the building through the back door. What happened to the alarm?"

"I'm sorry, Judge, but we don't turn the alarm on until seven thirty p.m. every day. That hallway is usually where I'm stationed until the alarm is set. I was asked to monitor that door from up here because the receptionist left early due to a family emergency."

A half-hour after viewing the tapes, I picked up Buster's cousin Alvin. He and I drove around the city for quite a while in search of my runaway resident. I was more convinced than ever that Buster held the key to me getting Eugene Scott to open up about Sheila's murder.

The young man whom I treated like my very own son directed me to various locations where Buster was known to frequent. During our travel Cecilia's son emphatically dismissed any suggestion that he had knowledge of his cousin's criminal activities. My passenger insisted that Buster's sole objective when he entered Sheila's House was to turn his life around.

Alvin explained to me that his cousin had gotten off track and drawn into the life when he went to work, at seventeen, as a dope runner. Alvin went on to say that his cousin began using right after he was robbed making a delivery and pickup.

Buster was given two ounces of cocaine and he was told to deliver one to a location in the Brewster Projects, the same housing development where Diana Ross grew up. Alvin's cousin dropped one ounce at his house, then, so as not to look too suspicious, he took a bus to his drop-off point.

Evidently, someone had pegged him as a runner and followed him as he walked through the projects with a gym bag draped over his shoulder. They lay in wait for him to leave the apartment where the actual exchange took place.

After the robbery, Alvin realized that it had to be an inside job because they didn't rob him before he went into the apartment. They waited for him to leave. The crooks wanted the money rather than the dope.

While trying to think of a way to explain his situation to the dealer he worked for, Buster was persuaded by another runner to build up his courage by sniffing some of the powder from his second delivery. The young runner was told that sniffing cocaine was very helpful in those situations. Alvin told me that his cousin, on that night, sniffed cocaine for the very first time.

Buster confronted his boss and told him of the robbery—something that he never would have done had it not been for the cocaine. He would have tried to find a way to get the money and repay his boss rather than look weak by allowing himself to be robbed.

Upon learning of the robbery, the dealer and several of his crew took Buster back to the projects. They found the guys that committed the robbery, and shot them both. From that moment, Buster was hooked on the false courage that he had gotten from the white powder.

Buster grew up like I did.

Like my mother, his mother hauled his butt to church every week—but Buster went one step further than me. He sang in the choir, and from what I was told, he had a great voice. Our paths differed only because I never did cocaine, and, unlike him, I got caught doing my dirt and had to stand before a judge. Standing before Judge Kaufman was truly my saving grace because as a young hoodlum, if you don't get caught, you get caught up.

After riding around for a couple of hours looking for Buster, I began to feel that the search was futile. I took Alvin home and insisted that he contact me if his cousin were to reach out to him.

When I pulled in front of Cecilia's house, I said to her son, "Look, Alvin, the only way that Buster is going to be able to get out of this situation is if he allows me to help. Tell him that I need to know what he has on Eugene. I'll be available at any time."

"I'll make some calls and see if I can locate him. I'm sorry, Judge Mathis," Alvin said with all sincerity.

"Your cousin is a grown man. You shouldn't be apologizing for his actions," I said, assuring him that it wasn't his fault.

"I'll find him, Judge," Alvin said as he got out of the car.

While pulling from the curb, I remembered that I was supposed to meet with Darwin and Ron at eight o'clock. I checked my watch and realized that I was already running ten minutes late, and the sports bar where we were to meet was at least fifteen minutes from Alvin's house.

"Shit, I hope they wait," I whispered under my breath.

When I finally entered the Time Out Sports Bar on Plymouth Road, I was able to walk in unnoticed because the nine gentlemen seated in the front had their eyes locked on a game between the Tigers and Baltimore Orioles.

The place was loud.

The game caught my attention because the Tigers had the bases loaded with Cecil Fielder stepping to the plate. The first pitch to Fielder was high and outside. After he took that pitch, I scanned the establishment in search of my friends. My eyes veered back to the television just in time to see the next pitch nearly hit the Tigers's designated hitter. I turned my head and resumed my search, and that's when I saw them.

I proceeded to the far end of the bar where Ron and Darwin were seated.

"Hey, guys, what's up?" I said as I approached.

The guys said hello without ever taking their eyes off of the television. Cecil Fielder was digging in; the count was two balls and two strikes. I knew that my partners weren't going to fully acknowledge me until Cecil took his hacks, so I sat down next to Darwin and watched as the Tigers's number four hitter attempted to drive in the go-ahead runs, as the score was tied at one.

Suddenly, everyone in the bar got to their feet and threw their arms in the air. They cheered loudly as the ball that Cecil Fielder hit traveled deep toward the left-field bleachers. It wasn't until the ball cleared the fence that both Ron and Darwin turned their undivided attention toward me.

Darwin took a sip of his Heineken before asking, "What going on, Judge?"

"I'm really drained," I countered.

Ron chimed in, "I took care of that thing with your cousin-in-law. I arrested her and charged her with prostitution."

"Thanks…"

As usual, Ron could tell that I was deep in thought. "Anything we can help you with?"

"Buster Wright, the guy who played hero at the center. Well, he walked away from the program."

Darwin was shocked. "What do you mean, he walked away? There's got to be some kind of mistake. He was determined to complete the program."

The newspaperman felt that Buster was the genuine article, someone who really wanted to change. Darwin had spoken with Buster several times by phone after the rehab incident because he wanted to support Cecilia Wright's nephew. The journalist couldn't believe that Buster would jeopardize his chance at sobriety.

I didn't mean to mislead Darwin about Buster's commitment. The conversation seemed to get away from me before I could cover the details. I knew that the journalist had taken a liking toward Alvin's cousin, so it stood to reason that my vagueness about his situation would cause confusion.

"No...don't get me wrong. He didn't leave because he was refusing treatment. I think that he saw Eugene Scott in the lobby of Sheila's House, got scared, and took off," I stated.

Both Ron and Darwin seemed baffled.

The police commander was surprised. "Scott showed up at Sheila's House?"

Darwin's eyes veered back and forth between Ron and me. He had no idea what had taken place because he had spent the day with his cousins and the Johnson twins. Neither Ron nor I had had an opportunity to cover the particulars of the day's with the journalist.

"I thought he was locked up. When did he get out...and why would he go to the rehab center?" Darwin asked.

Ron was already aware of the circumstances behind Eugene's release. But he ignored the jeers and cheers that accompanied the Tigers's six-run fifth inning and hung on to my every word as if what I was saying was news to him.

When I finally began covering my encounter with the crime boss's nursery school henchmen, they both seemed to get a kick out of it. It wasn't as if they took the situation lightly; they just found the teenaged wannabes amusing. I think that was because of my comparing them to Abbott and Costello.

The next subject I would cover dealt with the conversation that I had overheard between the chief judge and the district attorney. Only four people knew that I was on to the chief judge's plot to entrap me—so, who told him?

"Have any of you heard from Gram?" I asked.

Darwin spoke, "He said that he was gonna be here. What's up?"

"The chief judge knows that I'm on to him. I can't figure out how he found out."

"How do you think he found out?" the police commander asked.

For several minutes we discussed the possible ways in which the chief judge could've come across information that was exclusive to four people. I didn't believe Darwin, Ron, Maggie, or Gram would ever betray my trust—so the only conclusion was that Gram had attempted to use some of his political clout to squash the chief judge's efforts to entrap me. And whomever he spoke with must have had strong ties to my supervisor. But all we could do was speculate, and since Gram didn't show up at the bar as planned, we couldn't question him.

The early start to my day began to catch up with me. I glanced at my watch—it was ten p.m. With the Tigers up eight to four in the bottom of the eighth, I felt that the game was well in hand, so I left the bar and headed home.

It took me fifteen minutes to get home from the bar.

The floodlights in the backyard were triggered as I pulled the Explorer up the driveway. I was glad that Linda had left the garage door open because the batteries in my door opener had died, and as tired as I was, I didn't believe that I had enough strength to open it manually.

When I entered the dark house from the side door, I could hear a teaser echoing from the television in the family room. A reporter from Channel Seven ABC Eyewitness News was giving a rundown of the stories that would be covered on the eleven p.m. broadcast. One particular story caught my attention as I made my way to where my wife was seated.

The only light in the family room came from the television, so I didn't immediately notice that my wife was curled up on the sofa in deep depression.

"Hey, baby…" I said, my eyes locked on the TV.

"Also, the body of Elliot St. Paul, the man convicted of murdering his wife and her lover, was found hung in his cell. All this and more, tonight at eleven…"

Not hearing a response to my greeting didn't hit me until a commercial followed the newsbreak.

I turned my attention toward my wife.

Her eyes were watering—she quickly wiped at them. Linda sniffled several times before she sat up. She pulled her robe closed and stared at me.

I walked over and sat next to her. "What's going on...what's wrong?"

It was as if she were in shock, as if every word went in one ear and out the other. So I took her hands into mine. I kissed them, and afterward, I used my right hand and gently caressed her face before saying softly. "Baby...whatever is bothering you...we'll work it out."

Linda lowered her eyes. "Tell me the truth. Are you cheating on me?"

Naturally, I was flabbergasted. "What...baby, come on. You're gonna have to stop this. Look, I love you. I'm not interested, nor do I have time to be cheating."

"I don't believe you," she whispered.

"Why?"

She buried her face in the couch. I could hear her crying. I eased my way over to her and sat. I caressed her back gently, before saying, "Come on, baby, you gotta stop this."

The ringing of the phone caught my attention. I reached over to the end table and picked it up while continuing to rub my wife's back. "Hello!" Gram was on the phone. He wanted to talk to me. He wanted to tell his wife about his affair. He claimed that the guilt was getting to him.

I wanted to excuse myself and speak with the billionaire in private. I wanted to tell him that I was aware that he'd had another tryst with Otto, but I didn't want to make my wife suspicious. I didn't want her thinking that I was fielding secret calls from some imaginary lover. "Look, I'm a little busy right now. Let's talk about this tomorrow."

HOW COULD YOU?

The grassy knoll, Martin Luther King Jr.'s assassination, John Wilkes Booth, and the many such plots that made headlines over the centuries had suddenly become a topic of conversation in the office. The debates surrounding these conspiracies were sparked by the chief judge's despicable acts of deception.

The leader of the 36th District judicial system was conspiring to bring down one of his own. His foolishness led to my clerks's conspiracy-theory mindsets. Because of the chief judge's actions, and after informing my legal assistants that someone had strolled into my chambers and installed some kind of recording device, both Maggie and David became super-protective of the office, and overly suspicious of anyone and everything that entered through the doors.

One of the precautions that they instituted was, during business hours, they would never leave the office unmanned, no matter what. The way that my truth-seekers felt about conspiracies, I wouldn't have put it past them if they had scanned the office for wires every morning before I arrived.

It was nine o'clock in the morning when I entered.

I didn't see Maggie or David, yet the door was open. As I headed toward my chambers, I could hear mumbling coming from within. But before I could grab the knob and enter, David exited.

He was startled when he saw me standing at the door. "Oh…!" The openly gay law student quickly placed his hands to his mouth as if he were a frightened female.

After he caught himself, I could see it in his eyes. He wasn't going to let me get a word in edgewise.

His tone was always filled with the happiness and delightful energy that would be expected from an individual who never spent one day in the closet. And this time was no different. "Hey, boss! The mayor is in your office." He tilted his head slightly, put a hand on his hip, and lowered his tone an octave as he continued, "I wasn't gonna let him sit in there alone…I don't trust nobody." He winked at me before sashaying to his desk with the grace of a queen strolling through a gay bar in an effort to get noticed.

David wasn't ashamed to let the world know who he was.

All I could do was shake my head. As nerve-wracking as he could be, my young clerk was a hard-working guy, and he meant well. He was just a little too over the top for me at times.

One thing for sure, no one could say anything about his professionalism when it came to his attire. The young man always covered his thin frame with a nice suit. There were occasions when I had to ask him to tone it down with his hair. No one should change hair color like changing under-wear.

When I stepped into my chambers, I immediately noticed that the mayor was standing at the wall that was adorned with plaques and certificates. Aaron Dennis had never stepped foot in my office—at least, not since I'd occupied it. So I was a little taken aback that the Top Dog had stopped by to see lil' ole me.

"What's going on, Mayor?" I asked while heading toward my desk.

"Impressive…" he mumbled, his eyes still locked on my accomplishments.

I laid my briefcase on my desk, removed the blazer to my blue suit, then walked over and hung my coat on the rack next to my picture window. "So, what brings you by?"

The mayor casually made his way over to my desk. "We have a problem." He made himself comfortable in one of my chairs before continuing. "Carolyn Otto stopped by my office at eight thirty this morning. I got in earlier than usual because I'm dealing with some issues with Gram. Anyway, she stated that she was sending police over to your center this morning."

"For what?" I asked as I sat down.

"To make an arrest."

"What!"

"Apparently, she's been working on a case. A grocery store was robbed a few days ago. The clerk was killed in the commission of that robbery. Well, it seems that one of the people involved is a patient at your rehabilitation center."

"You've gotta be kidding me!" I was blown away. I'd heard about the incident. I was familiar with each of the patients, so my mind was trying to sort and identify who I believed was capable of committing such an act.

"I wish I were kidding... But, that's not the worst of it," the mayor uttered. "Otto wants me to shut down the center. She claims that your rehabilitation center is where criminals go to take refuge from law enforcement."

"She's crazy..." Suddenly, I felt anger. I was not about to allow that to happen.

Who the hell did she think she was? If she thought that I was just gonna stand by idly and allow that to happen, she really was crazy. "So, what did you tell her?"

"I told her that she would have to prove her accusations. Look here, Judge, if she proves that you have registered patients that are being sought by police, then she'll be able to make a case to have that place closed. I would be compelled to use the power of my office to do so." He was serious. I couldn't believe that he would work with her in any way against me. I don't know why I was so surprised.

Shit, it was then that I realized what her racist ass was up to. This was another one of her attempts to discredit me. She had gone out of her way to fuck the mayor to put herself in a position to do just that.

"Okay, so you're telling me that you would back that witch?"

"I would have no choice."

"BULLSHIT! Don't try and run game on me...you know better than that. You don't have to back her any more than I have to vote for her in the next election." I got to my feet and walked around my desk before making myself comfortable on the edge of it. "What's this really about?"

"What do you mean? I told you what this is about..."

"Again, you're trying to feed me bullshit. This is about you and Gram. You both are trying to one up each other. This is political tug-of-war and you're trying to put me in the middle of it."

Before I could get into what I really wanted to say, Maggie entered. "Excuse me, Judge Mathis...you have a very important phone call."

"Thanks, Maggie!" I reached over and grabbed the receiver. "Hello!" The caller was quick and to the point. "Okay, I'm on my way."

❂❂❂

It wasn't late, about seven in the evening, in fact it was broad daylight—after all, the sun doesn't set during midsummer until about nine, so that made what they did outright bold.

She walked casually with a brown paper bag in tow.

He said that she wore a blue hospital smock and that her cocoa-brown, flawless complexion and jet-black hair along with the contented glee in her beautiful hazel eyes was what drew his attention to her in the first place.

He was very clear in his detailed account of actions described as being completely random. There were three of them occupying a van that pulled up next to her as she made her way from the bus stop at the corner of Chicago and Evergreen, which was only six blocks from her home. His version of that moment made it clear that she was completely oblivious that she was being targeted.

He went on to say that he and his two partners discussed how sexy she was. In the midst of that conversation, the two idiots who accompanied him insisted that she was the one.

"I tried to talk them out of it. I wanted her phone number, that's all," he whispered solemnly. He claimed that he demanded that they move on and choose another, after insisting that she wasn't the right person. "They wouldn't listen... We weren't supposed to be on that side of town, any-way. We made an unscheduled stop. On the way back, we saw her. They said that we should get her and save time—that she would do, that he could make his point with her."

I didn't interrupt him, although I was dying to know—*what point?*

He went on to say how the driver checked the front to make sure that the coast was clear, while he checked the back window to ensure the same. The third thug waited to open the van's sliding door so that he could make his move when he felt that the time was right. The guy responsible for the snatch made it clear that he wouldn't do anything until he had a clear path from the van to the sidewalk. In other words, he wanted to ensure that there were no cars parked at the curb before he would yell, "now," prompting the driver to stop.

They had gone over the plan numerous times prior to spotting her, so they were poised and ready—all they needed was a victim, and Sheila Morgan was the unfortunate choice.

"I tried my best to talk them out of choosing her. I swear, I only said something because she was so cute. I pointed at her as we were driving, and I said, 'Damn, she's fine.' I didn't say, let's get her. But it was my fault. I shouldn't have said anything. I shouldn't have even been involved in the first place."

He was wallowing in a state of self-pity. Yeah, I was glad that he was remorseful, but at the same time, at that point of confession, I wasn't at all moved by his feeling of regret.

I finally chimed in, "Buster…you're all over the place. Settle down and tell me what this is all about. Who killed Sheila Morgan…and why?"

"Before I get into that, I have to explain something to you," he said as he glanced over to his aunt who sat next to me on the couch.

Buster sat in a dining room chair that had been placed in the middle of the living room. He directed his attention back to me and then said, "It started with someone stealing dope. Eugene had several spots where he had naked women cutting up and packaging his drugs."

Cecilia's nephew sighed and cleared his throat before he continued, "Someone at one of his Eastside spots was stealing. No one could figure out how it was being done so Gene wanted to kill every last one of 'em… He lost it…He pulled out a gun and stuck it to the heads of the three women he felt were brave enough to steal from him. But those girls all swore that they would never do anything against him.

"Two of his boys got him to calm down. He paced around the apartment for a while, trying to gather himself. He didn't wanna take out his frustration on all the girls because they were already trained, and he didn't wanna take the time in training others. After several minutes of pacing, he had me, and the two knuckleheads who were with me in the van, to follow him into the hallway. When he had us alone, he insisted that since he couldn't tell who was involved with the missing dope, his objective was to send them a clear message."

I was baffled. "What are you saying?"

"That Gene wanted to use a woman off the street to make his point. He told us to grab any woman and bring her back to the apartment."

My face tightened. "You tellin' me that Eugene Scott murdered Sheila Morgan?"

"When we brought her back to the apartment, Eugene sat her in the corner. He then began to lecture the seven naked women that worked for him. During the lecture, Gene disappeared into the kitchen for a split second. He then returned with a fireman's ax. He had Stanley and Arthur—those were the two guys that helped me snatch her—blindfold her and sit her in the middle of the room. As soon as they stepped away from her, that madman gripped the ax firmly and then reared back and swung. I was sick to my stomach when I saw that woman's head hit the floor."

Cecilia placed her hands to her mouth in shock. "Oh my God...Buster Wright...how could you?"

"I didn't know, Auntie," he declared as his eyes welled. "I never thought that he would do anything like that."

She raised her voice an octave higher. "Boy...HOW COULD YOU...? What did you think that a dope dealer would do to a woman that he had you snatch off the streets? What did you think his point would be, fool?"

The realization of what he had taken part in was too much for him to bear.

Buster began to shed tears. The guilt had been eating away at his soul since the day he played witness to the horrific crime. He buried his face in his hands and cried out, "What did I do... Oh my God... I'm sorry." The emotionally wrecked accomplice to murder sniffled. "I'm so sorry..."

I was stunned.

Watching him cry only reminded me of the pain that Darwin would experience once he was told the truth. The journalist was truly sincere about helping Buster turn his life around, so much so that he'd volunteered to sponsor the drug abuser.

Cecilia walked over to Buster and began her awkward attempt at consoling. "You always found a way to get yourself into trouble." She rubbed his back. "Baby, how could you?"

I interrupted Cecilia, "Can I use your phone?"

"Sure, Judge, you know where it is," she said before turning her attention back to her nephew.

The kitchen phone would allow me privacy, so that's where I headed. Upon entering, I picked up the wall phone and immediately dialed Commander Daly.

When he answered, I said into the phone, "Ron, I'm bringing in Buster Wright."

The law enforcement officer asked, "Did he tell you what he has on Scott?"

"Yes...and it's solid."

Before I could continue my conversation, I heard several loud successive pops, which were followed by horrific screams. Suddenly, several people ran through the house yelling. "THEY WERE SHOT...SOMEONE SHOT 'EM!"

"Ron, let me call you back," I said with urgency.

The commander could hear the ruckus. "What the hell is going on over there?"

"I don't know... Let me get back to you." I hung up the phone and headed for the living room. It was complete chaos.

Three of Cecilia's children, along with six of their friends, stood unnerved as they peered out of the opened front door. I had no idea that they were even in the house.

"What's going on?" I asked as I entered the living room.

I didn't see her, but I could hear Cecilia screaming in agony, "OH LORD!... NOOO!... NOT MY BABY...!"

Her anguish, her pleas to God—I could feel her pain, but I couldn't figure out what had put her in such a state of misery. It was definitely life altering.

I had only stepped away for the few minutes it had taken me to make my phone call, so I couldn't imagine what could have happened that fast.

The children unintentionally blocked my attempt to exit so that I could see what the commotion was about. "Let me through... get out of the way, kids," I said as I physically forced my way past the congregation of panic-stricken youth.

The sunlight nearly blinded me when I stepped onto the porch. When I was finally able to adjust my eyes, to my surprise, laid out on the covered entrance, bleeding profusely from several gunshot wounds to the torso, was Alvin. Lying next to him, with a hole in his chest, was his cousin Buster.

"What the hell happened?" I asked in disbelief.

Crying uncontrollably, while holding her child in her lap, Cecilia managed to say, "It was a drive-by...they shot my baby."

I bent over Buster; he appeared to be losing consciousness. "Hang on..." I quickly gazed at the stunned teens. "Call nine-one-one!" I ordered in desperation as I kneeled beside him.

Buster coughed up blood. "Judge..." he said in a hush.

"Don't try to talk, son..."

I could hear the children around us crying. They were in complete panic. I wasn't sure whether anyone had actually phoned for emergency service. For Cecilia's sake, I certainly hoped, and prayed, that paramedics were on their way.

Buster wanted to speak—the more he tried, the more blood his coughed up.

"Take it easy...don't try to talk," I whispered consolingly.

She cried, and rocked, she rocked and cried. Cecilia held her child, not knowing whether it would be for the last time, so she explained to Alvin as she gazed lovingly. "I love you, baby...Momma is so proud of you and who you've become. You have such a wonderful heart." She cried out, "Don't leave Momma, baby...I don't know what I will do if you leave me."

I could feel her pain.

I myself was in agony—for the first time since my mother, I was looking into the eyes of someone whose life was slowly slipping away, and once again, there was absolutely nothing that I could do to prevent it from happening.

"Judge…" he whispered once more. It was obvious that he was determined to tell me something, so I leaned my ear closer to his mouth and listened as he whispered.

❀❀❀

The emergency room at Henry Ford Hospital was hectic, like any other day. When paramedics wheeled in both Buster and Alvin, the two were barely breathing. I could hardly see moisture on either of their oxygen masks. Buster was conscious, but Alvin looked to be flatlining. The paramedics and residents were feverishly working on both young men as they were being pushed toward surgery rooms.

I held Cecilia as tightly as I could as I led her to the waiting room. All of Alvin's siblings followed. I could tell that the children were torn; their emotional state had never been so conflicted. They couldn't stand to see their mother in so much pain—they weren't used to it. Cecilia Wright had always been so strong, they felt that she could weather anything. Now, to see her torn up emotionally, was more than they could bear.

Most of all, there was their brother and cousin, both clinging to life—no child should have to deal with what they obviously had to work through.

We sat and cried; we held one another in an attempt to console. It seemed like we had been in the waiting room forever. I could hear the children praying, and Cecilia—her eyes had been locked on a MetLife poster of children playing the entire twenty minutes that we waited. Every so often, I could see a tear ease slowly from her eyes and down her chubby cheek.

Without warning, she whispered, "How's Linda doing? She hasn't been herself lately."

She never took her eyes off of that poster.

"Linda's okay," I said softly.

Cecilia finally turned away from the poster. She turned toward me before asking with all sincerity, "Why did this happen? I told Alvin to stay away from Buster."

"Don't blame Buster. He made a mistake, but he was trying to do the right thing."

Cecilia managed a kindhearted smile. "I know…but that boy always found a way to get into trouble. Nobody except Alvin saw the good in him…"

I took Cecilia's hand before leaning over and kissing the tear that slowly crept down her cheek. Just as I began to wipe the moisture from her face, a surgeon entered the waiting room.

"Wrights… I need to speak to the parents of Buster Wright."

Cecilia got to her feet and said, "They're on the way. I'm his aunt."

The doctor's eyes were caring and very sympathetic, which prompted Alvin's mother to place her hands to her mouth in anticipation of having to disguise any wayward emotions.

THE CHIEF JUDGE

After leaving the hospital, I immediately drove over to 1300 to meet Ron Daly—we had a search warrant to execute. Ron agreed to put together a team capable of carrying out a successful raid. He also contacted forensics and requested that a unit meet us at the location identified under the warrant.

We couldn't afford any screw-ups if we hoped to gather enough evidence to bring the murderer of Sheila Morgan to justice.

Terrence Simmons was to meet both Ron and me at an apartment building on the Eastside of the city. I wanted the prosecutor involved every step of the way. Evidential change of custody was top priority. Having Simmons there to witness what was taking place was unconventional, but so was the individual who had committed the hideous murder of Darwin's cousin.

The assistant district attorney arrived as the police commander and I pulled up in front of the sixty-four-unit apartment building. There was a SWAT team and several marked patrol cars awaiting our arrival.

Several uniformed officers and the SWAT team leader approached Ron and me as we stepped from his cruiser. Everyone was primed and ready to execute the raid and search.

Ron asked the SWAT team leader, "How long have you guys been here?"

"Literally seconds before you," was Captain Ellis' response.

We all turned our attention toward the courtyard of the complex and watched as several uniformed officers gathered up the children who were playing in front of the neglected building.

As the courtyard was being cleared, the forensics team arrived.

"Okay, let's move." Captain Ellis directed his next request to the ADA and me. "Judge, you two have to wait here with the forensics unit until we give the all-clear sign."

Safety was SWAT's primary concern. On most occasions, the unit would have some sort of assault plan based on intelligence gathered from observation. But, there wasn't enough time for the team to truly strategize or conduct surveillance, so they were going in blind.

The prosecutor and I stood in the middle of the courtyard with several uniformed officers and watched as the SWAT team entered the building with military precision. We could only hope that no one had alerted anyone in apartment 57B that we were coming—after all, we were conducting the raid in the early afternoon during the middle of summer vacation.

"Judge…how did you get the tip?" the ADA asked.

"Buster Wright."

"Is he willing to testify…because if we do prove that this is the location where the murder took place, we're still going to need someone who witnessed him do it."

I ignored the prosecutor and began to slowly pace around the courtyard.

My mind drifted just that quickly.

The apartment that was being hit was on the fifth floor at the rear of the six-story building. All I could think about was whether Eugene would be there. I was hoping that he was because I needed to see him in cuffs. Not only did he murder Sheila, but I also knew that it was he who ordered the drive-by that resulted in the fatal shooting of Buster Wright. Eugene's madness also had left Cecilia Wright's eldest child, Alvin, clinging to life.

"Judge…did you hear what I said?" Terrence Simmons questioned as he tapped my shoulder.

His words were muffled. It was as if they were fighting with my thoughts for attention. "Huh… what…"

"I asked you…will your witness be prepared to testify…because uncovering the fact that this was the location where the murder took place is not enough to hand down an indictment on Scott for murder."

What Terrence Simmons had said was true. I also knew that with Buster's death we would have to try and convince someone else to testify that Eugene murdered Sheila.

"He's dead!" I mumbled.

The ADA responded in shock, "What!"

"My witness...he's dead!"

Simmons stepped in front of me before asking, "How...what happened?"

"He died from wounds sustained in a drive-by a little over an hour ago," I said solemnly.

"Oh my God...!" Terrence Simmons was truly stunned. "Look, Judge, I don't want to sound callous...but we need another witness. What about the kid that shot up your rehabilitation center?"

I was not in the mood to talk about anything after having spent much of the morning surrounded by tragedy. All I wanted was to see Eugene Scott being led from that building in handcuffs. It took me several seconds to realize it, but my selfish desires were for short-term satisfaction. If I really wanted to make that murderer pay, it was imperative that I snapped out of my funk. Seeing him led out in cuffs was not really going to be that satisfying.

"I hadn't had a chance to speak with the kid responsible for the assault on the center," I said. "Look, Buster left me a list of individuals who were present when Eugene murdered Sheila."

The ADA's eyes lit up. "Did you have a chance to speak with any of them?"

I said sarcastically, "With that kid literally dying before my eyes... right...!" I was outdone that he was so insensitive. "Buster Wright just lost his life..."

Simmons realized that he was being unsympathetic; he interrupted me before I could continue. "I'm sorry, Judge. I was totally cold."

"After this, I'm going to pick up the list and attempt to speak with the people on it. Believe me...I'll do what I need to in order to get someone to step up."

Our conversation ended when we both noticed the SWAT team leader exit the building alone, his firearm hanging from a strap around his neck. Captain Ellis didn't look too happy as he made his way toward us.

"It's clear...the place is empty. It's been painted and is ready to be rented," the team leader said. "If a murder was in fact committed in that apartment…forensics has its work cut out trying to prove it." Ellis directed his attention toward the crime scene investigators. "Hope you guys have a lot of luminol."

If a murder was committed in apartment 57B, I was confident that Detroit CSI would be able to find the evidence.

Dressed in white jumpsuits, the forensics team professionals were preparing to search the spotless apartment for blood. That particular residence had to be the cleanest in the entire building; it was obvious that something was being covered up.

The four-man crew began to cover the windows with dark cloths they carried with them—their intent, to get the room as dark as they could.

Tiny particles of blood will cling to most surfaces for years; no matter how good a crime scene has been wiped down. In order to uncover these atoms, they would have to be revealed with a light-producing chemical reaction. The oxygen-carrying protein in the blood called hemoglobin could be exposed using a chemical mixture known as luminol.

I provided the forensics team with the information about the murder as told to me by Buster Wright, so the first area that they were prepared to spray with the chemical was the living room.

After we discovered that a great deal of blood was in the area of the living room as described to me in Buster's story, I was conflicted. Knowing that Sheila was murdered in that apartment did absolutely nothing to relieve the stressful feeling that had been hanging over my head like a dark cloud.

I didn't know what I expected to feel.

Did I actually think that I would gain some sort of relief? That woman was snatched off the street and murdered so that some power-hungry degenerate could make a point. In addition, someone whom I attempted to help was partially responsible for her death—and his involvement had led to his own murder. People were dying because of one man's quest to be in control.

It made me sick to my stomach.

Was I too involved? How did I get so caught up in this case in the first place?

All of these questions overwhelmed my thoughts as I drove back to my office. Sorting through each for answers wasn't going to be easy.

❁❁❁

When I got back to the office, David was standing at a file cabinet that sat in the far corner of my two-hundred-square-foot reception area. With his back to the door, he didn't immediately notice that it was me who had entered.

"What's going on?" I asked as I headed toward my office.

David glanced over his shoulder. When he saw me, he immediately stuck the folder that he was holding into the drawer before turning his undivided attention toward me. "Judge! Boy, am I glad to see you." There was a nervous excitement in his voice. I could sense concern in his blue-gray eyes.

I stopped. "What's wrong, David?"

"It's Maggie," my clerk responded as he stepped around his desk and over to me. "She's confronting the chief judge."

"Confronting him about what?"

"The chief judge came down here…as he always does when he thinks that you're not around. He's always sexually harassing Maggie." David went into gossipy mode. "Ever since she changed her look…which I think suits her so much. I love that she let her hair down and got away from that librarian look. For two years I told people that that girl could be beautiful, but everyone thought I was crazy."

I had to interrupt him or he would have gone on forever.

"David!"

"Oh! I'm sorry. Anyways, he tells her that she's gonna come work for him as soon as he gets rid of you. Maggie didn't say anything…she let him talk. But after he left, she said that she felt like a victim…like he'd violated her. Judge…he didn't know that I was in the office. He told her that he wanted her. I can't believe that he would say something like that; it was totally unprofessional."

He was about to stray again, so I said, "David, just tell me what's going on!"

"The judge said that you two were getting too close. He went on to say something about Maggie wanting to work with you because of your integrity. He said that he was going to prove that you were as corrupt as a crooked cop. You gotta stop her before she ruins her career...you know that he's vindictive..."

David was right.

If anything went down that would shine a negative light on the chief judge, he would have his clerks write up a statement that would discredit anything that Maggie would say in defense of her actions.

"David, I need for you to do something for me while I go get that girl. Call Barbara Olson. Tell her that I need to speak with her as soon as possible. Then contact Sheila's House. Find out who the police dragged out of the center. Also ask what precinct that person was taken to," I ordered, heading for the exit.

It was hard for me to imagine how Maggie would approach the chief judge; she didn't come across as a very aggressive person when it came to defending herself. Frankly, I believed that she would have been more forceful if someone were trying to take advantage of me. But, at this point, I couldn't be sure what she was capable of doing because she was preparing to take the bar exam. She probably didn't feel as vulnerable because she wouldn't have to see him every day. What she didn't realize was that the man she was about to chew a new asshole had a long reach. I didn't want her actions to hamper her career aspirations.

As soon as I entered his reception area, there they were. The chief judge was about to lead my assistant into his office. That bastard didn't see me until one of his assistants, an elderly lady by the name of Phyllis, called out to him. "Judge, you have a visitor."

The chief judge turned, and upon spotting me, he blasted if he were on the street selling dope or something, "What is it that you want?"

My eyes veered toward Maggie. I could see that she was nibbling on her bottom lip. She didn't seem at all comfortable. I could tell that she didn't want to go into his office, especially alone.

As I walked toward my assistant and the chief judge, I calmly whispered, "Maggie, I need you to get downstairs." My next statement, although meant for my assistant, was directed at my pissed-off supervisor. "Please allow me to speak with the chief judge." I put my hand on her shoulder, and then whispered in her ear, "Please… let me handle this. David filled me in."

My supervisor was angered that I would override his order for her to go into his office. "I'm your boss. How dare you attempt to supercede my request that she and I speak…" His face was beet red, his jaw tight as a vise grip. It was at that moment that it hit me—David had said the chief judge wanted to prove to Maggie that I lacked integrity, and he constantly flirted with my assistant. I suspected that his fight with me had more to do with him wanting to get next to Maggie than me replacing his poker buddy on the 36th District.

I felt like I was in back high school all over again. I figured that the man standing before me had never been involved with a woman as attractive as Maggie—at least, not unless he paid for her. Now, I understood why my assistant made it a point to dress down. Her logic made complete sense, because, believe it or not, she had a look that apparently drove middle-aged, lonely, successful men to the brink of stupidity.

The chief judge and I went into his office, closed the door, and went at it. I had to let him know that if he continued to harass my clerk that I would ensure that it was brought to everyone's attention—including the press. I also told him that I wouldn't stand for his blatant attempts to sabotage me with his efforts to chip away at my integrity.

He told me that he was not in the least bit concerned about any outrageous accusations that I might make public. The chief judge assured me that he was not one to stand idly by while someone threatened to ruin his name and his standing in the 36th District.

I had things to do. I had totally forgotten that I had to find the list of people who had witnessed Sheila's death. That list was stashed in my office. I didn't have time to continue dialogue with that bastard, so I reminded him to steer clear of my clerk and stormed out of his office.

When I got back to my office, David immediately told me that the police had arrested Gwen Ellison. He also revealed the precinct she was taken to.

That girl seemed so genuine; it was hard for me to believe that she had involved herself with a robbery homicide. When she introduced herself to me outside of my cousin Darryl's house, I was convinced that she was truly looking for a way to change her life, not for a place to hide from police.

David also informed me that Barbara Olson had gotten my message about the threat to close Sheila's House, which I had left on her answering machine after my unexpected meeting with the mayor. She asked that I reach out to her as soon as I could.

Before he could say another word, I excused myself. As my clerk turned to leave, I said, "David, tell Maggie to take off for the rest of the day."

A thousand things were going through my head.

Buster had stashed a list in my office on the day that Alvin brought him in to see me. My mind drifted to him whispering into my ear as he lay dying before me.

"*Judge Mathis, I'm so sorry. You have to believe me. I watched as he murdered her, and I did nothing. For that, I'm ashamed...*"

I recalled moving closer because his whisper became even harder to hear.

"*I wrote down the names of everyone that was in the apartment, including the ones that dumped her body. It's in your office. I put it in the law book that I was pretending to read while we were talking. Third book, top shelf...*"

I don't think I will ever forget those words.

Thinking back to the day that he came into my office, I remembered how he walked around. Obviously his interest in photographs, diplomas, and books was a pretense—it was his way of trying to find the perfect place to hide something that he felt was important.

The difficult part of this ordeal was, how did I explain to Darwin that someone he took a liking to was responsible for randomly snatching his cousin off the street and handing her over to a murderer?

I walked over to my bookshelf and pulled from it *The Law's Two Bodies: Some Evidential Problems in English Legal History* by John H. Baker. Once I read the title, the corners of my mouth turned up. Was this irony or what—the book that he had chosen to stash possible witnesses in was a book on evidence.

I made myself comfortable before opening Buster's hiding place. There it was, folded in half—a piece of loose-leaf paper. I removed the paper and unfolded it. To my surprise, before me were the names, addresses, and telephone numbers of twelve people. It was clear-cut documentation. I was only expecting a list of names—but Buster made my job as easy as he could. Next to two of the names were the words, *DUMPED BODY.* I whispered, "Thank you, Buster…"

Now was the hard part. I folded the paper, picked up my phone, and dialed. "Darwin, I need to see you. Get over to my office as soon as you can," I said into the receiver.

The journalist, unaware of the events that had taken place, replied, "What's up?"

I didn't want to go into any details over the phone, so I explained that I wanted him to be with me when I spoke to some potential witnesses. After ending my call with Darwin, I dialed Barbara.

I sat down and waited for Barbara Olson to answer.

"Hello," she said.

"How are you, Barbara?"

"Not too good…I've been having chest pains. But I'm sure I'll be okay."

"You need to go get that checked out," I said with concern.

"I will," she replied solemnly. "What's this I hear about the mayor wanting to close Sheila's House?"

"As I stated in the message I left on your machine, he said that he got a request from the district attorney's office. Carolyn Otto claims that Sheila's House is being used to harbor criminals that are eluding law enforcement."

Barbara and I talked for ten minutes. She told me that she had asked Gram to use his influence with the mayor. I knew that Gram wouldn't talk with the mayor before his wife went into the reasons that her husband had given her. Barbara insisted that since Gram and the mayor were butting heads, she would reach out to the Honorable Aaron Dennis.

"I'll speak to him myself. I won't let anyone close Sheila's House," she insisted.

I could clearly sense that the heiress was in pain. "Barbara, I think that you should be more concerned with your health. Go to the doctor…you don't sound good."

PLEASE! HELP MY BROTHER

I must have sat at my desk and gazed at Buster's list for at least twenty minutes. So much was going on in my head. Buster and Alvin, Sheila's brutal murderer, my wife being upset, the tapes, my cousin Darryl, the chief judge, and everything else that I had to deal with over the last month or so.

I laid the list atop my desk before placing both of my hands to my face; mental exhaustion had finally taken a toll on me. After a deep breath, I released an exuberating sigh.

When I looked up, I saw that my door was opening. Darwin walked in and made his way over to my desk. Sheila's cousin made himself comfortable in one of my chairs before asking, "What's going on, Judge?"

I slowly shook my head, then slid the list across my desk and explained what it was and where I had gotten it. When he learned of Buster's death, and that Alvin was barely hanging on to life, the journalist was shocked. I told him of how Buster was ordered by his boss to randomly snatch a woman off the street. I went into the reason why the drug dealer requested that the indiscriminately selected female be brought to him in the first place. I could see through his mannerisms that he was really hurt to learn that Sheila's abduction was completely random.

Then came the part I dreaded.

It saddened me to see him lower his head solemnly after I repeated Buster's version of how Eugene had murdered his cousin.

Once again, in his normal fashion, the journalist put things into a perspective that only he could. He whispered, "Sheila gave her life to save someone else."

I was confused. "What do you mean?"

"If they hadn't picked up my cousin, they would have picked up someone else. So, my cousin helped to save a life," he said.

Most people would have looked at what Darwin said as being a bit morbid. But I had come to know the man—I understood what he was saying. Watching him interact with Sheila's children, the Johnson twins, and my four kids, I realized that he was something special.

After he spent several minutes in contemplation, he made it clear that he felt the same way I did—we had a break with Buster being wise enough to put together a list of witnesses.

The journalist was adamant about his inability to concentrate on anything, including the list that could provide the break that he had been praying for.

Alvin was on his mind—he insisted that he wouldn't be able to focus on anything until he saw that the teen was still alive. The newspaperman also wanted to pay his respects to Cecilia, and we both knew that she would be by her son's side.

I also wanted to check up on the family, so we headed for Henry Ford Hospital.

As we entered the crowded waiting room, Alvin's fifteen-year-old sister, Charlotte; and thirteen-year-old brother, Terriq, rushed up to us. I could clearly see that Cecilia's children were upset. Their stressful behavior triggered a helpless anxiety within every fiber of my being.

Sure, they were hysterical when Alvin and Buster were wheeled into the emergency room earlier that day, and even more so after being told that Buster had died.

Of course, I realized that they were young people dealing with horrors that would cause a grown man to buckle. But something else was toying with their emotional state. My first thought was that Alvin had passed.

Several irate individuals who were arguing with a nurse made it difficult for us to decipher what the two kids were babbling about. Neither Darwin nor I could make out anything that the teens were saying.

I moved my hands in a calming motion. "Take it easy...slow up and tell us what's going on. Is it Alvin?"

"No...it's not Alvin. It's Shannon," Charlotte said.

I was relieved to know that whatever had gotten under their skin was instigated by their sixteen-year-old brother, Shannon, and was not because Alvin had died.

Darwin chimed in, "What's up with Shannon?"

Alarm saturated her next statement. "He's gonna confront Eugene!"

"What!" Darwin and I responded in unison.

Both she and Terriq looked terrified; their eyes begged for us to go after Shannon. The children's sad puppy-dog gazes suggested that they were truly fearful for their brother's safety.

Charlotte offered, "Please...if my mother finds out that he's gone after Eugene, I don't know what she'll do."

"How's Alvin?" Darwin's question was his way of getting Charlotte to focus.

"I'm not sure... Momma hasn't been out here in a while."

Terriq explained to us that the surgeons were hopeful that Alvin would survive, but made it clear to the family that one of the four bullets was disrupting the lumbar nerve. The bullet was lodged between his L1 and L2, which ultimately would cause paralysis in his legs. So, if Alvin were to overcome the many surgeries that he would have to endure, his prognosis was that he would be paralyzed from the waist down.

I encouraged the children to stay strong—their mother needed them.

Darwin and I needed to get over to Eugene's place before the drug dealer had an opportunity to hurt Shannon Wright. There were two things that the newspaperman and I needed to know: When did Shannon leave the hospital? And exactly where was their brother headed? Eugene had several properties and I didn't want to waste valuable time going to the wrong location.

Not many people outside of his three top soldiers were privy to Eugene Scott's private world. There weren't a lot of folk who knew he had two children and a longtime girlfriend. He cherished his family and did whatever he could to shelter them from his life as a murderous narcotics dealer.

Buster had driven for Eugene on occasion. Cecilia's nephew shared a lot of what he had witnessed surrounding Eugene's personal life with his cousin Alvin—including what he claimed was the entrepreneur's secret home. He described it as being a beautiful baby mansion on a street called Parkside, located on the Northwest side of the city. Charlotte said that Shannon was present during most of the conversations between their brother and cousin, so he knew the exact location of the house. I was very familiar with the affluent street; it was located several blocks from the campus of the University of Detroit.

When Darwin and I pulled to the curb opposite Eugene's home, we noticed Shannon pounding on the door. I yelled to him from my open window just as the door was opened. We watched as he was immediately yanked inside.

The journalist and I got out of the car and ran across the street.

I rang the doorbell.

"Who is it...?" someone could be heard yelling from inside the house.

I responded, "Judge Greg Mathis..."

It took several minutes before the door opened. Two of Eugene's lieutenants stood before us—their imposing physiques would intimidate most. They slowly forced Darwin and I to take a few steps backward as they stepped from the house and onto the porch.

"Can we help ya'll?" one of the men's baritone voice resonated.

I stepped up to him before pointing toward the house. "I want the kid that just went in there."

"What kid?" he replied.

Darwin countered, "You know damn well what kid!"

Those two fools thought that flexing the muscles that were covered by their body shirts, while moving toward us in a threatening manner, was going to put us off. As we stood face to face, each of us refusing to give ground, I noticed Eugene escorting Shannon from the house.

With arrogance, the drug distributor insisted as he pushed Cecilia's son toward us. "Take this little bastard away from here before I put a bullet in his ass. No fuckin' body comes around my family."

Shannon stepped from the porch, turned around, and shouted, "You killed my cousin...and my brother is paralyzed because of you. You ain't gonna stop me from comin' back. Next time I'ma kill you."

Eugene tossed a little pocketknife at the kid. "With this...?" His next statement was directed to me. "Scoey, you better take that little bitch away from here," said Eugene as he motioned for his boys to get back into the house.

There was a demonic, vengeful determination in Eugene Scott's eyes.

Seeing that narcissistic display of evil being directed toward a sixteen-year-old teen was an urgent call for me to not only get that man off the streets, but to completely strip him of his power.

How could I have possibly foreseen that dealing with the chief judge would be the easiest thing that I would face the entire day? His foolish threats were something that I was already prepared to deal with on a daily basis. But, Buster being murdered, and Alvin barely hanging on to life, was not something that I anticipated would be a part of my day when I got out of bed.

Then there was Shannon Wright.

Here was a young teen determined to step up and seek retribution for the tragedies that had besieged his family in the span of a couple of hours.

If his older brother were to survive, he would clearly be unable to walk, so Shannon felt that he had to step up. The teen believed that he had to become the man of the family. And in taking on that responsibility, he was willing to do something that the hardest criminal element in the city was afraid to do—confront Eugene Scott.

At first, it was hard getting through to Cecilia's second child. He felt a rage that he had never experienced. He told us that he believed that the only way his family would be safe was if he killed Eugene.

It took a while, but we were finally able to convince Shannon that a real man finds a way to protect his family without the taking of a life. At first, we couldn't get the kid to agree to look after his family rather than jeopardize his freedom with a murder charge. Then Darwin explained to him that killing Eugene would only allow someone else the opportunity to take over his organization. The journalist went on to make it clear that if the dealer were brought down legally, his entire cartel would be crippled, and eventually fall, like a house of cards.

We drove Shannon back to the hospital. The teen promised that he wouldn't leave again; that he would stay put and look after his mother and siblings.

❀❀❀

He left an urgent message, which stated that he had something very important that he needed to share with me—he needed to see me right away. He insisted that the information would only be shared in the presence of law enforcement, which meant that I had another stop to make. I had to return his call because I needed to find out when, and where.

When I was finally able to reach him, I tried to get him to open up over the phone. Once again, he made it clear that he wasn't the least bit interested in speaking about his situation without police being present because what had to be said was a matter of life and death.

I didn't feel that I should push him; he was already extremely agitated.

James Redmond said that he was leaving his home and heading straight to 1300 Beaubien. He asked that I meet him there as soon as I could.

It had been since the first town hall meeting he had attended that I'd seen the man who had taken on the responsibility of raising his grandchild after his daughter and her husband were gunned down in a carjacking. He had given a very poignant speech to the assembly at Young Adults Asserting Themselves that day. He stopped by the mentoring program on two occasions to fulfill his court-ordered obligation after that memorable night, but I had arrived late and missed him on both occasions.

It was only 6:08 p.m. and I had already had a full day—having spent most of the morning at the hospital, then being present during the raid on the apartment where Sheila's murder had taken place, running after Shannon, and dealing with the chief judge's crap. So, I was rather exhausted when I pulled up to Macomb and Beaubien. If it hadn't been for James Redmond, I would have been on my way home.

For ten minutes I watched as people entered and exited the station.

James should have gotten to headquarters before I did. We agreed that we would meet in front of the desk sergeant. There were several people vying for the desk sergeant's attention when I approached.

"Judge Mathis, how you doing today?" Officer Roby asked.

One of the irate citizens attempting to get his attention was not at all pleased that the officer was ignoring her.

"What kind of shit is this...I been here for an hour and ain't nobody even tried to help me. This guy walks in, stands around for a few minutes, and then *bogarts* his way up to you...and now you wanna have coffee and donuts with him."

"Lady, I told you that someone is gonna be with you," he said to her before redirecting his attention back to me. "What's going on, Judge Mathis?"

"Not a thing, Officer Roby. You still thinking about running for Wayne County Sheriff?"

"Yes, sir..."

"Well, good luck with that."

"Thanks! What brings you to these parts at this time of the evening?"

"I'm supposed to be meeting someone. I guess he must be running late." I scanned the crowded station house once again. "Do me a favor. Check to see if Commander Daly is still in his office."

After he verified that Ron hadn't left for the day, I described James Redmond to the officer and asked that he direct him to the office of the Commander of Special Crimes when he arrived.

Ron was preparing to leave as I entered his office with my hand extended. "Hey there, Commander," I said as I stepped toward him.

The officer shook my hand. "What are you doing here?"

"Someone asked that we meet here in the station," I replied as I sat down on his couch and crossed my legs.

"Who?" my friend questioned.

"James Redmond...do you remember him?"

Daly sat on the end of his desk and folded his arms. "Vaguely..."

His inquisitive gaze compelled me to elaborate. "He's the guy that lost his daughter in a carjacking a couple years back. The guy that was picked up for destroying billboard signs, that promoted alcohol… Anyway, he asked that I meet him here."

Daly's phone rang. Before answering, he asked, "Why did he want to meet you here, of all places?"

My hunched shoulders silently answered his question, so he reached over the mound of paperwork on top of his desk and picked up the receiver. He promptly said, "Daly…"

The officer would listen before replying, "Send him up."

It must have taken him all of five minutes to get upstairs.

James and a teenaged female were escorted toward Daly's office. I stood and immediately greeted the grandfather as he stepped through the doorway.

"Hello, James," I said, shaking his hand.

"Hello, Judge Mathis." He nodded at Daly, who was still sitting at the end of his desk. "This is my granddaughter." His eyes veered toward the teen. "Stacy, this is Judge Greg Mathis."

I introduced both James and Stacy to the commander.

Her DKNY jeans and hoody were clean; her makeup, light and neat. The teen looked normal—not at all like she was described to me at the YAAT town hall meeting. She didn't have the appearance of someone who spent most of her time drinkin' and druggin' as advertised. She was attractive, and she appeared to be the type of young lady who was very concerned with her outer shell. Her hair was perfect, as if she had recently gotten it done. Her fingernails were polished and manicured. If I had run across her on the street, I would have never imagined that she was living the life she was.

I whispered to James, "Can I speak with you for a second?"

He nodded in agreement.

"Have a seat, Stacy. Excuse us for a second." I directed a hand gesture toward the police commander. "Give me a second, Ron," I said before escorting James from the office.

"Thank you for meeting with me," the grandfather whispered.

I replied quickly, "Anytime…now, what's so urgent?"

"It's my granddaughter."

"That's the same young lady that you told me about...the one that was abusing alcohol and drugs?"

"Yes..."

"She looks as if she's gotten past her problem...so what's up?"

"I'll let her tell you," he said as he headed back to the office. I followed.

Several minutes into her story, I found myself flabbergasted to discover what Stacy had to say. Daly was so intrigued with the story that he had to make himself comfortable in his chair. The teen's statement simply blew both of us away.

I needed to get Terrence Simmons involved—quickly.

After contacting the assistant district attorney, I asked that he get over to the commander's office as quickly as he could. He assured me that he would be in Daly's office within minutes.

"So Stacy, how are you holding up?" I asked the young teen who was seated next to her grandfather on Daly's couch.

She seemed frightened. "I guess I'll be okay."

"Would you like to check into a rehab center?" I asked.

The teen turned toward her grandfather and smirked. The man who had taken her into his home after the death of her parents smiled. He slowly nodded his head up and down several times.

"I'd like that..." she said as she returned her grandfather's loving grin.

Just as I was about to ask another question, I saw the ADA making his way through the squad room.

"Hello, everyone," the prosecutor said as he entered the office.

Both Ron and I got to our feet and greeted the prosecutor.

"Thanks for coming, Terrence," I said as we shook hands.

"Judge, I told you that I would do anything that I had to in order to get this guy." Terrence Simmons faced Ron. "How are you, Commander?"

While Ron and Terrence exchanged pleasantries, I positioned three chairs in front of James and his granddaughter. When the ADA finally directed his attention to our guests, I proceeded with the introductions.

"Assistant District Attorney Terrence Simmons...this is Mister James Redmond...and his granddaughter, Stacy."

The prosecutor shook the hands of both of our guests before making himself comfortable in one of the chairs that I had set up. Ron and I followed suit.

"So this is the young lady that's going to make my day?" the prosecutor questioned.

I looked at the teen. "Tell him everything," I said. I wanted Stacy to fill Terrence in on what she had told us.

The teen leaned forward on the couch. "It started out with me hanging out with a friend. She was a senior in high school and I was a sophomore. I wasn't dealing with the death of parents very well...and my friend recognized that depression had set in because I was talking about killing myself. She came over to my grandfather's house the day I told her that I had feelings of suicide. "

The teen continued once again to tell us how her friend took her to a house party in an effort to get her mind off of the tragedy of losing her parents. Stacy and her friend Joy entered the house party to the sound of MC Hammer's "U Can't Touch This." The place was packed—several people were holding cups of beer or wine while they danced in the crowded, smoked-filled living room.

Two guys were leaning against the wall and talking while smoking marijuana. They stopped Stacy and Joy as they attempted to make their way through the room. One of the men passed a joint to Stacy's girlfriend.

"It's good, girl...so be careful!" the JJ Evans lookalike said with a smile.

Joy took three pulls of the joint, then attempted to hand it to Stacy, but the sixteen-year-old quickly refused.

"Take this, girl...it's gonna chill you out. Come on, girl..."

Stacy went on to say that this would be her first time smoking weed. The young teen took us through every step of her free fall into the pit of hell. She went on to explain how her addiction to various drugs had gotten so bad that she began selling her body. James's granddaughter told us that it wasn't until her girlfriend got her a job working in one of Eugene Scott's drug houses that she began taking care of herself again.

"Just before my eighteenth birthday, Joy introduced me to one of Eugene's lieutenants."

She said that although she was making a little money and had gotten into taking care of herself again, she was still using. Her story culminated with the revelation that she was present when Eugene murdered Sheila.

"I stole the dope—with the help of one of his guards." A tear escaped her watery eyes. "She was murdered because of me."

She described that evening the same as was told to me by Buster. In fact, there was someone named Stacy Gordon on Buster's list. I didn't recognize the name or address because the teen used her last name—and not that of her grandfather. Plus, she lived with a friend.

After listening to the child give her account of that fatal night, Terrence and I agreed that we had our witness. It was time to put together an arrest warrant for first-degree murder.

My main concern was our ability to protect the teen. I struggled with the idea of hiding her in Sheila's House. I felt that Eugene would not have a reason to go back to the rehab center since he had already murdered Buster.

While we were discussing possible safe house options, Ron's phone rang. He answered, so Terrence and I continued our dialogue.

I heard something in the police officer's voice as he held the phone to his ear. His demeanor was solemn—he had gone into a sudden funk. With his eyes locked on me, I could hear him say, "I'll tell him."

Normally, I wouldn't have given his phone conversation a second thought, but he slowly shook his head as if something had gone terribly wrong.

SHE DIDN'T MAKE IT

I couldn't believe that I was once again watching medical professionals at the peak of their vocation. Nurses and doctors frantically ran about as they attempted to attend to an elderly lady complaining of severe head pain; a teen who was suffering from multiple stab wounds; a girl who had a mangled leg; and several other trauma cases in dire need of immediate medical attention.

Then there were the paramedics.

As I stood at the emergency room nurses's station my attention was drawn to the automated doors when they suddenly opened. I watched two emergency medical technicians hurriedly enter. One held an IV that was connected to a child no more than two years old, while through the chaos, the other maneuvered the gurney that she laid atop.

I could hear a nurse yelling for them to wheel the child into emergency room three. A few minutes later, I listened to something that made me feel uneasy.

"*Doctor Wineberg...Doctor Steven Wineberg...to emergency room three, stat.*" Hearing some woman bark out instructions over the PA system had become a little nerve-wracking. But, on this particular occasion, I didn't mind hearing her. I was truly hoping that Doctor Wineberg was the best in the business.

"*Crash cart team...code blue...emergency room three, stat!*" Her voice echoed over the speakers for the umpteenth time.

Seeing all the commotion literally made me forget why I had rushed over to Detroit Receiving Hospital in the first place. "Ms.! Excuse me, Ms…" I said in an attempt to get the duty nurse's attention.

With chart in hand, the woman in the blue cotton smock, whose attention I had been trying to get for several minutes, swiftly walked up to the desk. "Sir, you're not supposed be in here."

"I'm sorry, but I was told that Barbara Olson was brought here."

She never took her eyes off her chart when she responded, "You family?"

"I'm Judge Greg Mathis…"

The woman that I was attempting to get answers from didn't possess any bedside manner, whatsoever. "Well, Judge Greg Mathis…are you family?"

I realized that she was simply doing her job, but I was still a little perturbed with her attitude. "No, I'm not… I'm a very dear friend and a business associate. Can you please tell me how she's doing? Is she going to be okay?"

"Sir, if you go through those doors"—she pointed to the doors that led to the waiting room—"I'll see if I can find someone who can answer your questions."

I sat patiently for word on whether my day would get any worse. Death was all around me and I didn't know if I would be able to handle another fatal tragedy. To my left, grief; to my right, sorrow—everywhere I looked, someone was praying that his or her loved one would pull through.

I buried my face in my hands and prayed for Barbara Olson, and the little girl that I saw wheeled into the emergency room. As a matter of fact, my prayer went universal. I asked the Lord my Savior to bless each and every person who was under a doctor's care.

I had already witnessed the death of one young man, and seen the grief-stricken faces of his family after they had been told that their brother and son did not survive.

While I was in prayer, I felt a sudden gentle stroke. Someone was rubbing my back in a consoling manner.

When I looked up, there she was. Maggie was at it again; she was always trying to comfort me. My assistant stood next to me and gently caressed my back. My clerk's sympathetic eyes were a welcome sight.

Just before I could tell her how much I appreciated her support, I saw terror out of the corner of my eye. There was no doubt that she was going to take what she was witnessing out of context.

"Every time I see you…you got your hands on my husband!" Linda said with attitude as she approached.

Maggie quickly backed away from me as my wife looked to be moving with lethal purpose. "Mrs. Mathis, it's not like that. You have to believe me!" Maggie pleaded. Her eyes were filled with sincerity.

I got to my feet and immediately stepped in my wife's path. "Linda, relax!" I ordered, throwing my arms around her.

"Tell me why that woman has to always have her hands on you?" my wife asked. "What is she doing here, anyway?" Linda looked me directly in my eyes, and with a tremble in her voice, she asked, "How's Barbara doing?"

I pulled her closer and whispered in her ear, "No one has told me anything yet… I'm sure she'll be all right." I kissed my wife gently on the cheek. "Baby…I'm asking you to give Maggie a break. She's truly a very sweet and kind person. I mean that."

Someone tapped me on my shoulder while my wife and I shared an intimate embrace. I immediately directed my attention to the rear of me—his body language spoke volumes. Gram Olson's mouth hung open; his puppy-dog gaze was truly panicky.

"How is she?" he barely managed to ask.

My wife and I broke our embrace. To me, that was a mistake. It was as if I let a tiger out of its cage. The anger that Linda had toward Maggie paled in comparison to what she was about to unleash on the billionaire. My better half blamed Barbara's husband for her heart attack.

"Gram, I can't believe you did that to her. How could you?" Linda stepped up to the stunned businessman. "She loves you so much." My wife's eyes began to show signs of weariness.

Most everyone had his or her eyes locked on the commotion that was taking place between the billionaire and my wife. The one exception was a heavyset white man who'd had his eyes on me from the time I entered the waiting room. At first, I thought nothing of it—I presumed he was someone who recognized me from the election. He looked to be sizing me up, as if he couldn't make up his mind whether to approach me or not.

"What's wrong with you, Linda? What is it that you think I've done to hurt my wife?" Gram asked.

One of the nurses who passed us felt it necessary to send hospital security in our direction. But, it would be the surgeon responsible for attending to Barbara who would be the key in getting our attention.

All present immediately recognized the anguish that seemed to follow the physician—it was as if he were keeping company with the angel of death. The short Asian had a dark, lifeless expression that covered his face, which was revealed after he pulled his surgical mask down. When he stepped into the waiting room, I could see that everyone was a bit nervous. No one knew to whom he was bringing the tragic news.

Like everyone else in the waiting room, we stood frozen.

For some reason, I stepped up to him and asked if he was the surgeon caring for Barbara Olson.

"Yes, I am… Are you people family?" the doctor questioned. His gloom-filled eyes darted from me to Maggie before locking onto Linda, and then Gram.

Gram moved past everyone and announced, "I'm her husband."

The surgeon led the emotionally distraught businessman from the assemblage of heartache that hung over the area where we stood, and into the hallway.

Linda and I watched his facial expression through the glass window that encased the waiting area. The surgeon was definitely delivering bad news—my stomach was suddenly tied up in knots.

When my wife and I saw Gram lose control after being told that his companion of thirteen years had lost her brief battle and had succumbed to a fatal heart attack, Linda literally fell into my arms.

My wife was very remorseful for the way in which she attacked Gram. "I know that I shouldn't have come down on him today. I'm just so disappointed that he would cheat on her. She's dead, baby…Barbara's dead!" Linda cried.

I held her closely; she buried her head in my chest. I gently wiped away her tears while watching Gram pace the hall with his face masked behind his hands. My wife and I could feel his tortured heart.

Several Days Later

"Well done on passing the bar!" Pride filled my congratulatory remark. There was absolutely no doubt in my mind that she would do well. I hadn't known anyone who was more prepared. The girl was extremely versed on case law, both federal and state—hell, she prepared briefs for some of the public defenders as a way of keeping herself sharp. The biggest advantage that she had over most that took the exam was, she wasn't going in afraid to fail. Maggie ended up with the second-highest score ever recorded at the State Bar of Michigan.

My soon-to-be ex-assistant sat before me dressed in a very smart tan business suit. Although her attire was extremely professional, it still didn't camouflage her sexiness.

"Judge Mathis, I would really like to write the brief for Timothy Jackson's appeal," said Maggie. She had always shown an interest in that particular case. I believe that my first court argument was the inspiration behind her finally deciding to take an exam that she was so reluctant to take. Stories like that of Timothy Jackson would inspire most people interested in making a difference in our judicial system.

I was extremely proud of her.

"I can't believe that nearly six weeks ago, I was sharing a conversation with your alter ego. When I first met you, you appeared to be someone that doubted everything. But, appearances can be deceiving."

I smiled at her.

She could tell I was proud. Maggie quickly returned my smile before saying, "Thank you so much for everything that you've done for me."

"I didn't do anything...you don't have to thank me," I said.

The giggle was unintentional; I couldn't help it. Seeing her sitting in front of me, and knowing what she looked and acted like when I first met her, made me laugh. It was like she was undercover—trying to gain intel on the goings on around the 36th District.

"What's funny?" she asked. The innocence of her expression made me shake my head in wonderment.

"I still can't get over how you hid your beauty purposely. Look at you... Then, atop that when I first met you...you feared that you would eventually fall into the category of those that mocked the profession. It seems that you've gotten over your fears of becoming a non-caring legal representative." I smiled a prideful grin once again. "Look at you. There's a lawyer sitting before me, one I feel will make a positive impact."

My thoughts drifted.

The woman was no longer the nerdish, librarian type who seemed to lack self-confidence—she wasn't the same woman who had entered my office less than two months prior. But, one thing had remained the same: When I first met her, I knew that she was going to be my saving grace.

Being a judge, I was no longer able to invest enough time into putting together a proper legal strategy for an appeal. Hearing of Maggie's desire to dedicate time and effort to Timothy's petition made me feel great. She was coming to the aid of an innocent bystander who was trying to do the right thing in rescuing a frightened child.

As far as the vehicular homicide charge that was levied against him, Timothy Jackson was not guilty. He was not driving the car when it struck and killed that child's mother. And, I was glad that Maggie had found that case worthy of her time.

My clerk brought me out of my brief state of contemplation when she said, "I've already dug up some of the information surrounding the case, but I wanted to talk to you before I proceeded."

"I'm really happy that you choose to devote your energies into helping Timothy Jackson. That kid is certainly in good hands."

There were hordes of files in my possession that I wanted to pass on to her, but before I could tell her about them, David entered. "Judge Mathis, Commander Daly of the Detroit Police Department is here to see you."

Maggie got to her feet. "I'll speak with you later, Judge."

"Okay...and again, congratulations." I turned to David as Maggie headed out. "Send him in," I ordered.

Several seconds later, David escorted Ron Daly into my chambers. I got to my feet and extended a hand to my friend as he approached my desk. "Hello, Ron. What's going on, my friend? You've never stopped by here before...must be important."

The commander was as serious as I had ever seen him. He took my hand into his—his grip was firmer than usual.

"Hello, Judge," Ron Daly said. The law enforcement officer relaxed before reaching into the inside pocket of his brown single-breasted suit and then removing a notepad. He flipped open the pad and continued, "We got a serious problem."

"What?" I questioned with interest.

He responded reluctantly, "An arrest warrant has been handed down."

For a brief moment I sat in silence—I didn't say a word because I thought that he would be continuing his statement, but he sat there staring at his open pad. I'd never seen him at a loss for words—it was obvious to me that he was searching for the best way to go into details surrounding the arrest warrant. My curiosity was building. He'd never stopped by to see me at work, and he never really discussed random cases with me. Whatever was on his mind I felt had something to do with me.

"What's going on, Ron?" My monotone was of a serious nature.

He took a deep breath, and then looked me dead in my eyes. "Barbara Olson's autopsy report indicates that traces of oleander were discovered in her system."

"Oleander!" I had no idea what that was.

"It's a toxic evergreen shrub indigenous to the Mediterranean region. It's one of the most poisonous plants known to man...very toxic to the heart."

I was stunned. "Are you saying..."

Before I could finish my statement, the police commander offered, "Barbara Olson was murdered. The warrant is for her husband."

"You gotta be kidding!"

"I wish I were." He closed his pad and placed it back into his breast pocket. "I came by here to see if you wanted to go with me when I serve him with the warrant. As a courtesy, Monahan wanted to keep this under the radar for as long as he could."

"With the mouths in his office...there's no way that he can keep this quiet."

"He didn't say anything to anyone in his office."

I sat completely dumbfounded at my desk for several minutes. At the same time I was trying to convince myself that Gram would never commit murder. I knew that I wasn't going to be able to mentally rest unless I could prove that my old law school buddy had nothing to do with knocking off his wife. I had to speak with Gram, so I was more than willing to accompany Ron to the Olson estate.

The officer told me that he was waiting on a search warrant, and that we had to go pick that up first.

When Ron and I opened the door to my chambers, I was completely stunned to see my wife and Maggie hugging. After so many weeks of Linda displaying resentment toward my assistant, I was relieved to see the two of them in an embrace. Wow!

"What's going on?" I questioned with delight.

The two broke free of what I looked at as a show of understanding: Maggie understood why my wife felt the way she did, and Linda realized that even if my clerk had a crush on me, she was always respectful.

They both directed their attention toward me, but before either could respond, Ron quickly stated, "I'll meet you out front."

Not a word was said until the police officer exited my reception area.

"I had to apologize to Maggie for my behavior," Linda stated. She gazed at my clerk before continuing, "I realized that it wasn't right that I allowed someone else's insecurities to shape the way in which I trust. And, I do apologize to everyone in the office if I made you feel uneasy in any way."

Before she could go on with her heartfelt apology, Terrence Simmons entered my reception area. "Judge Mathis! Just the man I wanted to see."

"I'm on my way out the door. What's up?"

"I wanted you to know that Geoff Sanders has taken over the Scott case. We had two other witnesses come forward. With those odds...everyone knew that Sanders was going to take over."

Terrence then joked about Sanders putting himself in a position to be the next victim of the venomous Otto, due to him snatching Scott's case from under her. Frankly, I could not have cared less who prosecuted Eugene Scott, as long as he went down for what he had done.

I thanked the prosecutor for his help. I then turned to my wife, Maggie, and David. They were all huddled up at Maggie's desk. "Hey, guys, I have to make a run."

Linda motioned for me to meet her in the hallway.

When my wife and I stepped from the office, she immediately hugged me before whispering, "I owe you an apology. Baby...I'm sorry that I acted so insecure." She kissed me.

"That's okay. We'll talk about this later. I have a few things that I have to take care of."

"Before you go, I need to tell you about a phone call that I received earlier."

"Okay, what's up?"

"It's Evelyn..."

My wife went on to tell me that my cousin's wife was crying about how she missed her child—how she would do anything to see her again. She claimed that she didn't want to disrupt her child's life, and she understood that her daughter staying with us was the best thing for the little girl.

Evelyn was seeking our help—realizing that Gail was better off with us made it clear to me that she was ready to be helped. I told my wife to reach out to both my cousin and his wife. However, it shocked me to learn that Darryl wasn't interested in being helped.

✪✪✪

Ron and I didn't head out to Gram's affluent neighborhood until later that evening because there was a delay in the search warrant. As we made our way through Bloomfield Hills, I couldn't help but reminisce about the last time I had visited the palatial estate. I remember pulling into the circular drive and being in awe—the twenty-one-room estate, which was surrounded by beautifully manicured acreage, was absolutely stunning.

I remember seeing seven or eight people doing various things: cutting hedges, mowing grass, planting flowers. At that moment my thoughts were that the Olsons had to employ a great deal of people to maintain their property.

It also amazed me that someone with so much money would be so willing to help the less fortunate. My perception of the *haves* was that they would try their best to distance themselves from the *have-nots*—but Barbara was different. I felt blessed that my family and I were able to call her a friend.

Barbara Olson was the personification of class, grace, and generosity. She gave of herself; that woman was not deserving of her fate—especially at the hands of someone who claimed to love her to no end.

When we pulled up to the circular drive, which was well lit by the ground lamps that surrounded it, I noticed a brand-new, red Monte Carlo, with vanity license plates: "BLK WDW1." I couldn't quite put my finger on it, but something about that car struck me as being familiar.

I stepped from Ron's cruiser and stood with the door open. For several seconds I allowed my eyes to scan over the grounds. That house, in all of it magnificence, was a sight to behold at night. With the moon, and the lights that bordered it, the house sparkled like a radiant chandelier.

After I broke the hypnotic hold that its beauty, which encompassed my thoughts, appeared to have on me, I glanced back at the Monte Carlo and remembered.

"I've seen that car before," I said to Ron as he got out of the driver's side and made his way to where I stood.

He was curious. "What!"

I could tell that me making a comment about a car at a time when a friend was about to be arrested, was confusing to him, so I said, "The person driving this car broke into my house and left me a provocative tape."

We headed to the door, and I pushed the bell.

It didn't take long before Edward, Barbara's faithful English butler, answered, "Good evening, Judge Mathis, sir...do come in."

"How are you, Edward?" I asked as we stepped into that beautiful foyer.

"I'm fine, Sir. Master Olson is in the library... I'm sure he wouldn't have a problem if you were to go right in."

"Thank you so much, Edward." As we headed toward the library, I turned to the English gentleman and said, "Once again, I'm so sorry about Mrs. Olson."

"Thank you, sir..."

When we stepped to the partially opened door, we could hear Otto and Gram.

"I told you that no one does me like you did!" Carolyn Otto's anger was evident.

Before Ron and I could enter his study, Carolyn came storming out. She immediately spotted both the law enforcement officer and me. The evil heifer didn't say a word. She stared for several seconds, then rudely forced her way past us.

When Ron and I entered, Gram was standing by his desk with his arms crossed.

"Gentlemen, to what do I owe this pleasure?" the billionaire asked.

Ron stepped up to him and I stood by the door.

The police officer went right into Miranda. "Gram Olson, you have the right to remain silent."

Barbara's husband was shocked. "What the hell are you talking about, Ron?"

"Gram...you're under arrest," Ron replied.

"For what?"

"Murdering your wife," the law enforcement officer whispered.

Ron's eyes veered toward me. "Mathis, what the hell is going on?" It was obvious that Gram was shaken. His bewildered expression pleaded for me to explain.

I walked over to the both of them. "Gram, Barbara didn't die from cardiac arrest...she was *murdered!*"

EPILOGUE

She was the wealthiest woman in the state, and because the mayor had revealed to Monahan that Gram was in fact, cheating on her, the district attorney felt that there was enough circumstantial evidence to issue a warrant for his arrest. It didn't help that a small oleander plant was found when police conducted a search of his estate.

After speaking with Gram for half the night, I was totally convinced that he had nothing to do with Barbara's death. But, if I were going to figure out who murdered his wife, I had to first consider who hated Gram enough to frame him; thus, my visit to Mayor Aaron Dennis.

The mayor attempted to convince me that he was caught between a rock and a hard place. "I realize that you blame me for his arrest, but what did you expect me to do?"

As far as I was concerned, he tried too hard to persuade me that he had no choice, that he had to do his part in assuring that Gram would pay for what he had allegedly done.

"Barbara meant a lot to this community...there's no way that I was going to let him get away with murdering her."

I wasn't really interested in any of his excuses.

"Look, Aaron, Gram could have exposed you for your adultery...but he didn't. He had a tape on you..." I knew that he had other motives, so I directed my attention toward his honor before saying, "You yourself have reasons to want Gram put away."

He was perturbed. "What are you saying?"

"He interfered with your plans and got the city council to back him. And, you must also be thinking that as long as Gram has legal woes, he's less likely to reveal the tape that he has on you. But believe me, if he finds out that you had something to do with convincing the DA that he murdered his wife, he's going to release that tape."

From the expression on his face, I could tell that he hadn't completely thought about the consequences of his actions.

"Look, Aaron, he already knows that you told his wife that he was having an affair with Carolyn." I continued as I approached his desk, "I still can't figure out what motivated you to do that."

The slow movement of his head from side to side as he rubbed at his eyelids with the index finger and thumb of his right hand made it obvious that he was trying to clear his thoughts.

I made myself comfortable in one of the chairs positioned before his desk. I then whispered, "Tell me something…"

He never looked up. "What?" replied the mayor as he continued rubbing his eyes.

"How did you find out that Carolyn and Gram were having an affair?"

Aaron made eye contact with me before saying, "When I found out that he had that tape on me…I had recording devices planted in his car and home. I didn't know what I expected to get on him, but I knew that I was going to have to get something because I didn't know what his plans were for that tape. All I knew was that he had something that could affect my reelection bid."

"So, you thought that you needed leverage?" I asked.

"Actually, Carolyn gave me that idea."

"What?" That bit of information hit me like a ton of bricks. It also got my mind back on events that I hadn't bothered to address.

"Yeah, she reminded me that he would be trying to take my job, and that he would eventually use that tape against me."

I was outdone. "Aaron, did it ever occur to you how Gram got that tape?"

"What do you mean?"

"The tape of you and Carolyn was recorded in her home," I said in an effort to get him to see, what to me, was obvious.

"I assumed that Gram planted devices in her home."

"No...she was recording you guys. She was evidently ensuring that she had something on both of you. Gram told her that he wasn't going to be involved anymore. He was trying to get free of her web...but she manipulated him into that second encounter...the one that your device captured."

When the mayor informed me that Carolyn was behind his thinking of exposing Gram's affair to Barbara, something suddenly occurred to me. "Look, Aaron, I gotta go, but I want you to know that you screwed up, period. There is no way in hell that you should have told Barbara. It wasn't your place. I could see if you were doing it out of friendship with her, but you were doing it to hurt him because he's been using his power to influence the city council."

I left the mayor's office with the intent of enlisting some help in my effort to prove Gram's innocence.

My first stop was Wayne County lockup.

Gram's attorney was trying desperately to get his client released on bail, but the prosecutor's office said that he was a flight risk. After all, he was facing first-degree murder charges, and he no longer had any ties to the community.

For the very first time since we were acquainted, the billionaire wasn't sporting expensive attire. I never thought that I would see the day when Gram Olson, businessman extraordinaire, would be led into a visiting room in county orange. Even in law school, Gram could have won any best-dressed competition across the country.

Seeing him without his winning smile was heartwrenching. Gram looked defeated when he entered the visiting area with his hands cuffed in front of him.

"Hey guy...how you holding up?" I questioned as he sat across from me.

He rested his cuffed hands on the small table that separated us. "Greg, you gotta get me out of here."

"I'm working on that, my friend." I gave him a sly grin. "I have a few more questions to ask."

"Go ahead...ask your questions."

"Did you know that Barbara had changed her will?"

"When we first got married, I signed a pre-nuptial. She added me to her will at that time. That's the only time that I know of her doing anything to it."

"Well, on your tenth anniversary, she changed it again. She increased the amount of assets that was to be left to you. Two weeks ago, she eliminated you from the will completely."

Gram looked bewildered. "So, she knew about the affair…"

"My wife said that Barbara had hired a private investigator. Your wife did suspect that you were cheating."

"I guess that information is going to be damning." He dropped eye contact before saying, "I didn't kill her…hell, Greg, I made a mistake…but I wouldn't kill her because she cut me out."

"Tell me something, did you know that oleander was deadly?"

He made eye contact again. "Hell no…I only had it for a few weeks."

"How did you come across that particular plant?"

❂❂❂

After leaving Wayne County lockup, I headed to the district attorney's office. The purpose of that visit was to find out who would be prosecuting Gram's case, and to see someone who had become an ally. I felt that I was getting close to being able to prove that Gram was innocent, but I still needed some help.

ADA Terrence Simmons was just as shocked as the others in his office when it was finally revealed to them that Gram Olson had been charged with murdering his wife.

He sat as the edge of his desk. "I'm blown away, Judge Mathis," the assistant district attorney said. "So, I take it that you don't believe that he did it…"

"I know that he didn't do it. Tell me something, who's going to prosecute?"

"Monahan said that Carolyn begged him for the opportunity. So I think that she's got the case."

I paced his office in an effort to gather my thoughts. I knew that what I would ask of him would send him into a frenzy, so I had to be tactful. "Terrence, I need your help again."

"What do you need?"

I stopped pacing and stood before him. I told him my thoughts, and why I had come to the conclusion that I had. I also laid out why Carolyn shouldn't be given an opportunity to participate in the case. Then I asked him to do something that could have put him in the cross-hairs, especially if we were unable to come up with the evidence that would exonerate Gram Olson.

Just as I figured, he was reluctant to get involved with my plan. He was only willing to go so far in sticking his neck out. But when he heard the entire story, he realized that to do nothing meant that he wasn't at all interested in living up to the oath that he had taken.

❋❋❋

Room 219 was my next stop.

I once again found myself in Karla Kelly's courtroom (five minutes before court was to adjourn for the day). This time I wasn't there to see Geoff Sanders at work—it was his partner in crime that I was interested in. Carolyn Otto was prosecuting a case in room 219 and I intended to speak with her before she made it back to her office.

I sat in the back of the courtroom as the spectators cleared out. Otto didn't notice me until she turned to say something to the defense attorney, who was on his way out.

"Edward, you should take my deal," she said. Her dark-blue skirt and white linen jacket looked nice. If I didn't know the woman behind the flattering attire, I would have thought her to be very professional.

"I'll pass!" said Edward before leaving the courtroom.

"What the hell are you doing here?" she asked, putting the last of her documentation into her blue leather attaché case and closing it. No one was left in the courtroom with us except an elderly female stenographer.

As calm as I possibly could, I said, "First you screw 'em, then you fuck 'em, now you wanna prosecute 'em."

The court stenographer tried to act as if she weren't listening, but I could see the corners of her mouth turn up. She'd obviously been around the courtroom long enough to know Otto's ways.

The prosecutor angrily snatched her briefcase off the table and made her way up the aisle and toward the exit. Her gaze was laced with vindictive intentions. I stood in her path—and didn't allow her access to the door.

"I need to speak with you for a second." My request was stern.

She stopped right in front of me. That woman sent chills up my spine—her eyes seemed to dig at my soul. "What do you want?"

"I have proof that you broke into my house and left a package."

She attempted to appear stunned. "What! What the hell are you talking about?"

"You know damn well what I'm talking about. You're not the only one that captures things on tape." My next statement was a flat-out lie, but she didn't know that. "I have several cameras set up on my property. You entered my home from the side door and left a package containing a tape on the coffee table in my den. You then exited and got into that brand-new Monte Carlo that you drive. The one with the vanity plates...I must say, the plates are very befitting: Black Widow One."

Otto was unflappable. She didn't care one bit whether I had her on tape or not. "You don't like *me*...and you know damn well I don't like *you*. If you had anything on me, you would have already addressed it." Arrogance filled her response. With her briefcase firmly gripped in her right hand, she attempted to force her way past me.

I grabbed her by the arm. "I'm on to you."

She gazed at the hand that firmly gripped her wrist. A second later, her eyes veered toward me before she whispered emphatically, "Take your hands off of me!"

"You've been playing games with people's lives...this is gonna stop."

She snatched her arm from my grip, and then pushed her way past me. What she said as she exited—"you're next..."—made me realize that if I weren't successful in doing something about her, that bitch was coming after me with everything she had.

✪✪✪

With files in hand, he nervously allowed his eyes to scan the common area to ensure that no one was paying attention to him. To his left, he saw several people congregated at a secretary's desk. To his right, two interns were passing files to each other. No one was the least bit concerned about what he was doing, so he slid into the office, closed the door, and immediately drew the blinds. He then went to the file cabinet and began digging—drawer by drawer.

He had no idea what he was looking for, but he knew that whatever it was, he had to find it in a hurry, because he couldn't afford to get caught.

The office was immaculately kept so he needed to ensure that he didn't leave anything out of place. After going through the eight drawers that made up the filing system, he turned his attention to the neatly kept desk.

He made his way over to the traditional executive L-shaped desk. The three side drawers were locked, so he opened the middle one in hopes of finding a key. His search proved to be unsuccessful.

He then turned toward the desktop computer. He didn't seem at all surprised that the screen saver consisted of a large spider web. A black widow looked to be putting an end to the life of a fly that was caught in a silky trap.

When he pressed the enter key, he saw a title and picture that he was greeted with on a daily basis. In the upper left-hand corner, *Welcome to Wayne County, Michigan* appeared on the screen, along with a picture of District Attorney Joseph Monahan.

Terrence Simmons was computer savvy so he was able to discover several files that he felt would be of interest. He also told Ron Daly and me that he found EINet Galaxy, a search engine that Otto had used frequently.

"I discovered a site that covers the effects of oleander." The ADA's statement was directed toward the police commander that sat next to him in my chambers.

Ron replied quickly, "All that proves is that she is preparing for the case."

"So you're telling me that she started her research on this case six weeks ago?" Terrence countered.

Both Ron and I were taken aback.

The prosecutor continued, "According to her searches, she visited these sites six weeks ago. Atop that, I checked the calendar on her desk because I remember her going away for several days. She went to Morocco after doing her research…"

I guess the expressions on both Ron's and my face prompted him to say, "Morocco is a place that oleander is indigenous to." His eyes veered from Ron and over to me. He continued in a shaky voice, "Judge, she almost caught me…"

"I tried to delay her in the courtroom…but she wasn't havin' it," I said. "What happened?"

Terrence seemed a little agitated. He sat forward in his seat like an anguished preschool kid. "I was sitting at her desk flipping through her calendar when I heard someone ask her how it went in court. Boy, you talk about nervous energy. Anyway, I had to get off her computer, put her calendar back to where it was, and then check to make sure that I didn't leave anything out of place…because, she is extremely meticulous. I had to do all that in a matter of seconds. When I stood and pushed her seat in, I realized that I had left the files that I was to use as cover on top of her file cabinet. I got the files, and placed them on her desk. As I reached for the doorknob, she entered, so it looked as if I were leaving as she was entering."

Terrence sat back before he continued, "She asked me what I was doing in her office. I pointed to her desk and said that I had brought her information on Gram Olson. I was scared. As I told you before, the bitch scares the hell out of me."

Ron said, "Sounds as if she was none the wiser."

"I don't know," Terrence whispered.

I asked, "What do you mean?"

"When I left her office and she closed the door…I suddenly remembered."

"Remembered what?" Ron asked curiously.

The prosecutor gazed intently at both the law enforcement officer and me. He was really building up the suspense. "I left the blinds drawn."

Ron shook his head knowingly. He thought that to be a none issue. "She probably thought that she left them like that herself."

"I thought that, too, until she opened them and glared at me standing in front of her office. She knew. I could tell how she stared at me through the slits."

My chambers went silent. Everyone took turns making eye contact.

Ron broke the awkward silence when he said, "It's on you, Judge."

I sat in silence for several seconds. I was going over everything in my head, and then it hit me. "Okay, this is how this will play out. We'll use the recording as a way to execute a search warrant of her office and home. We'll use her arrogance also. Her asking Monahan to prosecute a man who she was trying to blackmail will work in our favor. So I'll sign off on the search warrants."

❂❂❂

Ron ensured that simultaneous searches were conducted. Several detectives went through her home, while a few others checked her office and computer.

Monahan was not at all pleased that one of his own was being treated like a criminal. I had to explain to the district attorney that Carolyn Otto had given Gram an oleander as a gift upon her return from Morocco. I also told him about the tapes and that I felt she was going to use them to blackmail high-ranking public servants, including the mayor.

It wasn't until her diary was discovered that the DA realized he had a very sick individual working in his office. Otto's diary laid out her escapades, starting with a detailed list of the people whom she planned to ruin, and her reason for her vindictive wrath. The list captured Monahan's attention—because he was named.

❂❂❂

"I'd like to thank the Detroit Police Department, and Commander Ronald Daly. I'd also like to thank Assistant District Attorney Terrence Simmons for his diligence. I've made a lot of mistakes in my life…but none that has ever affected so many others, the way that my unfaithfulness has," Gram Olson said as he addressed a contingent of reporters who had congregated on the steps of Wayne County lockup.

Ron and I stood on the top step and watched as Darwin Washington maneuvered through the horde of reporters and positioned himself at the very front.

Gram looked over his shoulder and made eye contact with me before he would say, "My freedom would not have been possible without a true friend's belief in my innocence. I'd really like to thank Mr. Street Judge himself… Thank you so much, Judge Greg Mathis, for ensuring that I didn't go down for killing the love of my life."

I mouthed, *You're welcome.*

ABOUT THE AUTHOR

Greg Mathis became a national success story and a symbol of hope for urban youth by being a committed civil rights activist, public servant, and the youngest elected judge in the state of Michigan. As cofounder of Young Adults Asserting Themselves (Y.A.A.T.), a non-profit youth agency, Mathis is dedicated to helping troubled youth both in and out of the courtroom. His journey from a teenaged street youth and high school dropout to his award-winning career as a judge is chronicled in his autobiography, *Inner City Miracle*. He appears weekdays in his nationally syndicated television show, *Judge Mathis*. He lives in Detroit, Michigan.

Visit www.askjudgemathis.com or www.judgemathistv.warnerbros.com.

NATIONWIDE RESOURCES TO EMPOWER YOU

I have found in recent years that the Internet has become a great source of knowledge and discovery. If you know me, you know that I truly believe that knowledge is the key to lifelong success. No matter what age you are, ten to ninety-eight years old, there's information on the web that will empower you. With that said, within the next few pages, you will find websites that will inform and educate you on topics that I feel we, as a community, should learn and understand. Even if none of these sites pertain to you at the moment you are reading this, I encourage you to get on them, surf around and see what they have to offer.

While I don't personally endorse any of these sites, I do endorse growing knowledge of the world and all it has to offer.

SITES WITH FEDERAL AND STATE RESOURCES

www.usa.gov
Offers listings for federal, state, local and tribal agencies in all areas including but not limited to employment services, healthcare, finance and housing.

www.govbenefits.gov
GovBenefits.gov is a partnership of federal agencies with a shared vision—to provide improved, personalized access to government assistance programs.

SMALL BUSINESS

www.sba.gov

The U.S. Small Business Administration (SBA) was created in 1953 as an independent agency of the federal government to aid, counsel, assist and protect the interests of small business concerns, to preserve free competitive enterprise and to maintain and strengthen the overall economy of our nation. We recognize that small business is critical to our economic recovery and strength, to building America's future, and to helping the United States compete in today's global marketplace. Although SBA has grown and evolved in the years since it was established in 1953, the bottom line mission remains the same. The SBA helps Americans start, build and grow businesses. Through an extensive network of field offices and partnerships with public and private organizations, SBA delivers its services to people throughout the United States, Puerto Rico, the U. S. Virgin Islands and Guam.

www.score.org

SCORE, "Counselors to America's Small Business," is a nonprofit association dedicated to educating entrepreneurs and the formation, growth and success of small business nationwide. SCORE is a resource partner with the U.S. Small Business Administration (SBA).

SCORE is headquartered in Herndon, VA and Washington, D.C. and has 389 chapters throughout the United States and its territories, with 10,500 volunteers nationwide. Both working and retired executives and business owners donate time and expertise as business counselors. SCORE was founded in 1964.

We are America's premier source of free and confidential small business advice for entrepreneurs.

YOUTH

www.youthdevelopment.org

IYD is a non-partisan, non-profit organization that promotes a comprehensive message to youth in the U.S. and around the world to avoid five harmful risk behaviors that are inextricably linked: alcohol, drugs, sex, tobacco and violence. IYD believes that children and teens, provided with consistent and sound messages, are capable of making the choice to avoid these risk behaviors altogether, especially if they are empowered by strong parent and family connections.

This website is designed for both professionals in the field of youth development and for mothers, fathers, and teens looking for current information and advice.

www.helpingamericasyouth.gov

Helping America's Youth is a nationwide effort to raise awareness about the challenges facing our youth, particularly at-risk boys, and to motivate caring adults to connect with youth in three key areas: family, school, and community. As the leader of the Helping America's Youth effort, Mrs. Laura Bush is highlighting programs, which are effectively helping America's young people. Research has shown that supportive relationships are crucial to youth well being. President and Mrs. Bush believe that parents and family are the first and most important influence in every child's life. By becoming actively involved in the lives of young people in their community, teachers, mentors, clergy members, neighbors, coaches, and others can support parents and help youth make better choices that lead to healthier, more successful lives.

www.ojjdp.ncjrs.gov/

The Office of Juvenile Justice and Delinquency Prevention (OJJDP) provides national leadership, coordination, and resources to prevent and respond to juvenile delinquency and victimization. OJJDP supports states and communities in their efforts to develop and implement effective and coordinated prevention and intervention programs and to improve the juvenile justice system so that it protects public safety, holds offenders accountable, and provides treatment and rehabilitative services tailored to the needs of juveniles and their families.

www.acf.hhs.gov

The Administration for Children and Families (ACF), within the Department of Health and Human Services (HHS), is responsible for federal programs that promote the economic and social well being of families, children, individuals, and communities.

CONSUMER RIGHTS

www.ftc.gov

As a consumer or businessperson, you may be more familiar with the work of the Federal Trade Commission than you think.

The FTC deals with issues that touch the economic life of every American. It is the only federal agency with both consumer protection and competition jurisdiction in broad sectors of the economy. The FTC pursues vigorous and effective law enforcement; advances consumers' interests by sharing its expertise with federal and state legislatures and U.S. and international government agencies; develops policy and research tools through hearings, workshops, and conferences; and creates practical and plain-language educational programs for consumers and businesses in a global marketplace with constantly changing technologies.

HOUSING

www.hud.gov

HUD's mission is to increase homeownership, support community development and increase access to affordable housing free from discrimination. To fulfill this mission, HUD embraces high standards of ethics, management and accountability and forges new partnerships—particularly with faith-based and community organizations—that leverage resources and improve HUD's ability to be effective on the community level.

HEALTH

www.hhs.gov

The Department of Health and Human Services (HHS) is the United States government's principal agency for protecting the health of all Americans and providing essential human services, especially for those who are least able to help themselves.

The Department includes more than 300 programs, covering a wide spectrum of activities. Use this site to help find information on healthcare, immunization for kids, financial assistance for low-income families, maternal and infant health, care for older Americans and more.

www.hrsa.gov

The Health Resources and Services Administration (HRSA), an agency of the U.S. Department of Health and Human Services, is the primary federal agency for improving access to health care services for people who are uninsured, isolated or medically vulnerable.

Comprising six bureaus and twelve offices, HRSA provides leadership and financial support to health care providers in every state and U.S. territory. HRSA grantees provide health care to uninsured people, people living with HIV/AIDS, and pregnant women, mothers and children. They train health professionals and improve systems of care in rural communities.

EDUCATION

www.ed.gov

U.S Department of Education was created in 1980 by combining offices from several federal agencies. ED's mission is to promote student achievement and preparation for global competitiveness by fostering educational excellence and ensuring equal access.

FINANCIAL AID

www.studentaid.ed.gov

Federal Student Aid's core mission is to ensure that all eligible individuals benefit from federal financial assistance—grants, loans and work-study programs—for education beyond high school. The programs we administer comprise the nation's largest source of student aid: during the 2005-06 school year alone, we provided approximately $78 billion in new aid to nearly 10 million postsecondary students and their families. Our staff of 1,100 is based in ten cities in addition to our Washington headquarters.

This site also offers information on grants as a secondary source of financial aid as well as valuable information regarding paying back your loans once you have completed your education.

www.fedmoney.org

FedMoney.org is the most comprehensive free full-text online resource on all U.S. government grants and student financial aid programs. Here you will find detailed and up-to-date information about (1) who can apply, (2) how to apply, (3) full contact info, and much more...for over 130 government grants and loans (scholarships, fellowships, traineeships) related to education.

www.staffordloan.com

The federal student loan programs offered at StaffordLoan.com are a service of the Student Loan Network. As part of the full suite of student loans and financial aid services, the Student Loan Network offers Stafford Loans for undergraduate and graduate students and federal loan consolidation services for recent graduates.

www.coenet.us

Our nation has asserted a commitment to providing educational opportunity for all Americans regardless of race, ethnic background or economic circumstance.

In support of this commitment, Congress established a series of programs to help low-income Americans enter college, graduate and move on to participate more fully in America's economic and social life. These programs are funded under Title IV of the Higher Education Act of 1965 and are referred to as the TRIO Programs (initially just three programs). While student financial aid programs help students overcome financial barriers to higher education, TRIO programs help students overcome class, social and cultural barriers to higher education.

EMPLOYMENT

www.dol.gov

The Department of Labor fosters and promotes the welfare of the job seekers, wage earners, and retirees of the United States by improving their working conditions, advancing their opportunities for profitable employment, protecting their retirement and health care benefits, helping employers find workers, strengthening free collective bargaining, and tracking changes in employment, prices, and other national economic measurements. In carrying out this mission, the department administers a variety of federal labor laws including those that guarantee workers' rights to safe and healthful working conditions; a minimum hourly wage and overtime pay; freedom from employment discrimination; unemployment insurance; and other income support.

The Department of Labor's Employment and Training Administration (ETA) supports a wide variety of programs to ensure that all youth have the skills and training they need to successfully make the transition to adulthood and careers.

www.usajobs.gov

Use this site to search for jobs within all types of industries across the country.

EQUAL OPPORTUNITY/DISCRIMINATION

www.eeoc.gov

The Equal Employment Opportunity Commission (EEOC) is the federal agency responsible for enforcing employment discrimination laws.

EEOC does not only deal with race discrimination, but it also deals with discrimination against age, disability, pregnant women, sex and religion, to name a few.

This site offers valuable information that will help you file a charge of discrimination claim, and it is also a great resource to help you learn and understand employment laws.

If you are an employer, the Training Institute provides a wide variety of training programs to help employers understand, prevent and correct discrimination in the workplace.

LEGAL

www.lsc.gov

The Congress of the United States entrusts the Legal Services Corporation with a dual mission: to promote equal access to justice and to provide high-quality civil legal assistance to low-income Americans.

The main source of funding for civil legal aid, LSC gives grants to independent, local programs—in 2007, 138 programs with more than 900 offices nationwide. Grants are awarded through a competitive process. Generally, the size of the grant is based on the number of people living in poverty in a given state or service area.

NUTRITION

www.frac.org

The Food Research and Action Center (FRAC) is the leading national nonprofit organization working to improve public policies and public-private partnerships to eradicate hunger and undernutrition in the United States. FRAC works with hundreds of national, state and local nonprofit organizations, public agencies, and corporations to address hunger and its root cause, poverty.

This organization also helps with food stamps, nutrition within low-income homes and school meals for homeless children.

http://www.fns.usda.gov/wic/

WIC provides federal grants to states for supplemental foods, health care referrals, and nutrition education for low-income pregnant, breastfeeding, and non-breastfeeding postpartum women, and to infants and children up to age five who are found to be at nutritional risk.